The
Liar

ALSO BY AYELET GUNDAR-GOSHEN

Waking Lions

The
Liar

AYELET GUNDAR-GOSHEN

TRANSLATED FROM THE HEBREW
BY SONDRA SILVERSTON

Little, Brown and Company

New York   Boston   London

Copyright © 2018 by Ayelet Gundar-Goshen
English translation copyright © 2019 by Sondra Silverston

Little, Brown and Company
Hachette Book Group
1290 Avenue of the Americas, New York, NY 10104
littlebrown.com

First North American edition: September 2019
First English-language edition published in Great Britain by Pushkin Press: March 2019
Originally published as השקרנית והעיר in Israel, 2018

Published by arrangement with The Institute for the Translation of Hebrew Literature

Little, Brown and Company is a division of Hachette Book Group, Inc. The Little, Brown name and logo are trademarks of Hachette Book Group, Inc.

The publisher is not responsible for websites (or their content) that are not owned by the publisher.

The Hachette Speakers Bureau provides a wide range of authors for speaking events. To find out more, go to hachettespeakersbureau.com or call (866) 376-6591.

ISBN 978-0-316-44539-9
LCCN 2019937207

10 9 8 7 6 5 4 3 2 1

LSC–C

Printed in the United States of America

PART ONE

1

THOUGH IT WAS the end of summer, the heat still waited outside front doors along with the morning newspaper, both boding ill. So sequestered in their air-conditioned homes were the people of the city that, when it came time for the seasons to change, they didn't feel the newly autumn-tinged air. And perhaps autumn might have come and gone unnoticed if the long sleeves suddenly appearing in shop windows hadn't announced its arrival.

Standing in front of one of those windows now was a young girl, her reflection looking back at her from the glass—a bit short, a bit freckled. The mannequins peering at her from behind the glass were tall and pretty, and perhaps that was why the girl walked away quickly. A flock of pigeons took flight above her with a surprised flapping of wings. The girl muttered an apology as she continued walking, and the pigeons, having already forgotten what had frightened them, returned to perch on a nearby bench. At the entrance to the bank, a line of people snaked its way to the ATM. A deaf-mute beggar stood beside them, hand extended, and they pretended to be blind. When the girl's gaze momentarily met his, she once again mumbled an apology and hurried on—she didn't want to be late for her shift. As she was about to cross the square, a loud honk made her stop in her tracks and a large bus hurtled angrily past her. A poster on the back wished her a happy New Year. The Rosh Hashanah holiday was still a week away, but the streets were already filled with promises of big sales. Across the street, three girls her age were snapping pictures in front of the fountain, their laughter ricocheting off the paving stones. As she listened, she told herself over and over again, "I don't mind walking alone, I don't mind it at all."

She crossed the square quickly. Inside shops, red-haired saleswomen said, *It looks lovely on you,* adding, *If I were you, I'd take two,* as they stole glances at the clock. Bladders bursting, they could barely wait for their breaks. A charming young man stood at the counter, ringing up sales on the cash register with fingers that had run through his boyfriend's hair earlier that morning. Customers left the shops, their swinging bags twisting around each other, creating an urban rustling that was as much a harbinger of autumn as the rustle of leaves falling from treetops.

In the ice-cream parlor next door, the girl went behind the glass counter and began handing spoons of ice cream to those who wanted to taste, knowing that the summer vacation was about to end and no one had yet tasted her, the only girl in her class still a virgin, and next summer, when the fields yellowed, she would be wearing a soldier's army green.

Now she handed an ice-cream cone to the little boy standing in front of her and tried hard to smile as she said for the thousandth time that week, "Here you are." The next person in line asked to taste the fig sorbet. Nofar knew right away that he wouldn't buy fig sorbet. He would only taste it, along with ten other flavors, and in the end he'd ask for chocolate. Nonetheless, she handed him a bite of fig sorbet on a plastic spoon and glanced quickly at the clock above the counter. Only seven more hours to go.

At that very moment, the door opened and they stepped inside. She had been waiting the entire summer for this moment and had even written about it in great detail in her notebook: Yotam would come in and be surprised to see her there. She would offer him ice cream free of charge, and in return he would offer her a ride home on his motorbike. She would say that she still had a few hours left in her shift, and he would say that a few hours wasn't a long time to wait. But when the moment finally arrived, three days before the end of the summer vacation, Yotam didn't come in alone. He was surrounded by his crew of friends. And one of them was Shir, who, until four months ago, had still been Nofar's friend. Nofar's only friend, to be precise.

The five of them stood there, and although they weren't particularly good-looking as individuals, standing there at the counter they seemed to Nofar to be incredibly beautiful. They shone with the glow of being a clique, as if the fact that there were five of them made each of them appear at least five times more beautiful. They examined the row of flavors spread out before them, trying to decide, and for a moment Nofar dared to hope they wouldn't recognize her. But finally Yotam raised his beautiful eyes from the ice cream to the counter, frowned slightly, and said, "Hey, you go to school with us." The others looked up. Nofar fought the urge to avert her eyes. "You're in Shir's class, right?" Moran asked as she pulled her hair back into a ponytail in a gesture that was as ordinary as it was charming. Nofar nodded quickly. Yes. She was in Shir's class. In fact, she had sat next to Shir since the second grade, until that morning four months ago when she arrived at school to find that Shir had fired her without even a letter of warning.

There was a moment of silence before Yotam said, "So, I'll take cookie dough." Nofar had already begun piling ice cream into a cup when he said, "In a cone." And that, in fact, was all Yotam said to her, because immediately after that the others began telling her what flavors and toppings they wanted, and Moran added in a tone brimming with insincere amiability that they needed to get their ice cream in a hurry because the movie they wanted to see started in twenty minutes. And all the while, Shir stood silently looking at Nofar, a small expression of guilt on her face, until she finally said she'd have vanilla. She didn't have to say it—Nofar knew what flavor Shir liked. Five minutes later they were already outside, on their way to the movie. Nofar looked at the sorbets displayed under the counter in flowering layers of red and orange. Dozens of fingerprints covered the glass partition in front of her, all made by fingers pointing at the ice cream, never at her.

The glass door opened and a gang of noisy children burst inside. When this day was over, she'd play music she liked, not the songs that Gaby insisted attracted customers. She'd still have to pick up all the napkins people had dropped and the sticky spoons parents hadn't felt like throwing away after their kids finished their ice cream. She'd still have to wash the floor, scrub the fingerprints off the partition, and take out the garbage, but it would be her music in the background. Then she'd fill a Styrofoam box with ice cream and take it to the homeless guy who stood near the fountain. Or maybe she'd just put it down not far from him, because the last time she went up to him he had shouted some garbled words at her that she didn't completely understand.

She'd been daydreaming too long about the homeless guy and the ice cream, and about the gang at the movies without her, because when she looked around she saw that the kids had taken off with their ice cream without paying. Gaby would deduct it from her salary. A large lump of misery filled her throat and she took a deep breath and swallowed it whole. Six and a half hours to go. If only this day would end already.

She didn't know that this day would end differently from all the days she had known before, that this day would change all the days that followed, that this was absolutely the last day she would be nothing more than a drab ice-cream server.

She weighed seven and a half pounds at birth. Beyond that, there was nothing to say about her, simply because a moment before that she hadn't existed. The people who, a moment earlier, had been called Ronit and Ami were now called Mom and Dad, and looked at her through a haze of emotion. The birth had taken nineteen hours, and at its conclusion Ronit's vocal cords were almost as frayed as Ami's eardrums. The newborn baby girl lying between them was very red and very wrinkled, but the delivery nurse told them it was only temporary. "She'll be beautiful!" she said. "Like a flower!" It wasn't clear what the source of the nurse's prophetic confidence was, but the parents accepted her words as fact. Ronit picked up the baby gently, astonished at those seven and a half pounds that only a short time earlier had been part of her own body weight and now existed on their own. "We'll call her Nofar," Ronit said in a hoarse voice, "and she'll be beautiful!" Ami was quick to nod: "A flower!" The nurse went off to other rooms and other deliveries. And so, before she was ten minutes old, the baby girl had a prophecy and a name that meant "water lily."

Choosing a baby's name is no small matter. The first tiny cells are only just beginning to divide in the womb and the parents are already divided in their opinions: one wants Tamar and the other demands Daniel. One insists on Michal and the other decrees Yael. It would be better to wait for the cells to mature into an actual creature so that the name is born from the person instead of the person being born into the name.

But parents, unable to control themselves, are driven by their hopes and expectations to plunge ahead, and hopes and expectations have a way of outdistancing reality, creating so large a gap that the child is left behind, forever running to catch up to her parents' dreams for her. Nofar wasn't ugly. Far from it. But the delivery nurse had said "Beautiful!" and that prophecy had pursued her from infancy. She grew up to be a timid, withdrawn young girl who lived in the world as if she were an uninvited guest at a party. Now, standing behind the counter in the ice-cream parlor, she recalled that moment when Yotam and his friends had come in and he had recognized her. "Hey, you go to school with us." It was clear to her that he hadn't known her name. And that he hadn't cared enough to ask.

When the stream of customers in the ice-cream parlor slowed to a trickle, Nofar took the key that was hanging on a hook like a suicide and hurried outside to the employees' bathroom in the alley. A pair of alley cats stopped copulating for a moment to glance angrily at her, and then, with a wave of their tails, went back to their business. Nofar squeezed into the narrow stall and closed the door quickly, as if it weren't two cats she had just seen copulating, but, heaven forbid, her parents.

When she left the stall, she straightened her blue dress with a trembling hand. She had borrowed it from her sister at the beginning of the summer. How hopeful she had been then that it wasn't only the dress she was borrowing, but also the charm required to carry off wearing it. Her younger sister moved with such grace, such fluidity, that the city's traffic lights blushed with pleasure whenever she approached. The already traffic-congested streets grew even more congested because the lights became flooded with such a red wave of lust that traffic was forced to a standstill. And so Maya strolled from one pedestrian green light to another without ever having to wait, not even at the busiest intersections. But for Nofar it was different. She always waited.

When they were infants, people couldn't tell them apart. Nofar was less than a year older than her sister, and Maya closed the gap with the speed of a gazelle. She was born prematurely, and though the doctors attributed that to Ronit's emotional state (her husband was called to active reserve duty when she was in the last stages of pregnancy), the birth was actually premature because the baby inside was so eager to be equal to the one outside. The timid ice-cream server was not the least bit timid then. On the contrary. Plump and smooth as butter custard, reaching out with tiny hands to clutch any finger extended to her, the world was hers to grasp and taste. The word *daddy* was sweetening under her tongue, ripening slowly, a first gift to her parents, to be given at the right moment. But when that moment came, her father was gone and her mother, who at first had been as bright as a summer dawn, now flitted around the house like an agitated bird.

Nofar knew the story well. Family members told it regularly, and just as she learned at school to stand at attention when the national anthem was played, she followed the rules of the ritual whenever she heard that family anthem, listening with her head bowed at the sound of the familiar words and mumbling "thank God" at the appropriate times. *Thank God* that when the ambulance took Mom, the neighbor called Dad immediately. *Thank God* that Dad managed to get to the phone a minute before the ground operation began. *Thank God* that when the commander heard about Dad's new baby girl, he gave him a twelve-hour pass, and—here saying *Thank God* was not allowed; she'd fallen into that trap once and her mother had shot her a withering glance—*who would have believed it,* right after Dad left, his tank crossed into Lebanon and everyone was killed. *Thank God Maya's birth saved Dad.* As the years passed, the last sentence became slightly shortened to simply *Thank God, Maya saved Dad.* Not Maya's birth, the medical event. Not the commander, who had given him a pass. Maya had saved Dad. Everyone knew it and everyone talked about it, and when Nofar finally said the word *daddy,* they barely noticed. Because that's just how it is. All babies eventually say *daddy,* but not all babies rescue their fathers from a burning tank.

On her first day of work at the ice-cream parlor, Nofar left her house wearing Maya's dress, in better spirits than usual. For the first time in her life, she had a chance to begin everything anew, and there was no better place for it than the ice-cream parlor, that wonderland of flavors and colors, as if someone had managed to trap a rainbow, attach a door at the front and a cash register at the back, and place it on a street corner. Her parents had praised her for deciding to work during the summer vacation, but she hadn't done it only for the money. It was for the people that she went there, a fifty-minute ride from her house in the suburbs. It was for the welcome eyes of strangers who didn't know what the neighborhood knew about her: that there was nothing to know about her. That nothing had ever happened to her. No adventures. No misadventures. A marginal, harmless existence that was now seventeen years old.

Even the pimples on her face weren't enough to make her unique. There are teenagers who have truly exciting geological formations on their face: deep craters, unforgettable hills and valleys. Nofar's sebaceous glands, however, behaved moderately, satisfied to appropriate only her forehead and a small enclave on her nose. But the pimples, though they bothered no one else, bothered Nofar herself quite a bit. In her mind, she called herself "zit face."

Names and nicknames are very dangerous things. Lavi Maimon, who lived on the fourth floor of the building that housed the ice-cream parlor, could tell you that. Despite all the scoops of chocolate that had rolled around in his stomach, he was still as skinny as the bars of the bicycle racks the city installs on the streets. Perhaps he could have borne the humiliation of his existence if his parents had given him a name that was easier to live up to than Lavi, which means lion, but he carried the burden of the king of the jungle on his skinny shoulders. As a child, Lavi had waited for the mane to grow in and the muscles to develop under his skin when he finally reached his teens. But the years passed and the hair refused to grow. He had only fourteen hairs on his chin—he counted them in front of the mirror every night—and as for the muscles, well, forget it. His father, Lieutenant Colonel in the Reserves Arieh Maimon, ran his business with the same iron fist he had once used to command his soldiers. And just as Arieh Maimon's soldiers had kept climbing the hill because they were less afraid of the terrorists shooting at them from above than they were of their hot-tempered commander below, so the stock of the company Arieh Maimon had founded after his discharge also continued to climb well beyond every economic forecast because it feared the fiery glance of its commander.

Lieutenant Colonel Arieh Maimon did not give his son the name Lavi. That decision was made by his wife, a beautiful young woman who admired her husband, the country, and her Pilates teacher, not necessarily in that order. Since she was especially fond of the name Lavi, her husband generously allowed her to make the choice. As the boy grew into a teenager, it was clear that he did not possess even a smidgen of his father's predatory charm. If there was any connection between him and the world of large felines, it was only as a potential meal. In his son's early years, the father still roared at him and pierced him with the same look that had once driven his soldiers and then his stock upward. But after a while he stopped doing even that. Lavi began to miss the loud reprimands, even the roars. Anything was better than the silence, the quiet that followed the disappointment.

In the evening, as his mother made her ablutions in preparation for her Pilates class and his father purred contentedly in front of the TV, Lavi opened his bedroom window and looked down at the street. The urban river rushed by below him, gangs of teenagers on summer vacation bobbing and lurching in the current. Hearing their laughter, he asked himself whether they would keep laughing if his body landed beside them, a dull thud on the paving stones. Whether the girls would bend to help, run slim fingers over his short-cropped hair, the disappointing mane. Whether they would finally look at him—if not with compassion, then at least with interest—take out their mobile phones and snap a picture of the sprawled body, its arms embracing the street, arms that had never embraced a girl.

And so, every evening the city adorned itself with the glitter of streetlights and Lavi Maimon stood at the window contemplating his death, thinking about the many faces that would look at him when he landed near the entrance to the ice-cream parlor. He would have tried his hand at that sort of flight a long time ago if the summer military operation on the southern border hadn't begun, flooding the city with sirens and filling all the newspapers. To be buried somewhere on the back pages was not what he wanted. He preferred to wait for the fighting to end. And thank God, it never did: it stopped in the south only to begin again in the north. Lavi woke up every morning and saw that the newspaper was filled with the same stories that had filled its predecessor the day before. How would they find room for the story of his failed attempt to fly? So he postponed his death from day to day, and though the military operation cost many lives, it did at least save the life of one city boy.

As Lavi groaned under the name of the lion crouching on his shoulders, Nofar Shalev also buckled under the burden of her name. Why in the world had she believed that here, in the ice-cream parlor of all places, she would finally blossom into a different Nofar? Every morning she stood behind the counter. Summer came to the city, had its merry, sweaty way with it, and now that autumn was approaching, everything had a facade of respectability once again. In another few days, Nofar would go back to school without a single exciting story from the ice-cream parlor in the city except for the ones she wrote in her notebook. How much she had hoped for a brazen love affair with a student, or a tourist, or a heavily pierced bad boy. When she returned to school, he would wait outside the gates for her, she would run to him, and everyone would see. Including Shir. And Yotam. Nofar had been prepared for anything but entering her senior year with empty hands, with fingers that had never touched a boy's except to give him change. If only she had at least found a girlfriend here to replace Shir. Anything to be the entire focus, even for a moment, of someone's gaze.

On the fourth floor, Lavi Maimon stood looking down at the street. In the alley stood Nofar Shalev, her hands straightening her dress, neither one aware of the fact that they were not alone in suffering the humiliation of a name they could never live up to. It might have been easier if they had known that somewhere—on the other side of the planet, or four floors away—someone was enduring the same pain. Or it might not have been easier at all, just as someone with a toothache feels no relief at hearing the moans of the person sitting next to him in the dentist's waiting room.

Although Lavi Maimon and Nofar Shalev knew nothing about each other, they both sighed forlornly at precisely the same moment. The only difference between them was that Lavi continued to stand at the window while Nofar, suddenly realizing that she was late getting back from her break, rushed back inside. She ran, almost as if she knew that it wasn't only to the ice-cream parlor that she was hurrying now, but to the moment when everything would change, to the fate that already awaited her on the other side of the counter.

2

OVER THE LONG days she spent behind the counter, Nofar had developed a habit—she looked into the customers' faces and tried to guess which of them had come into the ice-cream parlor by accident and which were there by design. The accidental visitors were nicer: people strolling leisurely down the street, sailing along like fish until the ice-cream parlor's welcoming sign appeared and reeled them in on its line. The ones who planned to be there were totally different, people for whom the ice-cream parlor served an actual purpose: compensation for a hard day's work, the desire of a crushed heart. She saw it in their darting eyes, in their tight mouths that insisted on tasting more and more flavors, all of them unsatisfying. That kind of customer gulped down an ice-cream cone as if it were a headache pill: quickly, so it would have an immediate effect.

Nofar could easily see that the customer now waiting at the counter belonged to the intentional group. It wasn't a leisurely stroll that had led him there, but rather a disastrous day. She said good evening and wasn't surprised when he didn't reply. She asked what she could get for him, trying hard to smile even though she was exhausted from her dash across the alley and from the barrenness of the summer. The guy looked her over impatiently and grumbled that he'd been standing there for ten minutes already. How long did a person have to wait for service in this place?!

That wasn't accurate. He hadn't been standing there for ten minutes. In fact, he'd been standing there for less than five. But during those five minutes, he'd received a text from his agent saying that the TV bigwigs had thought it over and decided they didn't need another talent show. What his agent didn't say was that even if the bigwigs had been convinced that they did need such a show, they still didn't need the services of a singer whose glory days were behind him. Seven years behind him, to be precise. It was unbelievable how quickly seven years could pass. Only a minute ago he'd been riding high, his picture on the front pages of newspapers, one and a half million texts sent to him on that amazing night, an entire country sending him its love. Now he was here, in this pathetic ice-cream parlor standing in front of this pathetic girl who waited to hear what flavor he wanted, and there wasn't the slightest hint of recognition on her face. She didn't know who he was.

Later, when the echoes of the scandal died down a bit, Avishai Milner would wonder whether it had all started at that moment. A girl looking at him with blank eyes from the other side of the counter, and in that blankness he lost his soul. There he was, sinking, drowning in the darkness of anonymity, in the abyss of ordinariness. Across the counter from the girl, Avishai Milner couldn't breathe. With his last ounce of strength, he fought to remind himself that he wasn't just another customer, he was Avi-shai! Mil-ner! That was how the presenter on the finale had introduced him, slicing his name as if it were hot, fresh bread, lengthening the syllables for the pleasure of the studio audience, Avi-shai! Mil-ner! And the viewers at home had applauded with one million votes. For the next several weeks his name was on everyone's lips. Beautiful women swooped down on him in pubs and clubs, wanting to taste him, wanting to be tasted by him, and he made love to them, but even more to himself. He screwed Avishai Milner's brains out, and every nymph who sighed *A-vi-shai* in his ear was merely echoing that unforgettable moment when his name had been announced, when the presenter had opened the envelope, looked at the name with his kind, generous eyes, and in front of the huge audience in the studio and at home, crowned the young small-town man: Avi-shai! Mil-ner!

There's no way of knowing what went wrong after that. Avishai Milner was neither a better nor a worse singer than Eliran Vaknin, who had been crowned by the same presenter the previous year and appeared on all the top charts to this day. Nor was he less good-looking than Assi Sarig, who was crowned the following year and had already played a tormented doctor in a TV series, a tormented soldier in another TV series, and the tormented father of an autistic child in a soon-to-be-released feature film. The fact that there was no reason for it, no personality defect that could be blamed, no lesson to be learned—that was what tortured Avishai Milner more than anything. The total arbitrariness of his fall terrified him because it implied that his rise had also been arbitrary, not the product of his talent, but of a random set of circumstances.

Avishai Milner received his agent's text after long weeks of anticipation. Since submitting his proposal to the TV bigwigs, his days had been suffocating and his sleep sporadic. Like a wild bull, Fame had tossed him over its shoulder and then kicked him as he lay on the ground. He had to find a way to rise again. The longer the bigwigs took to give their answer, the more nerve-racking it was. The presenter came to him in his dreams and said that after the commercial they would sing a duet together, but to his horror he couldn't remember the words and the microphone turned into a terrifying snake in his hand. In short, he really did deserve ice cream. But when he went into the ice-cream parlor, he found it empty. Outside, customers were sitting and eating happily, but behind the counter there was no one.

Someone who receives bad news in the middle of an ice-cream parlor—what does he need? A steady hand offering him a variety of chocolate comforts. A smiling face waiting patiently for him to speak. Eyes that look into his and confirm that yes, despite everything, he still exists. But when Nofar returned to the counter, she didn't recognize Avishai Milner, and although she did her best to smile, her smile couldn't hide the sadness that popped out from beneath it, the way a too-small shirt she had once tried on couldn't cover her embarrassed flesh. Avishai Milner didn't know that the dress the girl was wearing belonged to her more beautiful sister. He didn't know that she had made her way there every day that summer in the disappointed hope that she would be rescued from ordinariness. All he knew was that he'd already been waiting ten minutes to be served here. And that was inacceptable.

"This is inacceptable," Avishai Milner said to the girl standing opposite him, and to emphasize exactly how inacceptable it was he slammed his hand on the glass partition.

"Unacceptable," the girl said.

"Excuse me?!"

"The word is 'unacceptable,' not 'inacceptable.'"

As the oldest daughter of a language teacher, Nofar knew very well that people hated nothing more than having their words corrected. No one would open a friend's mouth while he was eating, pull out the food, and demonstrate the right way to eat. And words, like food, belong to the tongue on which they rest. But then this customer had come into the ice-cream parlor and stood across the counter from Nofar. A nasty guy who banged on the glass partition, leaving another greasy handprint. But not to point out a flavor. The hand that slammed on the glass wasn't pointing to the mango sorbet or French vanilla. The guy wasn't making a choice, he was asserting control—he banged on the glass partition simply because he could.

Nofar was seventeen years and two months old on that evening, and in all her days on earth it had never occurred to her to bang on a counter. That's how it is. There are people who bang on counters and there are people who wait behind counters and ask, "What'll you have?" But something burst inside her that evening. Yotam and Shir's crew on the way to the movies. Her sister's dress. The humiliation of that depressing summer. She didn't need this guy's complaints. But if he insisted on complaining, then he should use the proper language. Otherwise it was unacceptable.

Avishai Milner looked in astonishment at the server who had corrected him. He'd never seen such chutzpah before. He had always considered himself a man of words. He'd written the lyrics to his songs himself. Now he mobilized all his skill to ram his words into the girl's flesh. "You pie-faced moron! You stupid cow! You should tweeze your eyebrows before going out in public. And those pimples, didn't anyone ever tell you not to squeeze them? You just need a few olives on your face and they can sell it as a pizza. But forget the face, what's with that stomach of yours? Didn't the owner of this place tell you that if you eat too much, you'll look like a hippo? Who would ever want to fuck you, huh? I'll take one scoop of cookie dough." He handed her a 200-shekel note and Nofar, standing on the other side of the counter, automatically reached out to take it, like a chicken without a head that keeps running around for a few seconds. Her limbs repeated routine actions, taking a cone and scooping the ice cream into it, until the realization hit her that she had been decapitated, that the man had removed her head, her selfhood, and she threw down the cone and fled.

3

THE PAIR OF alley cats screeched a few mating calls and had renewed their recently interrupted copulation. But at that moment the ice-cream server burst into the alley and dashed past them, heading for the bathroom. Eyes blazing with anger, the long-tailed creatures observed the flight of the sobbing invader, but she was too agitated to notice them. The customer's words still thundered in her ears. Tears rose in her throat. Her nose. Her eyes. To think that he had really said those things to her, that she had really stood there listening mutely and had almost served him ice cream. How pathetic she was. There was only one thing she wanted now: to disappear. The most terrible things she said to herself had just been said to her by a stranger: that she was ugly. Hairy. Pimply. Fat. That no one would ever want her. And though she was, in fact, quite nice-looking, the rejected little girl inside her was still certain that the customer at the counter had said aloud what everyone thought—the customers at the table, her classmates, her father, her mother, her sister. With her last ounce of strength, she looked for a place to hide, and the only one she could think of was the foul-smelling cubicle she had stepped out of a short time earlier. She was about to enter that tiled womb and squeeze between the garbage can and the raised toilet seat when, suddenly, a strong hand grasped her.

In the weeks to come, Avishai Milner would be asked again and again what had made him follow that underage girl from the ice-cream parlor to the bathroom. He, for his part, would continue to insist that he wanted to demand change for the 200-shekel note he had given her and believed she took with her when she left. The simple facts would not help Avishai Milner: the girl had not taken the money, but had left it on the counter. Though he would steadfastly claim that he did not see the bill when he went out after her, that claim, like most of the facts in the incident, would be eclipsed by the enormous impact of the scream the girl emitted when Avishai Milner grabbed her.

The cashier in the dress shop raised his head. The red-haired saleswoman stopped in the middle of folding a blouse. In the neglected alley, the pair of alley cats scurried off. And Lavi Maimon, sitting on his fourth-floor windowsill, realized that he would have to postpone his jump once again. Nofar Shalev looked at Avishai Milner, who had insulted her and was now clutching her hand, and screamed her heart out.

Some changes occur slowly. Geological erosion, for example, sometimes goes on for tens of thousands of years. Water and wind do their job, and gradually, bit by bit, a mountain ridge becomes a valley, a sea turns into a desert. Time, like a giant anaconda, crawls along lazily, swallowing up the tallest mountains. Some changes erupt all at once, like a match bursting into flame, or the "let there be light" of creation. The change that happened to Nofar was apparently of the second kind. She had walked the earth for seventeen years and two months and had never thought to pound on counters, much less to scream in alleys. But now, in the presence of that man who had said those horrendous things to her, Nofar's very soul shuddered. She ran out to the alley determined to disappear, but when the customer grabbed her hand she was suddenly overwhelmed by the opposite urge—to be heard.

She screamed out the humiliation of the words he had hurled at her. She screamed out the humiliation of the words she had hurled at herself. She screamed out the disappointment of that summer and the summers before it. She screamed and screamed and screamed, and didn't hear the police sirens arriving in response, or the fire engines that joined them, because so it goes—one jackal howls and one hundred jackals respond from the darkness. Nofar Shalev screamed and the city responded with screams of its own.

The entire street hurried to see what was happening there, in that neglected alley, and since Nofar Shalev was the one it was happening to, everyone looked at her. The dreamy-eyed cashier. The red-haired saleswoman. Neighbors from their balconies. Two traffic cops. Even heavily pierced members of street gangs, the sort that never show an interest in other people and are never the object of other people's interest, came to see what was happening. Nofar's body was awash in the kind of light that radiates from fondly gazing eyes, and that light was now focused—wonder of wonders—on a girl who had never before attracted a lingering gaze. A pretty girl soldier, her blond hair pulled back in a ponytail that burst from the rubber band like a fountain of light, held Nofar in a kind embrace and said "Everything's fine" with such certainty that it seemed she had the authority to say those words, not only in her own name but in the name of the entire defense establishment. Nofar gave herself over to the warm embrace, feeling as if she had never been hugged that way before. The light fragrance of the perfume worn by the fairy godmother in uniform enveloped her, along with another more masculine scent, that of the officer who only a moment earlier on the street had encircled the girl soldier's waist with his arm before hurrying with her to the alley when they heard the scream.

As she held Nofar in her arms to comfort her, the officer and two traffic cops held Avishai Milner and demanded to know what he had done to the girl to frighten her so badly.

"Nothing!" he shouted. "I didn't do anything!" And the poor girl trembled in the kind embrace because she knew it was true. He hadn't done anything to her. That dirty-mouthed customer hadn't done anything to justify the presence of two traffic cops and an army captain. A citizen of the country was certainly permitted to skewer the heart of another citizen with his words. In another moment, she'd have to say that to the gentle-eyed girl soldier, to the audience looking at her with the sort of affection she had never before experienced. Everyone was so friendly, so interested—what would they say when they discovered that nothing had actually happened, that they had run all the way there for no reason? They would turn their backs on her instantly. The policemen would certainly rebuke her for causing such a fuss, and she would bow her head in submission, as she always did. Then she would return to the ice-cream parlor to serve the waiting customers, wipe the glass surface, and ask, "Cup or cone?" and "What can I get for you?"

And in truth, she would have been willing to accept all that if Avishai Milner hadn't opened his filthy mouth again. It seemed that he hadn't vented all his fury. Or perhaps it had been recharged, like those almost dead phones that are suddenly revived by a newly found source of power. So it was with Avishai Milner. People's glances replenished him. How much he had missed that audience, young and old, soldiers and policemen—as the presenter used to say, the entire country is here with us. Suddenly he was filled once again with the familiar, addictive feeling of being at the center of things, the object of frenzied public attention that exploded all around him. But the fact that the attention was negative—no one threw flowers to him, no one applauded him—shook him to the depths of his soul. The audience's affection was lawfully his. He couldn't let that hippo who had kept him waiting at the counter, who had dared to correct his language and had run off with his money, steal what was rightfully his.

Once again, he snarled his nasty words at the girl, and words, like hot-air balloons, take off when the flame under them is lit: "You disgusting hippopotamus, I wouldn't touch you with a ten-foot pole," and a host of other pejorative words and phrases. The girl's eyes filled with tears. First he had insulted her when no one else was around, and now he was ridiculing her in front of everyone. In despair, she moved out of the pretty girl soldier's embrace, began to cry in earnest, and covered her face with her hands. Beyond her hands rose a monumental brouhaha. Everyone was asking questions at once, but, deafened by her own sobs, Nofar didn't hear, and it wasn't her fault that observers took her sobbing as confirmation. They asked, "Did he touch you?" and the covered face trembled—that is, replied in the affirmative—and each additional sob was further confirmation, each additional sob was the next day's headline. Suddenly, miraculously, the following story emerged from a neglected alley: refugee from reality TV accused of attempted rape of minor. And everyone looked at the newborn story and saw it was good.

Alley cats stand up a few days after emerging from the womb. Foals manage to stand up about an hour after birth. Only human babies, slow creatures that they are, cannot stand on their own two feet until many months after they are born. In contrast to the slowness of the human newborn is the incredible speed of the human story: a person brings a story into the world, and if it contains a whiff of scandal, it immediately stands on its feet. One minute it clings to its creator, and the next it breaks into a run. The question is not where it has come from, but where it is going, and how far it will go before surrendering to the law of nature that halts all runners.

The terrible story about the famous singer and the underage ice-cream server came into the world at 6:49 in the evening in the month of August. For a brief moment, the newborn story remained where it was and breathed the perfumed evening air, but then it was no longer willing to wait even one minute longer in the alley. It galloped far into the distance, and the alley, which had filled so quickly earlier, now emptied out with the same speed. The traffic cops and the firemen; the golden-haired girl soldier and her lover, the officer; and of course the proud parents—the once-famous singer and the minor from the ice-cream parlor—all went on their way. It was now impossible to know whether they were leading the story or the story was leading them, but either way, the alley was already too small for them. For their present size they needed a larger living space, such as, for example, the police station on the main street.

4

IN THE POLICE station on the main street they gave her water and tea, then Coke as well. They cut her a slice of the honey cake one of the dispatchers had brought. They offered her a seat, and when her bottom touched the chair, Nofar sighed in relief. She had been standing on her feet without a break all summer. She stood when she served the customers who flowed into the ice-cream parlor, and when they left she hurried to clean the glass counter, but the moment it was shiny again the customers were back, and the cycle began again. Now, with her legs stretched out in front of her, a glass of cold Coke in her hand, its bubbles fizzing merrily, she was asked once again what had happened.

The pleasant woman across from her leaned forward. She had beautiful, delicate hands with nails polished a lovely, subdued color so light it was almost transparent. The pleasant woman said her name was Dorit and that Nofar was probably finding it difficult to speak and answer questions. But in fact, it wasn't difficult at all. It was harder when nobody asked you anything, when you spent an entire day, an entire week, an entire summer without speaking to anyone. The woman asked, Nofar replied, and it was all incredibly simple. All she had to do was repeat what had already been said, just like in a history exam. She was very good at memorizing. There was a reason she was an outstanding student. The words flowed effortlessly. The woman across from her had all the time in the world. Her kind eyes were fixed exclusively on her, no distractions, and, faced with such attentiveness, Nofar found herself opening up. The delivery nurse's old prophecy was coming true: her body forgot its awkwardness. Her cheeks reddened. Fire ignited in her eyes. Her usually pale, stammering lips grew suddenly as red as a rose. A stranger who happened into the room and was asked to describe her by the way she spoke would undoubtedly say "blossoming."

That was her mother's word: *blossoming*. When Nofar completed primary school, her mother promised she would blossom in middle school, and when she completed seventh grade, her mother said that the transition to middle school was always difficult, but now, in the eighth grade, she would really, really blossom. And so she moved from class to class, dragging behind her a trail of buds that would open any minute now. How strange it was to discover that the change that had been so late in coming when she entered middle school, even when she began high school, occurred one evening in a small room in a police station—and the more she spoke, the more she blossomed.

Finally she stopped, though she could have kept going if she had wanted to. Dorit, the detective with the pleasant face and delicate hands, said, "You're a very brave girl."

In a side room on the police station's second floor, Avishai Milner banged on the wooden table. "I'm telling you I didn't touch her!" The two detectives sitting across from him were not especially impressed by the banging, and even less impressed was the wooden table. It had already been pounded on so much in its life, sometimes by suspects, sometimes by detectives, that it had long since lost hope of being rescued. Its production-line brothers had been placed in public libraries and post offices, and one of them had even risen to the census bureau office, but fate had doomed this table to be shipped to the police station on the main street. Now Avishai Milner banged the table in fury once again. Because it was unbelievable—an hour ago he had left his house, headed for the ice-cream parlor, and now he was looking at the street through a barred window. That enraged him so much that he had no choice but to bang on the table, proclaiming over and over again that it was unbelievable!

The gray-haired detective glanced at his watch. Through the barred window, he heard the groan of the city engulfed by its perfumes. People who hate the city criticize it for being nothing but a mixture of honking horns and soot, but on the days before the New Year's holiday, countless perfume bottles in a rainbow of colors are opened all at once in shops in an intoxicating urban flowering. The detective's nose, the nose of a seasoned hunting dog, recognized his wife's singular fragrance in the profusion of scents rising from the street. He wanted to leap out of his chair and hurry outside to her, but first of all he needed the truth. Without it, this day's work would not come to an end. So he looked hard at the suspect and said, "I remember you. My wife voted for you in the finals."

Avishai Milner softened instantly. Like the cookies that people dunk in their coffee cups, he couldn't withstand the heat that enveloped him. This man knew him. His wife had voted for him in the finals. For that dear woman, he was still Avi-shai! Mil-ner! The gray-haired detective continued to ask him questions and he replied willingly, almost enthusiastically now, just as he used to reply to reporters' questions in the past. He no longer saw a reason to bang on the wooden table. A meeting with old fans should take place in a congenial atmosphere. He leaned back. Relaxed. Gave an occasional bright smile. When the question about touching the pathetic ice-cream server inappropriately was asked again, he allowed himself to reply jokingly, "Yeah, right, I'm completely into pimply-faced sixteen-year-old girls." That was enough for the gray-haired detective. His partner asked a few more questions, and the suspect replied with the same sarcasm. But sarcasm is a dangerous ally, much like the perfumed notepaper young girls buy: after a while the fragrance evaporates and only the paper remains. And in truth, in only a few hours the sarcasm had evaporated and only the confession remained.

In the first-floor interrogation room sat Nofar Shalev, growing increasingly bewildered. In the second-floor interrogation room sat Avishai Milner, spinning the web in which he would entrap himself, like a spider that has lost its mind. Standing outside the police station was the deaf-mute from the square, trying to decide whether to go inside. He especially liked these pre-holiday days because, during the rest of the year, he had to work very hard to make a living. He didn't play a musical instrument as well as the Russian woman at the mall entrance, and he didn't have white hair to help him as did his colleague from the bustling street. White hair reminds hurrying people of their aging relatives. People in a hurry who think of their grandfather grow sad, and since they don't like to be sad, they buy deliverance with a coin. With his black hair, the deaf-mute never reminded anyone of their grandfather, which is why he barely eked out a living.

When the deaf-mute had first arrived in the square, he was afraid he would be found out. He thought it would be very unpleasant if someone discovered he wasn't a deaf-mute. He thought, What if someone asks me how to get somewhere and I answer by mistake, or someone just says hello to me? But after a while he noticed that no one asked him how to get somewhere, and of course no one ever just said hello, so the deaf-mute gradually forgot how to speak. That frightened him so much that he decided he had to begin speaking again. In many ways it was like riding a bike again after twenty years, and though everyone always says that you never forget how to ride a bike, anyone who has tried knows that your body might have a vague memory of the bike, but it remembers the fear of falling much more clearly. In the end, he succeeded. When a man hurrying by handed him a coin, the deaf-mute opened his mouth and said thank you. But the man was in so much of a rush that he didn't hear the words, and the deaf-mute remained standing there with the coin and the words all that evening. And so the deaf-mute from the square became mute once again. This time for real.

Now, standing in front of the police station, the deaf-mute recalled what he had seen in the alley. How surprised he had been when, pissing contentedly in a far corner of the yard, he was interrupted by the sounds of running and sobbing. A young girl in a blue dress was heading straight toward him, but, blinded by tears, she didn't notice him urinating in the bushes. A moment later a furious-looking man arrived. Then everything happened with dizzying speed. The alley filled with a huge crowd of people. The man spewed the venom he spewed, the girl said what she said, and then everyone went off to the police station. No one noticed the sole witness. But the deaf-mute knew: the traffic cops had come for nothing. The pretty girl soldier and her lover, the officer, had come for nothing. Because the only thing that had happened in the alley was an inconsequential act of cruelty, death on a small scale—one person stepping on another.

Now the deaf-mute sat down on the wooden bench on the street corner and remembered the tortured face of the young girl. Then he thought of the scandal and laughed to himself. No one else knew but him. And if, until that moment, he had been forced into being a deaf–mute, silent simply because no one bothered to listen to him, now he became mute by choice, his mouth shut in defiance. Bats hovered above him in the branches of the ficus tree like ministering angels. He was filled with a rare sense of joy. If he wished to, he would speak. If he wished to, he would remain silent. The young girl's life was in his hands, and she didn't even know it.

5

NIGHT FLOWED ONTO the city in a large wave of darkness and washed the streets, submerging the city dwellers on its way. First it closed the eyes of the children. Then it put their parents to sleep. In the bars, the last of the revelers clung to the shoals for several more hours before they too dropped off. One by one, eyelids fell, until there remained only the glow of the streetlights' constant stare and the red eyes of the all-night kiosk owners. The city slept like a large woman sprawled on her back, the darkness kind to her, concealing her wrinkles. A large, old city is like a large, old woman—easy to love in the dark, difficult in the light. Later the night ebbed, darkness retreated slowly, and the noise of garbage trucks thundered through the streets. Quiet and agile, the workers leaped down to collect the bins—like egrets on a hippopotamus's back, they foraged through the city's folds of fat to clean it.

In those early-morning hours, Nofar was still asleep in her bed. And truth be told, she slept quite soundly. On those bleak summer nights, the black TV screen had been a constant, loyal companion, lessening her loneliness with police investigations of rapes in San Francisco, murders in New York, and elaborate combinations of both—rape followed by murder, murder followed by rape, mostly in Chicago. In her teenage years, TV was for her what her teddy bear had been in her childhood—a shield against the terror of the night, a fortification against loneliness. But that night she did not reach for the remote.

What was the point of watching other people's stories when she finally had a story of her own? It was that sense of fullness, the clear knowledge that her life was no less interesting than the lives of the characters in the box, that enabled her to sleep so peacefully.

When the next day finally arrived, the ice-cream server opened her eyes and saw that everything was as it had been. The sun still rose in the east. Her sister was still prettier than she was. But the story appeared on the fourth page of the newspaper, with a prominent reference to it on the front page in letters as red as raspberry sorbet. "Famous singer suspected of attempted rape of minor." From behind her cornflakes her mother shot her a worried look. Late the previous night Ronit had been summoned to the station and informed of what had happened. She had cried a little, hugged a lot, demanded justice. When Ronit was a child, a neighbor had thrust his hand under her skirt, and to this day she remembered the paralysis that had seized her body. The previous night she had asked Ami to drive home from the police station so she could sit beside Nofar in the back seat. She held her daughter's hand the entire time, something Ronit hadn't done since Nofar was a child. The next morning, she looked searchingly at her—had the trauma left scars? But Nofar ate more heartily than usual and said that she had to go to work.

"Are you sure? After the . . ."

"Yes," Nofar replied, "I'm sure."

On her way to the bus stop, the bus passed her. And she, instead of accepting her fate submissively and waiting patiently for another forty minutes, raised her arm in a gesture of entreaty. There are people who can stop the entire world with the wave of a hand. Maya, for example. If her younger sister were to order the earth to stop spinning in its orbit, it would undoubtedly obey. And now, to Nofar's great surprise, the driver stopped for her thirty feet from the bus stop. To her ears, the rattle of the motor had the catchiest beat she had ever heard. Any moment now the passengers might stand up from their threadbare seats and start dancing. With the greatest of ease, the bearded ultra-Orthodox man and the eighty-year-old woman would move to the rhythm, the soldier and the girl reading Psalms would begin to boogie. Even if she got tired momentarily from standing throughout the long ride, a quick glance at the local paper was enough to reenergize her. Because her story was printed on the fourth page. Just one look at it filled her with secret pride. She could barely stop herself from ripping the paper out of someone's hands, leaping onto a seat, and shouting, "Me! That's me!"

It was finally time to ring the bell, and she stepped off the bus to the accompaniment of a cheery ding-dong. On her way to the ice-cream parlor she passed two kiosks and one supermarket, and from all of them the newspaper winked at her like an old friend. What a beautiful day it was. How beautiful the people were, and the billboards and the laundry that waved like flags from apartment balconies.

But how dirty the ice-cream parlor was. She had left it hastily the previous evening, barely remembering to lock the cash register before everyone moved on to the police station. Now she looked at the sticky plastic spoons left on the counter. The floor was decorated with a mosaic of used napkins. The air conditioner had been on all night and a small lake had formed on the floor under it. There were also coffee cups to wash and plates to clear away, empty ice-cream containers to refill and a counter to be polished yet again. She decided to empty the garbage first. A bag in each hand, she silently intoned her usual prayer—please don't let that sticky liquid drip on me—in vain. All it took was a few drops touching her flesh for her to revert to her previous self: a clumsy, pimply-faced girl. A foul-smelling liquid dripped from the bag onto her ankles and trickled into her shoes, where it would remain for the full eight hours she stood, sweating and repeating the same question, "And what can I get for you?"

How lovely it is to see a young girl blossom. How sad it is to see her wither. And just as Nofar was beginning to wonder if she had bloomed the night before only to wither this morning, the TV arts reporter walked into the ice-cream parlor and asked for one scoop of chocolate.

"Cup or cone?"

Cone. Of course a cone. A cone you can eat, but a cup serves no function the minute you finish the ice cream. The arts reporter didn't like things that had no function. She was just as purposeful about her eating as she was about her work and her sex life. Efficient, focused striving for maximum fulfilment had made her a valued professional in her field and a much-desired partner in bed. As she ate, she appraised the girl. The story did not seem credible to her. She had known Avishai Milner from his Avi-shai! Mil-ner! days. She had known him inside and out, and mainly from above. She preferred to have sex with men she didn't consider important so she wouldn't have to meet their eyes when she came. The arts reporter studied the girl, trying to decide whether her source had been right to send her to this ice-cream parlor, of all places. She looked at the plain girl behind the counter and wondered if there was anything about her that could arouse desire. She had almost decided that there wasn't when the door opened again and the red-haired saleswoman and the delicate cashier came in. They went over to the girl, who was drowning in her ordinariness, and said, "We came to see if you're all right."

And here was that change again, as rapid as a sunrise. One moment darkness, the next, light. As crunchy as an ice-cream cone on the tongue. One moment Nofar was standing there feeling the wetness of the garbage bag on her leg, and the next she was telling her new acquaintances—she remembered them from the alley yesterday—everything she had said at the police station. And as she spoke—how strange—her eyes became bluer. Her lips grew fuller. Her shoulders, usually stooped, suddenly spread like wings. And her breasts, usually concealed by those drooping shoulders, now appeared quite attractive. In fact, her figure was lovely. Her movements were graceful. So it is: the truth becomes some people, and others are made beautiful by falsity. Water plants need the heat of summer in order to blossom. And Nofar Shalev needed the excitement of the story to redden her cheeks. The moment they reddened, there could no longer be any doubt: the arts reporter swallowed the last bite of her cone, all set to land herself an exclusive interview.

Nevertheless, there was one other person who knew. Standing shyly near the glass door was Lavi Maimon from the fourth floor. He stared intently at the ice-cream server as she told her story, noticed how her skin glowed from the pleasure of being looked at, observed the dark flame in the depths of her eyes, and knew. He recognized that flame from his own home, saw it ignite whenever his mother flew off to her Pilates lesson. His father sat on the couch in front of the TV news, explaining to the commander in chief of the army and the government ministers exactly what they should do. His mother took the dishes to the kitchen, poured peanuts into a bowl, planted a quick kiss on the back of his unmoving head, and left. His father barely noticed her. He just wanted to watch in peace, one hand in the bowl of peanuts, the other on his testicles. But from his perch on the windowsill, Lavi saw the change that came over his mother from the moment she left the building. Her face was suddenly different. And her gait. Though she had always been beautiful, she was suddenly a thousand times more so. Her secret life pulsed within her like another heart. The hidden woman who lived inside his mother was walking along the street, and one look was enough for Lavi Maimon to know that it wasn't a Pilates class she was headed for.

At first, he had thought it was love that made her beautiful. But that love turned out to be a multitude of small loves. A calculated foray into his mother's mobile phone revealed months-long affairs, as well as one-night stands, and Lavi gradually realized that it wasn't a specific person who was making his mother's skin glow. It wasn't love that was blazing on her cheeks, but rather the intoxicating freedom she took for herself when she turned her back on his father and went out into the street. Now Lavi looked at the ice-cream server and recognized the same fire—the joy of knowing what others didn't.

Lavi didn't suspect or assume that the girl wasn't speaking the truth—he simply knew it. There are some things that people inherit from their parents. Lavi had his mother's eyes. Nofar's forehead came from her father. But in addition to those physical features, something else is passed down from one generation to another. Not the traits that parents transmit to their children, but rather a reaction to them: obsessive neatness in someone who grows up in a messy home. Compulsive cheerfulness in a person whose mother is always sad. A rare ability to sniff out untruths in someone whose mother constantly lies. That too is something parents pass on to their children.

After his discovery, Lavi chewed his mother's rice and swallowed the word *liar*. She asked how his day at school was, and in his mind he replied *whore*. After his discovery, he always thought she was hiding something behind her glance. Even when she said the most mundane things, such as "Come help me with the shopping," he examined her words carefully, like a detective in a film who checks his car for booby traps before turning the key in the ignition. And his perception of his father changed as well. Lavi had always thought his father was 5'9", though in reality he was barely 5'6". (No one knew that, neither his soldiers nor his employees, and it was difficult to see, even in photos, that the most powerful man in the picture was also the shortest.) Now Lavi suddenly looked at his father and saw his actual size.

He never tired of watching his mother lie to his father. It was like scratching an insect bite. He was fascinated by that contrast between the open expression and the secret it concealed—the lips that sang him lullabies spoke lies with the same simplicity. Because ever since his discovery, every sentence his mother uttered was like an overstuffed wallet inviting theft. Concealed beneath every ordinary sentence flowing on the surface of the conversation was another that dwelled below, in the darkness. How could the lieutenant colonel, that seasoned tactician, be such an idiot? Because the worst part of it all was that, since Lavi's discovery, he could no longer hate him as he had before nor love him as he had before.

That was why Lavi could recognize the ice-cream server's lies. He saw the gap between what she said and what had really happened. As soon as the others left, and the two of them were alone in the ice-cream parlor, he said to her, "I know you're lying." He thought she would cry, that she would be frightened. But she remained calm, a serene expression on her face, and instead of saying all the things she could possibly have said, she said only, "So what do you want?"

At that moment, he knew for certain that he was right. What had been only a feeling was now validated.

"I want you to talk about me during a TV interview. Say my name."

"What's your name?"

"Lavi Maimon. When they ask you how you had the courage to scream, tell them that your buddy, Lavi Maimon, taught you self-defense."

He spoke quickly, in a whisper, and when he said the words "your buddy" he lowered his voice even more, as if the phrase had dropped into a pit as he spoke it and he could barely pull it out. Nofar gave his words serious consideration. After all, she had never had a buddy before. Finally, she looked at the boy, saw that he was very skinny, that his curly hair and his eyes were black, and said, "My friend. I'll say that my friend taught me self-defense."

And so, even before the first hour of her shift had passed, Nofar Shalev had a friend.

6

THE NEXT SEVERAL hours passed quickly. The ice-cream parlor filled up with customers, some of them lovers of sweet things, most of them lovers of scandal, because although traffic in the city moved along sluggishly, the rumors in it moved along quite speedily. In consideration of the girl's age and the nature of the offense, the newspapers did not reveal her name, but everyone knew. Everyone denounced the offender. Everyone admired her courage. And wherever courage is admired, tips are given. By noon, the always empty glass left on the counter for tips was packed with coins. Nofar emptied it three times and it was refilled each time, as if it were an oil well that had finally found the place where the earth spills its bounty. At four o'clock, when the stony-faced boy arrived to take over for her, Nofar piled up the coins twice to make sure she hadn't made a mistake, and finally decided that she did indeed have 255 shekels in tips. Astounded by her good luck, she headed for the small square and went into one of the designer boutiques.

The saleswoman said, "What can I show you today?" but was in fact saying, "There's nothing here for you." It was clear from her tone, from the way she looked at the girl as soon as she entered. The boutique was petite and chic, while the girl was large and common. Well, not actually large, but definitely not slender. Wearing tights that did nothing to flatter her thighs, and a shirt that was disgustingly ordinary. But Nofar, instead of reverting to her usual mousy self, faced the urban cat with her manicured nails and pulled her by the tail.

"I need something for a TV interview tonight."

The words were spoken simply and confidently. Like *abracadabra*. Like *open sesame*. And in truth, after the saleswoman's phone call to the producer of the program, the shop magically opened for Nofar. The new collection was brought out from the storeroom. The head designer was summoned from the boutique in the southern part of the city. Try this one on, too, maybe in blue, have you already thought about shoes, shall we add a belt? And the designer immediately reached out to the mannequin in the window, removed the belt from its waist, and handed it to the stunned Nofar.

When she finally stood in front of the mirror, she was a different girl. The designer had wrapped her in lavender chiffon, which brought out the blue of her eyes. The neckline dipped just enough to hint at the hidden secret of her curvaceous breasts. Suddenly, she carried herself aristocratically. But a quick glance at the price tag made her face fall. After a discount, 2,000 shekels. And she had only 255 shekels in her bag. She still remembered how the coins had jingled when the saleswoman lifted her school bag so it wouldn't block the dressing rooms. How could she strap her shabby backpack onto her chiffon-caressed shoulders? How would she be able to walk with it in the shoes she would buy from the shop next door? She entered the dressing room to take off the dress and the saleswoman hurried in after her.

"Shall I wrap it for you?" Nofar was about to say no, but the saleswoman picked up the dress, folded it quickly, and put it into a brightly colored bag. "Just don't forget to tell the producer to list our shop in the credits."

And there she was on the street again, holding the bag with

the dress in it and 255 shekels' worth of coins still in her backpack, because it had never occurred to anyone to take them
from her. Her head spinning, she walked to the bus stop. She
didn't have to wait even a minute—just as she reached the
stop, a bus pulled up in front of her and opened its doors. It
was painted orange, as if it were a huge pumpkin.

Among the guests waiting their turn in the TV studio was a
retired general. He hadn't been called to serve in the armed
forces for twenty years, but he was called to appear on TV
news shows whenever the situation at the northern border
flared up. Sitting two seats away in the waiting room, a pointy-
chinned doctor mentally reviewed the main points she would
be discussing. It's important to vaccinate at the beginning
of autumn. Flu is especially dangerous for children and the
elderly. Actually, she was less disturbed by the prospect of a flu
epidemic than the general was by mortar shells exploding on
the northern border. What preoccupied her was the question
of whether Michael Shuster would watch the show, and if he
did, would he recognize her, and if he did, would he regret
having left her so abruptly eight years earlier. The general
ran his hand over his beard, hoping that the defense minister
would happen to watch the program tonight, and if he didn't,
that at least one of his assistants would inform him of the
astute, methodical survey the retired general had provided,
what an astute, methodical man he was, and that it was truly
a shame—the minister would realize—that he hadn't made
him chief of staff when he'd still had the chance. Standing
beside the coffee table with its stacks of paper cups stood
the third interviewee, an actress who would be performing a
one-woman show at the National Theatre the next day. She
was wondering if the Filipina health aide would remember to

switch on the TV at the time she had requested and would turn her mother's chair to face the screen so that the broadcast might ignite a spark in the old woman's memory, or perhaps even cause her to grumble, "Why don't you find yourself a serious profession?" The actress had learned to miss even those rebukes.

Nofar Shalev and her mother, the Hebrew teacher Ronit Shalev, sat among those people, embarrassed and silent. On the taxi ride over, the mother reminded the daughter, "Speak properly. Don't swallow your words." Ronit Shalev, normally a kind woman who had unwittingly relinquished her control of language and allowed language to take control of her, corrected her daughter constantly. Those frequent corrections had caused Nofar to score the highest marks in the history of the school in her language final. They had also caused her to barely speak. By the time the girl stepped out of the taxi, all her self-confidence had been washed away, dissolved under the torrent of rules of grammar and enunciation.

The producer, wearing headphones, welcomed them at the door. Authoritative young Amazons of that sort terrified Nofar's mother, who unconsciously did what she always did when feeling demoralized and corrected her daughter's posture even more vigorously. "Straighten up. Your shoulders are stooped. Chin in. Neck elongated." She ran a hand over Nofar's hair, pushed a stray curl back behind her ear, adjusted her bra strap, wiped off an invisible smudge on the sleeve of her dress. And the girl, the same girl who only a few hours earlier had stopped a bus with a wave of her hand, shrank slightly with each of her mother's words until she almost disappeared. There is no way of knowing what might have happened if the makeup artist hadn't suddenly appeared—wide hips, orange hair, a mouth permanently inhabited by chewing gum—and whisked the girl off to her mirrored room.

In the makeup room, surrounded by face powders and creams, Nofar looked bitterly at her reflection and quickly averted her eyes. The makeup artist, a woman with a heart as big as her hips, didn't have to ask. She knew very well: for some people, sitting in front of a mirror expands their chest, and for others it acts on their body like a jellyfish sting. She especially liked those. "Look at the wonderful cheekbones you have. And such lips!" Nofar mumbled something about pimples. "Those little things? Who can see them?! Come on, I'll perform some magic." Since Nofar avoided looking at the mirror, she didn't see how, with two strokes of a brush, the makeup artist made the humiliating red spots disappear. Then, opening a drawer, she took out a lipstick as delicate in color as hidden coral and applied it to Nofar's lips. After taking a moment to decide between peach-colored and apple-pink blush, she finally decided that the fresh hue radiating from the girl's cheeks was sufficient.

"So," the makeup artist asked, "don't you want to see?" Nofar raised her eyes hesitantly, expecting to see herself—a stooped, pimply, generally inconsequential person. But the girl in the mirror looked back at her in surprise. The mascara accentuated her eyes. Her lips were as pink as candy. Her cheekbones, normally covered with thick clumps of curls, were now revealed in all their chiseled glory. And above all: the pimples. The makeup artist, a hard-working fairy god-mother, had covered everything. The girl's eyes welled with tears of gratitude. The makeup artist said in horror, "Don't cry or it'll all be smeared!" Nofar nodded obediently and stopped the tears between her lashes and eyelids.

Then everything happened quickly once again. The

producer burst into the room and pulled her by the hand. Her mother, grayish and pale, was waiting for her beside the studio door. During the few minutes Ronit spent alone, she had managed to come up with many additional bits of advice to give her daughter for the interview. But when she saw Nofar, her truly lovely face now exposed, she was filled with a rare sense of satisfaction that kept her silent. The producer opened the studio door and pushed Nofar inside. Breathe, the girl told herself as they plugged in her microphone and sat her in the chair, breathe. But her body didn't listen, or if it did, it didn't obey. Her limbs froze. Her tongue dried up. Only her armpits, traitors that they were, perspired non-stop, pouring out rivers of fear. She was sorry now that she had agreed to the arts reporter's request to be filmed without having her face blurred. Earlier, the reporter had praised her courage and hastened to inform the TV news producers about her. After obtaining signed permission forms from the mother as well, she had been allotted a large segment of the broadcast, because when the victim has a face, the story is stronger. But though the story might be stronger, Nofar was overcome by weakness. She shrank, yearning for a compassionate hand to lead her back to the four walls of her sheltered room. But the hand did not appear. Paralyzed with terror, she heard the reporter introduce the next story.

"Attempted rape in an alley in the heart of the city. The suspect in custody is none other than the famous singer Avishai Milner, who confessed during questioning. The courageous young girl who has accused him is here with us in the studio. Tell us what it was like."

Nofar was silent.

The journalist tried again. Patiently. "You reported for your shift and..." She offered this sentence to the girl as if she were handing a paddle to a drowning person. Nofar just had to grab hold of it, but, as if she had decided to go under, she didn't reply. Orders were given from the control room: one more try, and if it doesn't work, cut to commercials.

Nofar cleared her throat. Swallowed. Took a deep breath. Then began to speak. And the words, wonder of wonders, rolled off her tongue, round and perfect. Like pebbles. Like dinner rolls. She hadn't watched endless episodes of TV series for nothing. It turned out that she had learned many things from the small screen, even things she didn't know she knew: how to express herself in brief, clear sentences, interspersed with short, meaningful breaks wrapped in doleful glances. How to lead her listeners down a winding but clearly marked narrative path with high and low points. No less important than the words themselves, however, was the face of the girl speaking them. It must be acknowledged that the makeup artist had outdone herself, and not because she had made the girl extraordinarily beautiful. Striking beauty sometimes strikes too hard. But Nofar, with her average face, was endowed with precisely the requisite amount of charm. The skilled makeup artist, wise enough to know this, had made the girl remarkably sweet, stopping before the sweetness became cloying.

As Nofar answered the reporter's questions, an image of Shir passed through her mind. Is she watching me now? Does she miss me in spite of everything? She thought about all the Friday evenings she and Shir had sat together in front of the TV, talking about the programs to keep from talking about the fact that all their classmates went out on Friday evenings except for them. To her disappointment, she suddenly realized that Shir, Yotam, and the others weren't even home now, but at some movie, with everyone. There was always an "everyone." The interview would be over soon and she would go home. The makeup would come off and her pimples would be there as always.

This time, there was no makeup artist to block her tears. Slowly they filled her eyes, round and heavy, and the reporter, who was about to wind up the interview, decided to wait a bit. The audience at home was having dinner now, watching and eating. And there's nothing to help you digest food better than the tears of an attractive young girl. The first tear was already rolling down her cheek, and along with it rolled the thousands of tears of the viewing audience and the photogenic tears of the reporter. Nofar's tears made her eyes immeasurably bluer, a bottomless sea.

The reporter began to shift her glance from the girl's teary face to the camera. But Nofar suddenly panicked: in the excitement of the interview, she had completely forgotten the black-eyed boy. There was no way of knowing what upset her more, the fear that he would expose her or the knowledge of how disappointed he would be if the interview ended and he was left out. So she dared to interrupt the reporter at the exact moment she was about to speak again.

"I just . . . wanted to say . . ."

"Our time is up."

"But it's important. The person who saved me. The one who taught me to scream for help in emergencies: my friend Lavi Maimon." And to end the interview well, she added, "He's going to join an elite combat unit."

"Thank you, Nofar Shalev. You are a very brave girl. When we return: the flu epidemic and the tensions on the northern border."

The news broadcast sailed on and Nofar, having done her part, was tossed unceremoniously off the deck. The reporter, the cameras, the army of producers—they all glided on their way in calm waters. Only the kindhearted makeup artist came out to wave goodbye before Nofar and her mother stepped into the taxi. And that friendly wave finally brought it home to Nofar: it was truly over. The interview had ended and she was being sent home to the wasteland of her life. The driver pulled away and Nofar looked through the window, committing every single detail of the place to memory, until the studio disappeared from sight.

7

IT WAS LATE when they arrived home from the studio. Maya stood in the dark hallway, her face illuminated by the dim light coming from the bathroom, the rest of her body concealed by shadow. "I waited for you." She went over to Nofar and wrapped her slender, tanned arms around her body. "You were wonderful." Despite the year that separated them, they were exactly the same height. "But what did they do to your face? You look completely different!" Even before their mother could protest that it was the middle of the night, they had already closed themselves in the bathroom to better examine the makeup artist's handiwork in the mirror. Standing next to each other was so pleasant—why hadn't they done it even once that entire summer vacation? "You look fantastic," Maya said, moving her face closer to Nofar's to see better, "and you spoke so well. I was really proud of you, proud you're my sister."

Nofar smiled. So did Maya. She had a gorgeous smile. Even when she was a very young child, people said she should appear in commercials—anyone would easily buy diapers or laundry detergent from her, even an expensive air conditioner in three installments. She didn't sell any of those things, which made them love her that much more. Even before she knew how to talk, she felt that love, which was so natural to her that it never occurred to her that it might end. It was like the sun rising, like night falling, the way of the world, and since she expected it with such certainty, people's love kept coming the way sunrise and nightfall keep coming, because when someone expects something, disappointing them is unthinkable.

When Nofar had left for the studio, Maya sat down in front of the TV and waited. Every few minutes the phone buzzed with another offer to go out, but she rejected all of them. Her big sister would appear on the news soon and she wanted to see it. She waited patiently while the newscasters talked about a crisis in the coalition and she yawned mildly at the protests of the opposition, and when Nofar's face finally appeared on the screen, she applauded enthusiastically with the generosity of a victor. But then Nofar was struck dumb, and her little sister's heart shrank. Nofar sat paralyzed in the studio and Maya sat paralyzed on the couch, the mortification she felt for her older sister like an actual physical pain. As the seconds of Nofar's paralysis ticked by, the pressure in Maya's chest grew unbearable. She had already covered her face with a pillow so she wouldn't have to look at her, when Nofar suddenly began to speak.

And how beautifully she spoke! When the interview was over, Maya hurried to send her recording of it to everyone she could. There was a slight bitterness on the tip of her tongue that she was only barely aware of. It took a while until she suddenly felt that her breath was sour. The younger sister was not used to that taste on her tongue. Having no choice, she told the boy who loved her not to come by that night—she didn't feel well. Again and again, she inhaled the air she breathed into her palm—perhaps that revolting sourness had evaporated. But instead of evaporating, the smell only grew stronger as she continued to look at her sister's face radiating from the screen. When Nofar came home, they became immersed in conversation in the bathroom, and Maya no longer felt that strange taste on her tongue. She thought it had passed.

In the middle of the night, Lavi lay on his back on the fourth floor. He had already tried lying on his stomach. And on his side as well. To no avail. He hadn't been able to calm down since the interview was broadcast, six hours and forty-one minutes earlier. How beautiful she had been as she told her story. How her eyes had glowed when she mentioned his nonexistent enlistment in an elite combat unit. And those tears that had rolled down her cheeks—he'd wanted to stick out his tongue and gently lick them off. And that frightened him, because, like most boys his age, he watched porn all the time, but it was that first tear and his burning desire to catch it with his tongue that suddenly shamed him so much, that gave him away.

Over and over again, he recalled the previous day's events. A four-minute interview. A miniature eternity. Over and over again, he returned to that sweet moment when the girl interrupted the reporter's summary and mentioned his name. She hadn't forgotten him. She had done what he asked. And though he knew he hadn't given her a choice, he nonetheless trembled to the depths of his soul.

Nofar got out of bed at dawn. The furniture in her room was as she had left it, and for some reason it surprised her that the desk, the bed, the wardrobe hadn't changed places because of what had happened the night before. She kept going over it in her mind. Four minutes turned into four hours because Nofar contemplated every second from every possible angle, expanding the moments in her thoughts. The commotion in her head was so loud that she didn't hear the sounds coming from the next room, where Maya was mumbling in her sleep.

Walking out into the hallway, Nofar feared she might bump into someone from the family, as if meeting their eyes might kindle a feeling in her that had been extinguished until now. But when she reached the living room, she found it empty. Couches, a rug, a TV set. Everything in place. Everything normal. She looked at the clock. At least an hour until the others woke up. An entire hour's pleasure reliving the joys of last night. Because so it is, sitting alone in the seam between day and night: dreams are still stronger than regrets, yearning overcomes inhibition, until the sun rises to shame us and drive our desires back to their burrows.

But when she sat down on the couch, she suddenly felt a pair of eyes on her. Grandpa Elkana was looking at her from his portrait on the wall. Nofar averted her gaze and tried to reimmerse herself in the wonders of the interview. The hero of the War of Independence stared at her angrily. Nofar might have been crowned heroine of the day in the TV studio, but Grandpa Elkana knew what a genuine heroine was. It was not for nothing that his name appeared in the third paragraph on page 184 of her history textbook. Sitting before the penetrating eyes of that hero in the early-morning hours, Nofar felt more insignificant than a flea.

The family always talked about his ability to shoot armed infiltrators from the nearby village while riding a galloping horse. What they failed to mention was his great love for the earth—how much he loved to walk barefoot through the fields and feel the soft grass on his feet in winter, the crisp thorns in summer, the kiss of centipedes intoxicated by the perfume of spring. When he went to bed, he left one leg hanging off the mattress so he could leap up at any sound, but mainly to feel the sleeping earth. He even made love to his wife standing up so he wouldn't have to break contact with his true love for even a moment. Elkana had refused to wear shoes even to his wedding. It was only at his son's bris that he deviated from his habit because the rabbi, having learned from his experience under the wedding canopy, threatened not to perform the ceremony if Elkana came barefoot again. His wife begged him, shedding endless salty tears, and he, perhaps fearing that the saltiness would damage the crops, gave in for the first and last time.

At night, on horseback, he waited in ambush for infiltrators and shot them to death. In the morning he would go out into the fields with two hoes, so that when one grew tired of working, he could replace it with the other. As long as Elkana was faithful to the land, the land was faithful to Elkana. But all that ended after the stroke, the moment his wife sat him in a wheelchair, spread a checked blanket over his lap, and straightened his feet on the footrests. She knew quite well, stoop-backed Delilah that she was, what would happen when he raised his feet from the ground. If not for that, he might well have recovered. People like Elkana don't die of strokes. A wave washes them off a pier. Lightning blackens them in a field. And indeed, the moment Elkana's feet lost contact with the earth, his final decline was only a matter of days.

Elkana had only one request in his will, and it surprised all the people on the kibbutz. The only one who would not have been surprised had passed away a long time before. "I want to be buried as far away as possible from Dvorkin."

In the days preceding the War of Independence, Eliyahu Dvorkin had been Elkana's closest friend. Elkana wept on Dvorkin's shoulder when, on a hot summer's day, his favorite field went up in flames, and it was Elkana's fist that freed the foal stuck in the womb of Dvorkin's mare. And the famous offensive in that war, the one that had earned Elkana the line on page 184 of the high school textbook—that too they carried out together, Elkana leading the forces and Dvorkin his second in command. But although they captured the fortress together, they withdrew from it separately. Dvorkin was the only person who knew that, surrounded by the roar of exploding shells, Elkana had shouted the order to retreat. The others didn't hear, and if they did, they didn't believe it. It was inconceivable that such a man could be frightened by the tumult of battle.

But there was no getting around it, he really had been frightened. The ground under his feet had been covered with a layer of pine needles so thick that he could barely feel the earth beneath it, and the sudden thought that this might be their last time together, separated by those damned pine needles, filled him with such terror that his mouth roared the word "Retreat!" After all, what difference did it make who won, or what the country would be called and what names would be given to the hills and valleys? Names don't make hills higher or valleys deeper, they have no effect on the direction of river currents. Dvorkin stood thirty feet away from Elkana, ready to pass his orders back to the troops. It's difficult to say that Elkana's cry of "Retreat" surprised him. For a long while he had suspected that his friend's love of the earth had become too literal. He turned back to the soldiers and gave the order, "Charge!"

The soldiers might not have followed him. He was a head and a half shorter than Elkana and lacked his charisma. But when Dvorkin gave the order, they all thought he was echoing Elkana's roar, and that was enough to get them racing forward. In their mad dash the soldiers carried their commander, frightened and trembling, along with them. It was only when the last of the enemy soldiers had fled that his heart began to beat normally. This did not appear on page 184—Nofar knew nothing about it—but historical accuracy requires mention of the fact that Grandpa Elkana did not receive the cut that graced his hand in the heat of the charge, but during an attempt to flee that was foiled by his second in command.

Elkana did not want to be a hero. He refused to tell the story of the battle. But the prime minister himself, all 5'3" of him, came to visit and reprimanded him for lowering morale. "We're not asking you if you want to be a hero, we're telling you that you are," he said. He added, "Just imagine if everyone here decided on his own what he wants or doesn't want to be." After all, not every lie is bad—some lies build countries. The first busload of visitors arrived that weekend, and Elkana was asked to tell them what happened at the fortress. And so it continued: tours arrived on the weekends, and during the week Elkana worked in the fields. Only at night did he hear the never-ending whisper, sharp and clear, cutting across the valley, sailing along the earth, that emerged from Dvorkin's house at the other end of the kibbutz: *Liiiiiiiii-aaaaaaaar.*

Now, at dawn in the living room, Nofar stood in embarrassment before the picture of Grandpa Elkana. The first rays of the sun danced on the glass frame, adding even greater majesty to the old man's beard. His sharp, dark eyes examined her silently, and there was no way of knowing whether the girl trembled because of them or because of the morning chill. As she left the living room to make herself a cup of tea in the kitchen, she thought for a moment that she heard a muted whisper: *Liiiiiiiii-aaaaaaaar.*

Guilt, when it comes to visit, can choose from any number of routes. It can suddenly appear from behind and sink its talons into your back. It can charge you head-on. But Nofar's guilt, like a Persian cat, rubbed her legs fleetingly, sat for a brief moment on her lap, then moved onward. It had no desire to stay longer than that. And so the girl spent twenty whole minutes thinking truly tormenting thoughts. She was about to call the detective with the delicate fingers and confess when, all at once, she stopped herself. She didn't owe that man with that filthy mouth of his anything at all.

8

LAVI MAIMON LOOKED at the first rays of the sun
filtering through the shutters and didn't move. He was utterly
exhausted. His heart had pounded furiously all night, not letting up even at dawn, as if a new branch of a twenty-four-hour
supermarket had opened in its chambers. He lay in his bed and
listened to his heart hammering until his head spun. Such loud
drums, such speed might be popular with the city's partygoers,
but they were more than a boy like him could bear. Someone
else with such a pounding heart might have wanted to dance.
Lavi wanted to die. Because he didn't understand that the pain
he was experiencing was nothing more than pleasure.

He heard the rustling of a newspaper on the other side of
the door. His father was sitting in the living room. Lieutenant
Colonel in the Reserves Arieh Maimon was an early riser.
Even on Saturdays, he jumped out of bed at exactly 0600
hours. The rest of the week it was his habit to ambush the
newspaper-delivery boys and scare the life out of them. He
listened surreptitiously at the front door, and after he heard
the footfall of the poor delivery boy on the steps, he waited
for the precise moment he tossed the paper on the mat—and
flung open the door. Arieh Maimon was very fond of the
element of surprise. During his military service, there was
nothing he liked more than to hide in the bushes behind
a hapless corporal napping at his isolated post, who would
wake up only to find his testicles being squeezed by none

other than the commander himself. After his discharge, the lieutenant colonel missed that sneaking around at night. He had tried twice to slip unnoticed into the conference room of the company he owned, but it wasn't the same.

Unlike his father, Lavi woke up late. He'd never had anything in his life worth getting up early for. His father didn't like that late rising, but there were so many things he didn't like about his son that Lavi saw no special reason to sacrifice his morning sleep. Until several years ago, he had tried, set his alarm clock to wake him early so he could say goodbye to his father before he left for work. But they passed those early-morning moments in silence. Wordless, embarrassing moments when they drank—Arieh Maimon his coffee, Lavi Maimon his chocolate milk—then parted with a nod. When the boy became a teenager, he stopped getting up early to be with his father. His father noticed this sadly, but didn't know what to say. It was easier to charge into the depths of enemy territory than to ask his only son why he no longer woke up early to be with his father. Arieh Maimon knew the map of Lebanon very well, but the hidden paths between the living room and the boy's room, the wadis between the hallway and the kitchen—those he wandered helplessly.

The father ate his breakfast bent over the op-ed pages. Then he moved on to the international weather forecast. Arieh Maimon was not someone who vacationed abroad. He was too occupied with his business. Perhaps that was why he loved the international forecast so much: all the continents were squeezed onto a small newspaper page, and one glance was enough to know that it was snowing on the Eiffel Tower now, and that the people walking on the streets of Tokyo were dripping with sweat. The ritual ended at 0730 in the morning. Arieh Maimon folded the newspaper with precision, the same precision he demanded of his soldiers when folding their blankets for inspection. He showered, shaved, kissed his wife's cheek on precisely the same spot every morning, and went out. The walls breathed a sigh of relief and stood at ease. His wife also seemed relieved. And Lavi stayed in bed a while longer because he hoped that maybe, miraculously, he would manage to fall back asleep. In the end he gave up, dressed, and came out of his room. His mother looked up from her cell phone and asked where he was going.

"To the ice-cream parlor."

"First thing in the morning? That's not healthy!"

While his mother changed lovers with impressive frequency, she was totally faithful to her balanced diet. Twelve years earlier, a popular dietician had devised a nutritional plan for her, and she had not deviated from it since, not even at moments of crisis. She was convinced that there was nothing like wheatgrass juice to give people the strength to face their day. She said that to her husband and her son at every opportunity, but they stayed with their respective coffee and chocolate milk, and she, through some sort of woman's intuition, understood that their united front against her was the only place they could bond, and let them tease her about her juices to their hearts' content. Now she mumbled something about sugar and empty calories, but Lavi shrugged and said he was going anyway.

He was overjoyed to see the girl behind the counter. She was wearing a pretty green blouse, and her breasts moved shyly as she bent to pick up a paper napkin left on the floor. If only he knew the torment she had endured that morning until she found that shirt. She had tossed the entire contents of her wardrobe onto her bed, a rainbow of cotton and tricot. Pink accentuated her pimples. She'd worn blue to work the day before, purple to the interview. The yellow one made her look pale. The white one was transparent. If she didn't make up her mind soon, she'd miss the bus, but she still couldn't decide. Finally she remembered Maya's green blouse. The one she had never dared to try on. The neckline had always looked too low to her. The style too unique. It was the sort of blouse that cried out to people on the street, "Look at me! Aren't I stunning?" Yes, it was stunning, and though a stunning blouse needed a stunning girl to wear it, that morning Nofar summoned the courage to ask her sister for it.

She thought about him all the way to the city, and never stopped to wonder why all the songs blaring out of the loud-speaker on the bus sounded so wonderful. Even the chatter between songs, which usually bored her, sounded remark-ably musical that morning. When the bus finally reached its destination, she hopped off, strode across the street, and took her place behind the counter. During the entire two hours that she waited for him to come, the passersby outside were quite beautiful, the songs coming from the loudspeaker were quite good, and her chores were quite effortless. If someone had told Lavi that he had the power to do such great things—make passersby beautiful, improve the quality of songs, and turn floor-washing into a pleasant pastime—he would not have believed it. Just as Nofar would have burst out laughing if someone had told her she had the power to keep a boy awake at night. But it was precisely that shyness of theirs, that inability to imagine how much they affected each other, that made the highly anticipated encounter such a fiasco. Nofar looked away from a customer and saw Lavi, and instead of saying "I thought about you all night," or at least "Hi" or "How are you?" she found herself reciting, in her usual tone, "And what can I get for you?"

The roaring lion that had leaped down the stairs earlier could not utter a sound now. The ice-cream server, who had spoken so well in front of the cameras, looked at the black eyes of the boy standing in front of her and was rendered totally speechless. Like the time she had been walking down the main street and suddenly discovered that her wallet had been stolen, except that now it was her words that had been taken, leaving her not a single sentence to utter. Just as she had looked at the shop windows then, she looked now at all the things she could have said to him, had she been capable of speaking.

Lavi Maimon could not bring himself to ask Nofar Shalev to be his girlfriend. She might say no. But a person lacking the courage to ask might very well discover that he has the courage to demand. The weakness expressed in a request is well hidden in a demand: when you ask someone for something, you are putting yourself in their hands, but when you demand something from them, you are crushing them in your own hands. Lavi, realizing he was unable to ask the girl for what he truly wanted, walked straight up to the counter and demanded that she meet him in the alley in exactly one hour.

"Or else I'll tell all."

Fifty-nine minutes began to tick by. Nofar looked at the clock and blushed. She had no idea what the boy would ask her for there, behind the garbage bins, in the wasteland between the fuel tanks and the bathroom shed. The possibilities filled her head. He could demand money. Or a yearly supply of ice cream under the counter. He could...her eyes widened in terror—he could demand *her!* She had already seen a similar case in one of her TV series. That had ended in murder, she didn't remember exactly whose, either the man doing the blackmailing or the woman being blackmailed. Anyway, it turned out later that the coffin was empty and the murdered man—or maybe the murdered woman—was still alive. Lavi Maimon wasn't the least bit like the people in the series, but if he'd been brave enough to walk into the ice-cream parlor and blackmail her in the light of day, there was no telling what else he was capable of doing. That "no telling" stirred Nofar's imagination, blurred her vision. Customers came and went, and she served them, but her mind was somewhere else, in a thousand different places. Her thoughts, like pizza-delivery boys on their motorbikes, reached the most remote streets.

At 11:30 she left the counter and the cash register for a moment and hurried to the shop next door for a quick look in the mirror. The red-haired saleswoman was delighted to see her. The sales clerk with the soft eyes cried, "We saw you on TV!" and told Nofar she had nothing stuck between her teeth and complimented her on her ponytail. She had to be back in the ice-cream parlor in a few seconds—it was almost 11:45.

Her knees were trembling and her throat dry, as they had been in the studio yesterday, only a hundred times worse. What if he demanded that she kiss him? What if he demanded that she fondle him? The poor girl was on the verge of tears, her breathing labored, and the customers who knew her story whispered to each other: after all she's been through, it's only natural for her to be upset. She tried to remember what the girls in her class said when they gossiped in the bathroom. Last year she'd heard one of them complain about the salty taste as her girlfriends giggled. If that was true, she had to be prepared for the saltiness. To be on the safe side, she took a bottle of Coke out of the drinks fridge. On second thought she shoved a moist cleaning rag into her pants pocket. The girls had said it was sticky, and she had quite a bit of experience with sticky things—after all, she'd spent the summer in the ice-cream parlor. But the saltiness worried her. She was afraid she wouldn't like the taste. She was afraid he'd be insulted. But more than anything, she was afraid he would discover her secret, would realize that this was her first time tasting, touching, living beyond the boundaries of her own body.

She spent the minutes fearing and dreading, and undoubtedly, if time were a more merciful master, it would have delayed its movement a bit. But the clock is an old bureaucrat, a grumpy clerk unwilling to deviate in the slightest from its routine—and so it happened that 12:00 arrived exactly at 12:00. Not a moment later.

On the fourth floor, Lavi sat on the windowsill, wanting to die. If he didn't jump then, it was only because he felt bad for the girl, who would have to watch his pathetic body slam onto the ground. He had no need to look at his watch. He knew that 12:00 had already come and gone. The second hand was beating in his heart. He should have gone down to the alley a while ago but he couldn't move. For a brief time after he left the ice-cream parlor he tasted the pleasure of the meeting in his mind, like a child licking an ice-cream cone. But before ten minutes had passed, his limbs began to tremble with anxiety, as if the child had been forced to eat an entire carton of ice cream—there is a limit to the amount of sugar a body can digest. Lavi's mother looked at his face and said, "I told you not to eat ice cream in the morning." What could he tell her? That his tongue was choking him, not because of what it had tasted, but because of what it still might taste? Not knowing what to say, he was silent, and his mother was about to suggest making him a glass of wheatgrass juice when he turned his back on her and ran down the stairs.

Nofar stood in the alley and bit her nails, a disgusting old habit that, unsurprisingly, had reappeared now. She stood there waiting for five full minutes. She had already sniffed her armpits. Thank God, her deodorant was still doing its job. She undid her ponytail. Redid it again. Undid it again. She certainly would have tied and untied her hair a dozen more times if she hadn't suddenly heard the sound of footsteps behind her. It was Lavi Maimon, almost wetting his pants, his fear so great that it drove away all desire. How sad that he was unable to ask simply if she was willing. Instead, he was forced to demand, to grab the girl by the shoulders and kiss her.

A lively fish, wet and fluttering, in her mouth, sailing along her gums, its fins brushing against her teeth, paddling up and down and in circles, a pink, sweet-water fish, tickling the inside of Nofar's mouth. So this is what it's like to kiss, so different from what she had imagined, because over the years she had seen thousands of kisses on the TV screen. But no one learns how to swim through a correspondence course, and no one can experience a kiss taking place on a screen. Only now, with the boy's tongue in her mouth, with her tongue in his mouth, did she learn how strange it is, how wet it is. Perhaps that is the magic of such a moment: that throughout it they think about nothing else. Not about kisses they've seen on TV, not about their classmates' groping. Other people's lives—better, worthier, more exciting lives—no longer pre-occupy them. Above them, on the second floor, a woman was hanging laundry. The socks dripped, and Nofar, her eyes closed, could almost believe it was raining. Beside the garbage bins, the pair of alley cats watched the drawn-out kiss in boredom. In the time it was taking, they could have finished copulating at least once.

When Nofar returned to the ice-cream parlor, it was buzzing with waiting customers. Most of them nodded patiently. Some who didn't make the connection between the girl behind the counter and the subject of the latest media frenzy burst into loud complaint. Nofar apologized distractedly. She scooped coffee-cardamom ice cream into the cone of a customer who had asked for chocolate mint. She gave a hundred shekels in change to someone who had handed her a fifty-shekel note. Six hours later she left the ice-cream parlor and stood at the bus stop. Two buses passed her by before she remembered to board one. And if her mother hadn't said anything at dinner, she might have forgotten that tomorrow was the first day of her last year of school.

9

THE FIRST DAY of her last year of school arrived. For the entire vacation, Nofar had feared this day. In previous years she had told herself that if nothing happened this school year, it would definitely happen next year: next year she would have a boyfriend. Next year she would skip classes to be with a carefree, irresponsible crew of friends. But now there would be no "next year" at school. During the long summer-vacation nights she had lain on her bed, watching teenage dramas. She saw lives full to the bursting point, sweet nectar dripping from the girls' laughter and the boys leaning over them to lick it up. The boys who walked in her school corridors weren't as handsome as those on the screen, but they too—she had no doubt—lived in the hidden world whose doors were locked to her. If she didn't find the key this last year of school, she would never enter it.

On the first day of her last school year Nofar arrived at school at five minutes to eight. Groups of boys were gathered in the front courtyard. She wanted to just walk over to one of them. That's what Maya always did. That's what Shir finally managed to do. But she was neither Maya nor Shir, so she leaned on the fence and buried herself in her phone, as if it were the most important thing in the world.

"Are you okay?"

Maya stopped beside her, her school bag over her shoulder. Only an hour ago they had tried on clothes together, but as usual, when they reached school, Maya was surrounded by her girlfriends and Nofar walked the last few feet of the pedestrian crossing alone. Now Maya had come back to stand next to her, and Nofar nodded quickly, yes she was fine, and she was somewhat surprised when Maya leaned over and gave her a long hug, the longest she had ever given her in or around school. A moment later Maya turned around and went inside, while Nofar remained standing in the yard. Again, she focused intently on her phone.

From the corner of her eye, she saw Michal and Liron arriving together. Instinctively, she recoiled until her back was pressed against the fence. Right before vacation began, during their last gym class, they had both made fun of how she looked in tights. Their voices dripping with venomous sweetness, a praline with a sharp knife inside it, they said, "Poor thing. You need to work on your thighs." What they hadn't said out loud, they whispered. Though she hadn't heard, she shriveled with humiliation, for that is the nature of whispers—it's not the content that matters, but the choice to lower voices. When the whispers during gym class became too painful, Nofar mumbled an excuse and escaped to the bathroom, where she sat on the toilet, hands over her ears, curled up like those dust balls the cleaner sweeps up at the end of the day.

A teenage girl who runs off to the farthest stall—what does she want? Not to be seen. An injured animal alone, hidden. No one there to smell the blood. But at the same time, a wish for the opposite burns inside her: for someone to comfort her. After all, the bathroom is the true heart of a school. That's where the truants hide to wait for the best time to slip away, listening intently for the sound of teachers entering classrooms. Where teenage girls rid themselves of extra calories straight into the toilet. Where Mayan Speiser went down on Amitai Zabari one evening at the end of an extended school day, and where Inbar Shaked didn't go down on Tamir Cochavi, even if the creep said she did. But most of all, a bathroom stall is a refuge for tear-filled eyes. Where girls can wipe away their tears and think about what to say. It's where especially tortured souls can cut flesh with a box cutter, the sharp, clear pain kind enough to dull what preceded it. During the last gym class in eleventh grade, Nofar had sat in a locked bathroom stall and waited for Shir to come looking for her. At first she had hidden only so that someone would find her. The minutes passed. The bell rang. And Nofar sat on the lid of the toilet, praying that no one would come and see her crying, despairing when she realized that, in fact, no one was coming.

"Hey, I saw you on TV."

In the three days that had passed since Nofar saw her in the ice-cream parlor, Shir had managed to get a haircut. Her forehead was still covered with curls, but the back of her neck was exposed, and it was pretty. Now she ran her fingers along that nape, clearly not yet accustomed to it, and asked what it was like to be in front of the cameras. "Is it true that the presenters only wear their suit jackets for the camera, and all they have on under them are boxers?" Nofar said no. Shir looked disappointed. Nofar tried to think quickly of something else she could tell her so their conversation would continue, but with her new haircut Shir suddenly looked like someone else, as if the Shir that Nofar had known for ten years had simply vanished and been replaced by a new girl. Moran and Yotam were waiting for Shir at the far end of the schoolyard, and a moment later, when Nofar could find nothing to say, Shir said goodbye and joined them. The three of them nodded to Nofar and went inside, together, and Nofar thought—as always—about all the clever, interesting things she could have told them and didn't. Idiot. She had stood there like a golem. And her head was already filling up with malicious whispers, not only about what she hadn't said, but also about the way she stood and the way she dressed, about her big backside and her pimply face. But, fortunately, she suddenly heard a different kind of whisper, the boy's whisper in her ear:

Be here tomorrow at six. Or I'll tell all.

Those were the last words he'd said to her yesterday. They were with her when she rode home on the bus after her shift. They were with her when she brushed her teeth before going to bed. They were with her when she woke up in the morning long before the alarm. And even though her head, as usual, was filled with whispers of self-loathing, she nevertheless heard another voice, the voice of Lavi Maimon as he blackmailed her. He was putting the squeeze on her, and she had the feeling that it wasn't just a metaphorical squeeze he wanted. And thinking about that made her smile.

Smiles have a way of catching a person's eye, like a red balloon gliding in the sky and drawing the glances of people below. A girl with cropped hair and a tattoo on her leg came up to Nofar and said, "That's some smile you have." Luckily, they immediately found a trendier subject to discuss: the girl's new tattoo. She told Nofar that she hadn't been able to decide on just the right one, and Nofar quickly assured her that the one she had chosen was perfect for her, but what exactly was it? Cropped Hair stuck out her chest proudly and replied, "*Anarchy*, in Japanese."

(It might have been *anarchy* in Japanese. The tattoo artist didn't really know. He had once been a rejected, pimply boy. Everyone had made fun of him, even though he never hurt anyone. When he grew up, he found a legitimate way to take revenge: he practiced the only profession that allowed him to hurt teenagers and take their money for doing it. With supreme concentration he pierced the tongues of teenage boys very much like those who had humiliated him when he was a child. With a steady hand he pierced the navels of teenage girls identical to those who had turned their backs on him in high school. And more than anything, he loved to tattoo the bodies of smug, self-important teenagers, promising them that, yes, of course this is the way you write *anarchy* in Japanese.)

Nofar admired the tattoo at length. In her heart she wished that Shir would come by again and see her talking with a new friend. Shir didn't come. The bell came instead. Nofar was so sorry the conversation was interrupted that she found herself asking, "What do you say we skip school today?" She had already begun to mumble that maybe that wasn't such a great idea when Cropped Hair shrugged and said, "Why not?" and when Nofar looked up in surprise, she saw that the girl had begun walking toward the bus as she asked, "Which number goes to the beach?"

10

MEANWHILE, AVISHAI MILNER. Like the girl from the ice-cream parlor, he too reverted to biting his nails. In the middle of the night, realizing what he was doing, he pulled his fingers out of his mouth and looked at them in horror. Until that moment he hadn't noticed he was doing it, but now, in the jail cell, he suddenly became aware that the long-buried habit had returned from the netherworld, covered in layers of dirt. Avishai Milner knew quite well that the habit was only the first messenger. The others were on the way. Everything he had buried, everything he had gone through, everything that had been covered with a marble gravestone in the shape of the newspaper interview he had given after winning first place: "Avishai Milner Tells All." Now that boy was suddenly here, biting his nails. And he thought he'd gotten rid of him forever.

He thought once again about the girl from the ice-cream parlor and clenched his fists. He had never felt such hatred. To keep himself from biting his nails, he began making lists in his mind: the ten biggest hits of the 1980s. The best films of the 1990s. During the most difficult hours, when despair crept toward him like a wet snail, he named the city streets in his mind, from north to south, struggling to remember every alley and lane.

Avishai Milner was scheduled to be released in a few days. The bail would be high, but feasible. There, outside, he could finally prepare for battle. First of all, he would shower and get some sleep, and then he'd call his agent. He'd been trying to reach him for days, but the bastard didn't answer. The minutes passed, and his thoughts wandered from the agent to the girl. He would grab her by the throat with one hand, and with the other he'd pull her slanderous tongue out of her mouth. When he closed his eyes, he could actually see that lying tongue flapping around in his hand like a fish out of water. He hadn't eaten meat for sixteen years, but he would be happy to feel that red tongue between his teeth.

He had never thought it was possible to hate so much, but of course, he had also never thought it was possible to spend three days in jail for something he didn't do. And since he had quite a bit of time to wait for his release on bail, he could continue to plan: where he would lie in wait for her, how he would hide all traces. He would maintain firmly that he had slept at his parents' house that night. Like Nofar, Avishai Milner had spent his nights watching TV series. Like her, he was well acquainted with the precise planning of a murder. Until, realizing how much preparation and attention to detail was needed to actually carry out the deed, he suddenly trembled. "Stop it right now," he whispered to himself, and when that didn't help, he shouted out the words.

The guard on duty came to ask if everything was all right. "Instead of shouting, why don't you sing something?" But Avishai Milner did not sing for an audience of one. The guard shrugged and went off, leaving him sitting in his cell, his face angry, his fists clenched. And the thought of her tongueless body, like a song he couldn't get out of his head, played endlessly on the strings of his soul.

11

ON THE FIRST day of the school year, the beach was left
to its own devices. Only the day before, vacationers had lain
on the sand, limbs spread, groggy from the heat. Suntan oil
had glittered on their skin, making them look like a school of
fish caught in a net, flopping around, scales glistening, mouths
open. But September had arrived. The beach-cleaners began
looking for other jobs. For four months they had spent their
days there without stepping even once into the water. Birds
spread their feathered wings and flew south, while tourists
flew west on their motorized wings. The last of the plastic
bags sank to the seafloor, twisted around a sea anemone, and
stopped moving. The sea and all that dwelled in it breathed
a sigh of relief, even the suffocating anemone. The dry land
would not bother them for a full eight months. The ebb and
flow of the tides occurs slowly over a period of several hours,
but the start of the school year happens all at once, the single
blow of a sword that decapitates the summer and brings the
beach season to an abrupt end.

But right then, four feet began splashing gleefully in the
surf, accompanied by screams and laughter. "It's cold!" "Stop
whining!" The girl from the ice-cream parlor and the girl
with cropped hair ran fearlessly into the waves, despite the
sign warning "No Swimming," or perhaps because of it, since
there is nothing sweeter than swimming in forbidden waters.
Until that moment, they had thought they were breaking only

their parents' and the school's rules, but now it seemed they were breaking municipal rules as well, and the knowledge made their bodies vibrate with excitement. In their underwear and bras they floated, abandoning their bodies to the gaping eyes of the clouds and the storks. They shivered because of the cold water and the excitement caused by their near-nakedness. When one of them thought the other wasn't looking, she took a quick glance at her friend's body. Silently, they made precise comparisons of rear ends and thighs, breasts and navels, and it was clear to both of them that what one was lacking, nature had given to the other, and vice versa. That discovery, instead of arousing envy, actually reinforced the fondness they felt for each other.

They floated on their backs and talked about the teachers they hated, about how they had sneaked onto the bus through the back door, and about everything they would do when they finished high school. Cropped Hair couldn't decide whether to live in London or Paris, and Nofar tried as hard as she could to help her make the decision, hoping her new friend didn't realize that she had never been to London and had spent only three days in Paris when she was seven. In fact, Cropped Hair had never visited London either, or Paris for that matter, but you don't need a passport to float in the sea and make plans. Each girl peed in the water when she thought the other wouldn't notice, and both talked about couples who did it without condoms right there, in the water, wondering whether they could get pregnant just from swimming near a couple like that, and decided they couldn't.

When they came out of the water they lay in silence on the soft sand, letting the sun warm their skin. Cropped Hair sat up and looked at Nofar. "You're very brave, you know." Nofar averted her gaze quickly. "What you did on TV...," and to

Nofar's complete surprise Cropped Hair burst into tears. In all the years they had passed each other in the school corridors, Nofar had never imagined that the girl with the cropped hair was a crier. She looked strong, always cheerful, and now she was crying right there in front of her. Nofar didn't know whether to look away politely or look directly at her, whether to reach out and touch the girl's hand as she dug in the sand or let her keep digging to the place where the sand ends and water begins, and even farther, to the beating heart of the planet. Her movements were so desperate that Nofar was convinced she would reach that place in the end.

Nofar was dumbstruck by embarrassment, but Cropped Hair welcomed the quiet. She was grateful for the silence that left room for her words, like an old man who approaches a bench on the street and sees the people sitting on it squeeze together to make room for him. Slowly she began to speak. "I understand," she said, "because it happened to . . ." Nofar was surprised to hear how differently Cropped Hair was speaking now. As if someone had tied a sack of lead to the end of every word and they plunged downward the moment they were uttered. "It happened to me, too."

A long while passed before Cropped Hair spoke again. Finally she talked about the shift manager in the café where she had worked the previous summer. He followed her every time she went into the storeroom. At first he just made comments, then he started touching her. At closing time one night he sent everyone home and remained alone with her. She didn't know why she didn't tell her parents. There was no reason. They're really okay. She didn't tell her friends either. And she broke up with the boyfriend she had at the time—she didn't want anyone to touch her. But what she really didn't understand was how she had stood there and let him. Why she didn't say anything, didn't scream, and not afterward either, when she could have said something. But she was ashamed. She didn't have the courage. What if they said she was making it up? She was so scared about what people would say about her that she didn't say anything. She had passed the place twice this summer, but she couldn't bring herself to go inside. Through the window she looked at the tight face of the waitress, who was about her age, and wondered if he was doing it to her, too.

Cropped Hair grew silent. A tear rolled down her cheek and fell into the sea. A tear rolled down Nofar's cheek as well, but she quickly wiped it away with her wrist. So it wouldn't fall into the sea and contaminate the pure tear of her friend.

12

LAVI MAIMON STOOD at the entrance to the ice-cream parlor and waited. It was 6:20 and she still hadn't come. Maybe she would never come there again. The thought made his stomach churn like the coffee-bean grinder in the café next door. The hours that had passed since he saw her the day before had left him with the taste of anticipated pleasure, a tingling in his body that, until now, he had experienced only when masturbating. But this time, there was another person involved apart from himself. A real girl. She might be less beautiful and less well built than the ones in his imagination, but that only made her a hundred times more exciting than they were. Her defects gave her presence. The secret he kept for her thrilled him. It was like holding a chick between his palms. Something soft and delicate vibrating between his fingers. He walked gingerly all day, saving it for her.

Lavi Maimon waited ten minutes. Twenty minutes. And there is no way of knowing what the poor boy's fate might have been if she hadn't suddenly appeared, running to the ice-cream parlor at 6:25, her face flushed and sand in her hair. She's sick, he thought, and her eyes were indeed glowing unnaturally. Hearing Cropped Hair's confession had been like swallowing a small ball of fire. Nofar had spent the afternoon wandering the city streets blindly. At 5:00 she received a message from her new friend. *It was so good to finally tell the secret,* it said, and the words were like a can of gasoline thrown on the small ball of fire in her stomach.

At 6:15 she headed for the ice-cream parlor. Not for a moment did she forget the boy and the threat he'd made the day before. She had held it close all night. But since this morning at the beach, the sense of shame she felt refused to abate. When she stood before him, he gave her a look he hoped would seem cold and said, "You were supposed to be here at six. You're late one more time and I'll tell everyone you lied." Nofar, having spent the day filled with the torment of a ball of fire rolling around inside her body, said, "So tell them."

Lavi cleared his throat. He didn't know what to say. His black curls shook slightly. Perhaps a gust of hot wind from the fire blazing under the girl's skin had reached him. Something wasn't right, but he didn't know what. All he knew was that the delicate little chick he had been cupping in his hands all day was teetering between life and death now. Nofar looked into his black eyes and burst into tears. Lavi touched her shoulder, and instead of calming her, that touch only intensified her weeping. Undaunted, he took her hand and led her to the nearby bench. Fifteen hours earlier a homeless man lying on it had dreamed mad dreams, but the bench was empty now, so they sat down on it and didn't speak. Finally, Nofar told him what had happened that morning. How she had gone to the beach with the girl with the cropped hair, how they had gone into the water, how she had applauded Nofar for the courage she didn't really have, and how the girl had told her a secret she didn't deserve to know. Because it was the word *liar* that had kept Cropped Hair from speaking, the fear that people would say she was making it up. How would Nofar be able to look her in the eye during break tomorrow? (In fact, Nofar wouldn't, but not out of choice. After that morning on the beach Cropped Hair avoided Nofar at almost any cost. When they passed each other in the corridor she averted her eyes, fearing that her secret would be reflected in Nofar's. The secret she had shared that had brought them closer that day on the beach would keep them apart from now on.)

It was almost seven. The cries of babies refusing to go to sleep came from the lighted apartment windows. Lavi Maimon was silent for a while, and then said, "But your story was good for her. She said so herself. It's only because of you that she finally managed to talk about what happened."

Nofar looked at him with large, stunned eyes as he insisted, his words coming in spurts: that even if it wasn't exactly what happened in the alley, it didn't necessarily matter. The people who are so strict about sticking to the truth are the ones who benefit from it. And there are people who benefit more from a lie. It's not their fault.

"You're not lying for no reason. You have no choice. Like, if you had a good enough truth, you wouldn't have to lie, right? It's like people who have enough food don't need to steal. Only someone who's hungry steals, and you wouldn't blame them for it."

That was the most Lavi had said to any girl, ever, and it was quite clumsy. For the first time in his life, he regretted having spent his days playing computer games. Instead of learning how to express himself, he'd been busy piling up bodies. He had walked along the city street, battling an army of dead people he had downed with his nimble fingers on the keyboard, but what good were all those dead people when he couldn't help one girl? If only he could take the cloud of thoughts gathering in his mind and squeeze rain out of them, one simple sentence: to tell her, for example, that lies are inseparably entwined with life. That the days are threaded on them like pearls on a string. Every round day has a small, dark hole in it where the lie that enables it to exist is strung. Such images were out of the question, and perhaps that was for the best—they tend to miss the mark. "The point is," he said, "that it's not a bad thing to lie when the truth is shitty. And Avishai Milner really is a piece of shit."

Nofar wiped away her tears with her wrist. She snuffled. The boy's awkward words had managed to calm the storm a bit. Lavi waited for her to start breathing normally. Then he stood up and glanced at his watch. Seven ten. He was no longer prepared to accept such chutzpah. She should go straight to the alley and wait for him.

"Or I'll tell all."

The first day of school was over. Maya sat in her room, presiding with nimble fingers over twelve text messages simultaneously. And all that time, silence thundered from the next room. Her parents had knocked on her door twice to ask if she had heard from her sister. Out of her sense of sisterhood, Maya told them there was nothing to worry about. They didn't have to be available twenty-four hours a day. But her stomach was churning. Twelve simultaneous text messages, and not one of them seemed as interesting as what was certainly happening to her older sister now.

When Nofar finally returned home, Maya stayed in her room. The younger sister heard her parents' questions coming from the other side of the door, questions that, until now, had been reserved for her: "Where were you?" and "Why so late?" and of course, "So why didn't you call?" But it wasn't her parents' familiar questions that concerned her—rather, it was the answers. They were remarkably brief, which is what made them so full. She didn't have to open the door to know that her sister had come home with the taste of a boy on her lips. That's why they were closed so tightly. After partaking of a superb dessert, you don't want to taste anything else so as to keep the flavor from fading, and after kisses in the dark you don't want to talk so as to keep the words from removing what your mouth wishes to hold on to.

Late at night, Nofar's hand groped for her notebook. She left the light off so she wouldn't see the words she was writing. Her fingers held the purple fountain pen she had received for her bat mitzvah. On the day of the celebration, she didn't understand why her grandmother hadn't given her a check like everyone else, but after her grandmother died the fountain pen carried the full weight of Nofar's longing to see her again. Ever since, she had used only that pen to write in her notebook. Now she picked it up and wrote everything down in purple ink. It's not true. Everything I said. I made it all up. And he's the one paying the price.

She didn't know whether she was writing to force herself to stop telling that story, or the opposite, to unburden herself of the secret on the pages so she could close the notebook and move through her life with a lighter step. When she finished writing, she wiped the tears from her eyes, put the notebook back in its regular hiding place, and got under the covers. She stared at the ceiling for a long time.

The next morning, Maya lay in her bed and waited—any minute now Nofar would knock on the door and ask to borrow something from her wardrobe. Though they both had to be in school at the same time, Maya always got up late, with the indifference of someone who would look wonderful even in a shower curtain. Nofar always knocked on her door half an hour before Maya got up, not only because she was concerned about being late, but also because of some unspoken anger. In the end, Maya would wake up and shout "Come in!" and Nofar would dash into the room and straight to the wardrobe. She would pull something out, unfold it, return it—but not exactly the way it had been—take out something else. Everything was too tight, too close-fitting. So it was each morning, and with every minute that passed, Nofar's resentment of her sister grew. It wasn't Maya's clothes that she coveted, but the body on which the clothes fit so perfectly. And then it would suddenly explode into the well-practiced accusations and shouts—"Let me sleep!" "Can't you help me when I ask you?" "Couldn't you have done that last night?"—until their mother came and ordered them to stop, and they both lapsed into angry silence.

But that morning, Nofar didn't come in to forage through Maya's wardrobe. Nor did she appear the next morning. At first, Maya was glad—at last she had her precious moments of sleep back. But over the next few days she found herself waking up earlier and earlier. An unknown force sent her to her big sister's room. Now it was Maya's turn to knock on Nofar's door and ask to rummage through the secrets in her older sister's wardrobe. Nofar was willing and happy, not to mention gratified, to open the door. And if the clothes were returned with new stains or an annoying crease, Nofar didn't care. But when Maya took the purple fountain pen to an exam and came back without it, the shouts rose to high heaven.

13

IT WAS AN omelet consisting of three egg whites that made Lavi realize his father knew. It appeared on the table four days after Nofar's interview on the news, and Lavi had already lost hope. Lieutenant Colonel Arieh Maimon had recently developed prostate problems, and he'd spent most of Nofar's interview trying to pee normally. He was nowhere near the TV when the girl from the ice-cream parlor talked about her friend, Lavi Maimon, who was training to be accepted into an elite combat unit. Lavi had hoped the information would reach his father somehow—after all, the news had so many viewers, someone he knew would certainly notice. But after a few days he sensed that there was no longer any chance. Not only did his father maintain his usual silence, but so did his classmates. Maybe none of them had been watching TV that day. Or maybe they had, but it never occurred to them that the "Lavi Maimon" the girl had mentioned was the same lackluster boy from the fourth floor. After four days of silence, Lavi gave up hope. And that was when the omelet consisting of three egg whites appeared on the table.

"What's that?" his mother asked in surprise. Lieutenant Colonel Arieh Maimon was not the sort of man who made omelets. "It's for the boy. He needs protein." He spoke the words from behind the op-ed pages, which is why he didn't see the flush that spread across his son's cheeks. Lavi dug his fork into the egg-white omelet his father had made and knew that the next taste in his mouth would be the taste of manliness. He remembered quite well his father's stories about the time he trained to try out for the unit. Every morning he would run six miles in the sand and do a triple-digit number of sit-ups before heading home, where he fried himself an egg-white omelet. There is nothing like it—so he said—for building and strengthening muscles. Arieh Maimon's mother had been a hard-working woman who struggled to put food in the mouths of her four children as well as that of her useless husband. The eggs, if there were any, were rationed, and the young Arieh would make his egg-white omelet with eggs he stole from the neighboring kibbutz. Those were his first operations deep into enemy territory, so even before he joined the army, Arieh Maimon had become highly proficient at boldly infiltrating a hostile environment. It is no wonder, then, that he passed the examination for the elite combat unit with flying colors.

When Lavi was a little boy, his father amazed him with stories of that period. Children's fairy tales never interested Arieh Maimon. He preferred to tell his son true stories he could learn from and, when the day came, repeat. To his father's great sorrow, the boy grew into a skinny, drab teenager, dashing the hopes he'd had for him. Although in front of the computer Lavi slaughtered many enemy soldiers, more than his father had killed during his years of outstanding service, real life was different. On the surface Lavi was an only child. He had never competed with a brother for looks and smiles. But in fact there was always another boy there, the one his father had dreamed of before he was born, and in the competition between them it was clear who the loser was. At one stage or another, most parents learn to give up the imagined child, but Lavi's father found it difficult, because for him the imaginary child was the firstborn.

And now the protein omelet had reappeared on the table. Behind the op-ed pages, Arieh Maimon was filled with satisfaction. He didn't ask Lavi about the combat-unit screening. The boy wanted to succeed on his own merits, without his father's connections, and as far as Arieh Maimon was concerned, that was definitely a commendable decision, appropriate for a soldier in an elite combat unit. Nonetheless, when Lavi finished his protein omelet and chocolate milk and stood up to get ready for school, the lieutenant colonel couldn't restrain himself. He lowered the newspaper with the same deliberate movement with which he had lowered his rifle sight in the past, and gave his son an eloquent wink, one that said, in effect, I won't say anything and you won't say anything, because that is what men do, but we both know what we need to know, and that's the important thing. Lavi left the table, his knees shaking. That was the first time his father had ever winked at him.

Some plants must be watered once a day. Others don't have to be watered at all—the more they are left alone, the more they thrive. That applies to lies as well. Some must be reinforced by a constant stream of words, others are better off left alone—they will grow on their own. Lavi Maimon's tests for an elite combat unit were of the second kind. Since Nofar had mentioned them on TV, no one had ever spoken of them again. Lavi Maimon didn't say a word. Arieh Maimon didn't say a word. But the protein omelet continued to appear on the table every morning, and after a week it was joined by new sneakers with special shock absorbers that were left on the threshold of Lavi's room. The boy examined the shoes, his happiness mixed with concern. The catalogue in the shoebox heaped praise on the sneakers' performance, and Lavi wondered if it was good enough to compensate for the pathetic performance of the feet inside them. Several days later he found a watch with a diver's compass on his bed. He put it on hesitantly, but the feel of the metal on his wrist suddenly reminded him of the feel of handcuffs, and he took it off quickly. He had to talk to his father today. Or tomorrow.

14

DETECTIVE DORIT HAD changed her nail polish from pink to red, and Nofar thought that was a bad sign. Her nails looked as if she had stuck them in someone's insides—maybe the last person she had interrogated. Nofar tried to imagine that person, whether it was a man or a woman, or a teenager like her. It was weird to think about how many people had sat on the chair facing Dorit before her, and what had happened to them since. But it was still better to think about that than about Avishai Milner. The night before she met with Detective Dorit, Nofar couldn't stop thinking about Avishai Milner. What would happen if he killed himself in prison? What if he escaped and came after her? The night before her meeting with Detective Dorit, she turned on the TV and hoped that Avishai Milner's face would just disappear in the clamor and she could finally go to sleep. But he stayed there, like the rattle of the fridge in the kitchen. Always present, even when other voices overpowered his. She didn't fall asleep until almost dawn. When her father came to wake her and touched her shoulder, she woke with a shout that frightened both of them.

The call from the investigation unit had come several days earlier. *Just routine,* a kind voice promised on the phone, a chance to go over her testimony before the file was passed on to the district attorney's office. Nofar had no reason to doubt the truth of that, but a person who deceives ends up seeing deceit everywhere. Nofar was terrified that the summons to the police department was nothing but a trap. The red nail polish on the detective's delicate fingers, the light filtering through the plastic shutters at an unnatural angle—it all seemed wrong to her. She was almost surprised when, after an hour and a quarter, Detective Dorit smiled at her and said, "Excellent, I think we've covered everything."

Had they really covered everything? Had she really sat there and repeated that whole story down to the smallest detail? On the other side of the table, Detective Dorit said something and smiled, then stood up to walk Nofar to the door. But the girl remained seated, frozen and staring into space. As soon as she left, Dorit would send an email to the district attorney's office. Nofar's words would be sent from one government office to another, and no one would suspect that there was nothing behind them, that the words did not describe what had happened, that only the words had happened, and now they were sewing Avishai Milner the striped jacket of a prisoner's uniform.

Detective Dorit looked at her and sat down again. Slowly. It seemed to Nofar that she was looking at her differently. The way someone looks at a hair she has just found in a plate of food she's been eating heartily. "Is there something you want to tell me?" Nofar was silent. Dorit placed both hands on the table and Nofar could swear that her nail polish was even redder than before. She opened her mouth to speak, but not a single word emerged. Dorit saw it, she saw her open her mouth, saw that not a single word emerged, and Nofar thought that Dorit must know that words not spoken are the best evidence there is. Dorit's silence continued. She was really good at being silent. She made you think she could stay silent for an eternity. Nofar didn't know if an eternity had passed before she herself said, "Maybe that's not exactly how it was."

Dorit was silent for another moment, and then asked, "So how was it?"

Nofar lowered her gaze to the floor and felt the tears rising in her throat. Without looking up, she spoke quickly, said that maybe she'd been confused, maybe she'd spoken without thinking, maybe she hadn't understood. Dorit listened without saying a word. She really was good at that. Gradually, her silence crushed Nofar until she too stopped speaking.

"So what should I believe, what you're saying now or what you told me earlier?"

Nofar didn't reply. She heard Dorit stand, but she didn't look up. She didn't want to see Dorit's face now. She heard the detective's steps as she walked around the table. She thought the door would open and Dorit would go out and return with policemen who would arrest her. But instead, Dorit knelt down in front of her.

"I think you're terrified, Nofar. I think you're suddenly afraid of the trial, of facing Avishai Milner after what he did to you." Nofar nodded, fat tears rolled down her cheeks and she didn't lift a hand to wipe them away. "But you don't have to be afraid. You didn't do anything wrong. He's the bad guy here, you have no reason to recant." The detective's fingers stroked her shoulder. She told Nofar about victims of sexual assault she had escorted to court, how much pressure the system brings to bear on the victim and how her heart had broken to see the monsters who had perpetrated the attacks walk away unpunished. She promised Nofar she wouldn't let that happen again. "It's not only your fight, it's the fight of all the other girls who went through what you did. You need to understand that Avishai Milner is not the important thing here, the important thing is to fight against the next shit who even thinks about behaving that way." Dorit said that she remembered very well how Nofar had come to the station the first time. It had been clear that she was traumatized, and Avishai's open-and-shut confession had to be added to that. *Really, there's nothing to be afraid of, sweetie.* Dorit's fingers stroked her hair, and as Nofar listened to the detective's words, she realized that she lied better than she told the truth.

But nothing I said was true. I made it up. Because he insulted me. Because he stepped on me. Because I've been stepped on a million times, and that time I couldn't take it anymore. At first it was by mistake. At first I just cried a lot, and everyone there thought he did something terrible to me, and he really did, but not that, not what everyone thought, and then everything happened so fast, with the newspapers and the TV, and the people who were so nice to me for the first time in my life, and I wish they could be so nice to you when you're not suffering from anything special, even if you're not the victim of a crime, just to be nice for no reason, but it doesn't work like that, it's either-or, either he's in jail and everyone's nice to me, or he's out and everything goes back to the way it was. Only worse, because then I won't be the girl everyone forgets, I'll be the crazy one. The monster. And I want to ask you, Detective Dorit, which is better, to hate yourself alone, quietly, or to have the whole country hate you?

Detective Dorit rang for the elevator and went down with Nofar. She offered to walk to the bus stop with her, but Nofar insisted that there was really no need. Nonetheless, Detective Dorit went with her. She lit a cigarette and said, "I can see that this is hard for you. That you're keeping your tears inside. But I promise you that soon it'll be behind you. Just hang in there until after the trial." Nofar waited for her to say that she was a very brave girl, but this time it didn't happen. Maybe Dorit had actually sensed something back in the interrogation room.

All the way home, Nofar's legs trembled unnaturally. So that's how it is. No one knows. Even the detectives, whose job it was to know, couldn't guess. And how good it was that she was still herself with the boy who was blackmailing her. Those black eyes of his when he looked at her and threatened her, they were the only eyes that truly saw her.

15

"AVISHAI MILNER ON the Crime He Didn't Commit."
"Jailhouse Rock—The Famous Singer Talks about His Suffering."

"Justice Will Out: Avishai Milner—From Criminal to Hero."

He polished the headlines in his mind constantly. He came up with a new one every day. And he didn't think only about the headlines, but also about the interviews and the pictures that would appear and what the captions would say. He spent hours thinking about the questions he would be asked and the replies he would give: sharp, damaging, moving. The scenario in his mind was written down to the smallest detail, so tangible that Avishai Milner was surprised each morning when he woke up in his cell and discovered that it still hadn't come true.

When Avishai Milner was a teenager, a storm covered the land. Later they would say that the writing had been on the wall, but that Saturday Avishai Milner hadn't been interested in writing or in walls, he was too busy learning to play the guitar. There was nothing like strumming to drown out the tumult of his parents arguing in the living room. He read the chords over and over again, tried to play them over and over again, until the coveted moment arrived—the lock opened, the song burst forth, and he took control of it. On the Saturday night when everything changed, the teenage Avishai Milner was sitting in his room and strumming away to his heart's content as he watched a movie on TV. But just as the plot was reaching its climax, a news broadcaster suddenly appeared on the screen. A horrified expression on his face, he said that someone had shot the prime minister. Avishai Milner began to shake. Not because of the prime minister, but because he had never seen the announcer so agitated before. He hurried into the living room, the last moment of the film still lingering in his mind, and found his mother crying and his father hugging her. Later, he realized that that was the only time he had ever seen his father hug his mother when she cried. Maybe because, for a change, she wasn't crying because of him.

The next day his mother took him to Kings of Israel Square. Sad, beautiful songs were playing on the radio, and Avishai Milner noted with satisfaction that he could play almost all of them. When they reached the square, he was shocked to see crowds of young people. Until that moment he had been sure that only mothers were affected. The enormous square, normally full of voracious pigeons, was now filled with young people in mourning. And like the pigeons, they too were hungry for something. Everyone's sorrow would be channeled into the national tragedy, and, finally, you could cry openly without being asked why.

Guitars rose from within that swamp of sorrow and blossomed like lotuses. There was singing everywhere. Circles. Endless circles, and boys and girls walked among them, sat down, stood up, lit candles, spoke a bit, wiped away tears, sang another song, wrote their phone numbers on a page they'd torn from a notebook. The next day Avishai Milner went back to the square alone, his guitar slung over his shoulder. The bus ride had taken more than an hour, and Avishai Milner spent the time preparing a first-rate list of songs, the sort that builds the sorrow gradually until it reaches its climax. But when he arrived at the square, his hands began to shake. He was surrounded by groups of teenagers in black shirts, lighting candles, their eyes melancholy. Would he really be able to fit right in with them? They could probably smell the loneliness on him. He'd put his father's aftershave on his face in vain. Desolation has a smell of its own. Like wet dog fur.

At home, he'd had a simple plan: join one of the circles and take his guitar out of its case. But now, in the square, all the circles seemed to be for members only. Since he couldn't summon up the courage to join any of them, he remained standing. Finally, when his legs began to hurt, he stretched out on the paving stones, alone and defeated. But before long he was surrounded by a group of girls, and, as if it were the most natural thing in the world, they sat down beside him, still humming a song they'd carried with them from another circle. Avishai Milner needed nothing more than that: he immediately took out his guitar and accompanied their singing, and followed them into their next song. Then, bit by bit, he took control, and even before one song ended, he was leading them into the next one, song joining song in a gradual, emotional ascent until the members of other circles began to feel that something special was happening in that circle, and every minute someone else joined its ranks. What had begun as a slow trickle became a massive upsurge, teenage boys and girls went to sit in Avishai Milner's circle, and just as he was thinking that nothing in the world could be better than this, the first TV camera turned on, its white light flooding his face, and he understood that the best was still to come.

But even national mourning must eventually come to an end. Genuine sorrow has an expiration date. Avishai Milner went back to the square the following week and the week after that, sang many songs, some of them his own, and there's no telling how much longer he would have continued if the day hadn't come when he realized that he was alone. Fresh grief, like fresh grass—how long can it last in such a hot country? The teenagers returned to their lives. Only pigeons and a homeless man who claimed that the banks were to blame for everything remained in the square.

The candles in the square were extinguished, but the flame that had been ignited in Avishai Milner's heart could not be put out. It burned even now, in the darkness of his jail cell. The desire to be seen, to be heard, to penetrate the flesh of the world like a thorn, that fire had begun to blaze inside him when he was a teenager in the square and it continued when he auditioned for talent shows, when he made his first album, when his second album flopped, when he appeared in a series of breakfast-cereal commercials, and when he was finally reduced to doing humiliating birthday-party gigs. Even in jail he never stopped planning his triumphant comeback for even a moment. Planning, or perhaps hallucinating. Because whenever he took a brief break from writing the headlines for his next interview, a clear image of the tongueless girl rose before him, and the more he told himself that those thoughts were only mad fantasies of revenge better left behind when the lock was opened and he was released on bail, the more deeply the image became embedded in his heart: one tongueless girl.

And in fact, why does no one take the trouble to point out the first lie? How eager we are to honor the first word, the first day of the first grade, the first kiss. Each of those is like the planting of a flag in a foreign land: *see how far I've come.* But we do not usually celebrate the first lie. Nonetheless, we can point to that moment—the first time it occurred to the girl that deceit is perhaps preferable to truth.

For example, on the way home from ballet class. Four girls who lived on the same street—it was only natural that they should go home together. It was expected that living on the same street would cause them to bond, and so it did, but only for three of them. Because even if all the mathematical permutations of the number four were applicable to the girls, for Nofar the calculations always had the same results—three there, one here. Perhaps to balance the slanted equation a bit, she added another one who wasn't there to the one who was.

His name was Yoni and it wasn't that he was nonexistent. That is to say, there was such a Yoni in the world, her mother's friend's son. She had met him twice, perhaps three times. Their mothers had chatted over coffee while they fidgeted awkwardly over their glasses of Coke. There was nothing about those boring encounters to support the stories she told her friends later at the community center. She extracted the little she could from the encounters—his freckles, his slightly hooked nose, his love for Dungeons and Dragons—and the rest, having no choice, she made up.

And then came that night. She sat beside her mother in the front seat. In the back, three little girls crowded together, their school bags on their laps, their ballet costumes dangling from them like pink tongues. Her mother asked how the class was, and after they said it was great, a strange silence filled the car. Netta spoke first. In a syrupy voice, she asked Nofar about Yoni. How long had they been friends, what did they do together? Nofar's tongue felt heavy in her mouth. An hour earlier, at the community center, she would have replied easily enough. But here, with her mother holding the wheel, a witness, blood flooded her face and her temples pounded. It felt as if the entire car could hear her swallow her saliva. She replied quickly, praying that her mother was concentrating on something else. The shopping list, let's say, or some task she had to do at work. But then Michal spoke, continuing to ask, and something about the wooden way she uttered the words made it clear to Nofar that they had planned this.

Michal recited a question that had been formulated in advance, like a fisherman spreading a net that had been woven earlier. How had she and Yoni met? Where did they see each other? Nofar replied slowly, carefully. Trying not to contradict what she'd told them at the community center. Trying not to say anything that would cause her mother to look away from the road. She didn't know what frightened her more—the girls ambushing her from the back seat or her mother's silence in the driver's seat. Ronit's fingers wound around the wheel in a movement that boded ill. A traitorous traffic light lengthened the ride another few minutes, and Nofar saw the fingers begin to drum on the wheel. Drum drum pause, drum drum pause. As if this was a message her mother wanted to send her. A long silence from the back seat, hands squeezing each other, small shoves. Until Yael opened her mouth. "So is he really your boyfriend?"

Exactly at the spot where her upper ribs were—that's where she felt it. As if someone had opened the door of the bathroom stall when she was inside, on the toilet, and now everyone was standing there watching. Netta. Michal. Yael. And her mother, which was apparently the worst. Her mother, who might or might not have been looking, her expression at the moment gave away nothing. Even the drumming stopped for a moment. She had no message to pass on to her daughter; and if there is anything worse than a mother witnessing her daughter's humiliation, it is a mother who refuses to be a witness, turns her glance away as if it has nothing to do with her, like drivers passing the scene of an accident and slowing down at first, then stepping on the gas.

That night Nofar swore she would never lie again. And the truth is that since then, there had been only little white lies, just crumbs. And so Nofar moved deeper into that forest, from one small lie to another, until she finally reached her gingerbread house, the ice-cream parlor where she was both prisoner and guard.

16

ONE MIGHT THINK that after that first kiss in the alley, Nofar and Lavi would kiss again. But for some reason, things went differently. When they met again, they were barely able to utter a sound. No word seemed good enough to speak. The miracle of their meeting felt so fragile to them that they feared a wrong move would destroy it. And so they sat, holding in the words they dared not speak. Fortunately, Nofar finally reminded Lavi that she was in his hands, whispered in his ear that if he revealed the secret, she was lost. That reminder of his power filled him with renewed energy—they were no longer embarrassed teenagers, but a blackmailer and his victim.

And indeed, there was some improvement over the next few days. Here and there, hands reached out to grope. There were clumsy mini-caresses, the unforgettable feel of her hand on his thigh, his trembling fingers brushing against her breasts. Of course, it was all as if by accident, in silence, both barely breathing, their hands supposedly not their hands. But no real kiss had reoccurred since the first one. Perhaps they had used up all their courage for that one and there was not enough left for another. The days passed, each beginning with perhaps today and ending with perhaps tomorrow, expectation as warm and fresh as the bread unloaded at dawn at the supermarket and thrown away, moldy and hard, in the evening. In the alley, crude awkwardness. The laundry that had dripped rain on them the afternoon of their first kiss had long since dried.

One day it was removed as surely as it had been hung, a hand reached out from the balcony and plucked the items one by one. As Lavi and Nofar watched from below, embarrassed, the circle of life in the apartment above them continued smoothly on its track while theirs remained frozen and clumsy.

It wasn't that she didn't want to kiss him: Nofar was so immersed in thoughts about the boy that even a stranger, glancing at her face, would immediately blush. The same was true for Lavi—his mouth was busy reliving the precise details of that kiss, and when he wasn't kissing her in the past, in his memory, he was kissing her in the future, imagining every possible kiss to come. Since the number of possible future kisses was very large, he could do nothing but kiss the girl. And so he spent his days kissing, not only the pillow on his bed—that's for beginners—but also his pen during English class, the gum he chewed, and the sabich sandwich he ate on his way home, anything that came into contact with his mouth tasted of her.

One evening, the alley cats took pity on them. They gave a full performance in front of them, wailing and meowing to show them that, here, this is how it's done. But watching the copulating cats only increased Nofar's and Lavi's embarrassment. "Idiot, why don't you do something?" he said to himself. "Jerk, why are you sitting here like a dope?" she said to herself. First, they ridiculed themselves, until soon enough they believed that everyone was ridiculing them, especially the laundry that was once again hanging on the line, dripping silent gray drops on them. The women's briefs looked truly monstrous to Lavi, a giant lace sail that hid the sun. When he finally looked away from the hanging underwear to the yard, he found that Nofar had moved closer and was now sitting a millimeter from his nose. He could feel her breath. He could almost hear the rustle of her eyelashes. *Do it,* the cats' whiskers vibrated. *Do it,* the laundry on the line pleaded.

Right then, the sound of a phone ringing split the air, so cheery it was painful. The producer of a morning program asked Nofar if she wanted to do an interview the following day. Lavi listened as the producer told her that she would share the taxi to the studio with a famous actor. And it was the thought of her in the taxi, totally forgetting him, the handsome actor probably sitting beside her in the back seat, their knees touching—it was that thought that finally opened his mouth. He reminded her that she was in his hands, that he knew what needed to remain in the dark. And the moment he mentioned the secret, there was no longer any choice, hands reached out, lips met, and a collective sigh of relief rose from all the residents of the alley: the pair of cats, the hanging laundry, the skinny boy, and the hesitant girl.

17

TWO RADIO SHOWS. A human-interest story in the weekend supplement. A six-minute interview on a red couch on a nightly talk show. As they spoke to "the girl who dared to scream," they bent their heads slightly in a gesture that became an emblem of sympathy and compassion. The viewers at home were glued to the sweet face on the screen the way cling wrap adheres to a sliced watermelon. They all pointed out that she was a very brave girl. In the neighborhood, people said hello to her. The sales clerk in the grocery store said she was proud of her. Without her knowledge, her name came up at a meeting of a lingerie company. Perhaps they would make her their next spokeswoman. That would undoubtedly echo in the public consciousness—the power of women, the spirit of youth, realistic body sizes. In the end the CEO went with an alternative option, an actress who had just returned from filming abroad.

Nofar wasn't disappointed—she hadn't known she was a candidate. And in any case, the center of her world was that neighborhood, that school. In the months that had passed since Shir dumped her, she had tried to leave for school to arrive just in time for the bell, to avoid those embarrassing moments alone in the schoolyard, focused on her phone and looking busy. Now, arriving at school in the morning was pure, unadulterated pleasure. Everyone came over to her, asked how she was. *I saw you on TV. My mother says you're a hero. Tell me what it's like in the studios. Did you see anyone famous?* And she (blushing slightly, her breathing somewhat accelerated, a bit embarrassed by the attention) said yes, she did see famous people. She told them about her conversation with the news anchor who came up to her in the corridor after the show and bought her a Coke in the studio cafeteria, where they were joined by lots of actors from the programs they all watched on Friday nights and other programs. She had thought they would be snobs, but they were really very nice. Her fascinated classmates, their eyes wide, asked *So what's he like in real life?* And she replied confidently: *Fatter. Skinnier. Better looking. Kind of ugly.* She hoped she wasn't confusing her answers with the ones she had given yesterday, or the ones she would give tomorrow.

Finally, Shir came over to her. It was on the day of her second morning program. Nofar knew that Shir would talk to her after that. She had slept over at Shir's house enough times to know that everyone there watched that program in the morning. Shir and her brothers ate their cornflakes while watching that program, shouted "Did anyone see my shoes?" while watching it, and demanded to be driven to school while watching it because it was too late to walk. And so it was, on the day of that program Shir waited for Nofar at the entrance to school and said, "You were fantastic on the show!" When the bell rang, they walked to class together, and when they arrived, Shir simply sat down next to her as if it were the most natural thing in the world. For nine years it really had been the most natural thing in the world, until that morning at the end of last year when Nofar arrived in class and discovered that Shir had moved to another seat. Now Shir sat down beside her again, and that would have made her happy if she hadn't been afraid Shir would sense the truth. Because if someone knew her well enough to know, it was Shir.

But maybe the most truly frightening thing was that Shir didn't sense it; not the next day or two days later. All that time Nofar waited for Shir to give her that piercing look, but it didn't come. Because after Shir came back to sit next to her, everything was as it had been before, but not really.

When she lied, her body perspired differently. Instead of that stickiness in her armpits, there was a dampness between her shoulder blades, the sort that appears after running. The smell was different as well. Not the usual embarrassing sourness mixed with deodorant spray. Actually, there was hardly any smell, but her shirt stayed wet for hours. The sweat of the unspoken words dripped down her back. The saliva she swallowed tasted different on her tongue. And why was everything suddenly sharper? Smells. Sounds. Boys' voices. Maybe the danger was making her senses more acute. After all, everything could turn upside down in an instant.

One day, she would open the classroom door and everyone would look accusingly at her. One day, she would go into the school bathroom and find new graffiti on the wall, "Nofar Shalev is a liar" written in huge letters. But the days passed, and every time she walked into class she was greeted by sympathetic faces. She found nasty new graffiti in the bathroom every morning, but none of it had anything to do with her. And still she was afraid. Children always find out. Perhaps, like whales, they possess a kind of sonar that calculates the distance between the story and the facts. The word *liar* is whispered, then spoken, then shouted across the yard. In the end, it is hung around the child's neck, like a collar.

18

AT FIRST, THE DEAF-MUTE decided not to say anything to anyone. In the morning he wandered through the cafés holding a cardboard sign that said "I Am a Deaf-Mute." The people of the city quickly raised the newspapers they were reading, the pages creating a screen between reading eyes and begging eyes that allowed the deaf-mute comfortably to scan the headlines: "Famous Singer Accused of Attempted Rape of Minor." There were pictures as well: the familiar face of the man he had seen, the sweet face of the girl. In the days that had passed since the event, the deaf-mute had begun to feel undue affection for that fragile young girl. He defended her constantly with his silence, like a noble knight defending a lady completely unaware of his existence.

The deaf-mute had indeed sworn an emotional oath to protect the girl's secret, but emotional oaths are no different from cottage cheese and eggs — they too have a sell-by date. At first, the excitement of the story warmed his nights and spiced his days. But gradually the secret began to make his skin itch. He wandered back and forth through the city, saw hundreds of people every day, and though every such encounter was another opportunity to lean forward and whisper, he persisted in holding his tongue.

But he soon discovered that secrets were not meant to be kept. On the contrary: they were meant to be whispered from mouth to ear, an expression of guilty excitement on your face.

The deaf-mute controlled himself for one day. He controlled himself for two days. But even as the days piled up on his back and the weight became too great, he continued to struggle, barely able to keep his mouth closed. In the end, on an evening not very different from those that had preceded it, he was unable to go on. He let the person walking toward him pass by, and then ran in the direction of the green garbage bin—he couldn't keep the secret in for another minute—lifted the plastic cover and exhaled into it: "It didn't happen!"

He felt better immediately, hurried to reclose the garbage bin and then stood beside it all night to make sure it didn't spill the secret he had buried in it. How relieved he felt when the garbage truck arrived and the secret was carried off to the hills of trash at the far side of the city, where it would stay buried once and for all.

When the truck vanished from sight, he breathed a sigh of relief. For a long while, he stood in the middle of the street as if paralyzed. He sometimes experienced such attacks of immobility. He stood somewhere unable and unwilling to move. In the all-night convenience store next door, a small TV broadcast the morning talk show, and he suddenly recognized the face of the girl, speaking to him. There she was, sitting on the designer couch, her sweet face remarkably serious. But the longer he watched her replying to the presenter's questions, the more surprised he was by the change in her. Her freckles had disappeared under the makeup. Her entire appearance bespoke confidence. Where was the fragile young girl he had sworn to protect? That evening in the alley, she had been so helpless and sad. Now, as he looked at her on the TV screen in the convenience store, he could barely recognize her. When he had seen her then, she was exactly like him, pathetic and invisible. And now everyone was looking at her, everyone was listening to her. He detected a jaded arrogance in her eyes, a look he hated so much in café customers. His affection for her grew cooler from minute to minute, and when the interview was over, he grimaced with distaste and decided that first thing in the morning he would go to the police station.

19

LAVI AND NOFAR quickly discovered that their secret wasn't the only thing that bound them together. Their similarities were truly amazing: both hated olives. Both despised red peppers. Both knew that superstition was ridiculous, but they preferred to keep their distance from black cats, and both agreed that if they had cancer, they would try all the drugs in the world because there was nothing to be afraid of anymore. When they talked about what they would take from their homes if they were burning down, they found their first difference: Lavi said he would go back inside to take his computer, while Nofar said she would go back for her notebook. "What notebook?" he asked, because with all due respect to homework, he wouldn't run into any burning house to get school assignments. Blushing slightly, Nofar said, "My notebook," and her embarrassment was downy and delicate, crying out to be stroked. Lavi sat down, too bashful to reach out, but he did try to soften his reply, saying that, for sure, if he had *that* kind of notebook, he would certainly choose it over a computer. Hearing those words, Nofar's eyes lit up as if it weren't theoretical burning houses they were discussing, but a real fire that demanded an urgent decision.

There were other similarities: both knew the best thing to take to a desert island was a TV set. They both agreed that if a goldfish gave you three wishes, one of them would definitely be to fly. They had both been equally upset a year earlier, the day of their national composition exam, when they were asked to write about what they did on their last summer vacation. Their classmates wrote enthusiastically, bent over the pages, and Lavi and Nofar watched them surreptitiously. If only it were possible, the way it was in a math test, to sneak a look at what the kid on your right was writing and copy the correct answer. Because what were they supposed to write? That they spent entire nights staring at princesses astride dragons? That they spent days watching a detective solve mysteries?

"So what did you do?" she asked.

"I decided to write as if I was Ido Tal."

"Who's Ido Tal?"

The first guy to have a motorbike. The first to replace computerized breasts with real ones, and the first to tell everyone all about it, two months before the event actually took place. Everyone knew that Ido Tal lost his virginity in the ninth grade, which had made it much easier to actually lose it in the middle of the tenth grade. Ido Tal was the sort of person who didn't bother to uproot stray rumors that grew in their yards. On the contrary, he let them grow wild. That way, the rumors thrived, put down roots, blossomed, and trailed around Ido Tal's feet, lending him an air of importance and superiority. They raised him to the sky, because after everyone whispered that he was going to be a pilot, he had no choice but to be accepted into the pilot training course.

"And you answered the question of what you did last summer as if you were Ido Tal?"

Lavi shrugged. What choice did he have? He couldn't fail the exam, and if he'd really tried to describe what he did over the summer vacation, he would have had to hand in an empty page, with the "enter" icon in the middle of it.

"And what grade did you get?"

"Seventy." It hadn't surprised him—he knew he didn't write very well. What did bother him was the way the teacher looked at him when she returned the composition to him, a slight wrinkle in her forehead. She often had that wrinkle when she looked at him. His composition teacher thought he was a pretty strange boy.

"But you really are a pretty strange boy."

He considered taking offense, but something in the way she said the word *strange* stopped him. As if it wasn't a bad word. As if she had said, "You really do have brown eyes" or "You really are five foot two."

"Besides," she added, "if there's something strange, it's those composition teachers who are always asking you what you did last summer. It just turns them on to hear who kissed whom."

They laughed out loud, and a bit too much, because the words "turns them on" glowed in the alley like fireflies. She told him about her composition teacher, Sigal, who very clearly wanted to be in high school herself. That's why she wore those stupid tight jeans, and that's why she always hung around during free periods and asked who was going out with whom. Once, when they were all complaining about homework, she said, "Someday you're going to miss the homework and the age you are now."

"Can you imagine? To miss being seventeen? If I could press a button that would send me to any other age, I would've pressed it a long time ago. I don't even care very much where it sends me."

Lavi almost told her that he wouldn't want to be sent anywhere else. He would choose to stay right here, where they were now: squeezed together on the second step in the alley, his back pressing uncomfortably against the third step, his hands sweating in the pockets of his sweatshirt from the mere possibility of them. But he didn't say anything, and when Nofar asked him what he would choose, a time machine that sent him into the future or one that returned him to whatever time he wanted, he didn't say, "I want to stay here." Instead he said, "To the future. That's where the best weapons are." She said that was a stupid answer, and he said he would forgive her only because she was a girl, and girls don't understand anything. Then she did the most wonderful thing she ever could have done: she hit him. Not really, nothing that actually hurt. She struck him the way girls in her grade always hit the good-looking boys when they were being annoying, a blow—a giggle—a blow, and he defended himself the way she had seen those boys defend themselves: he grabbed her hands so she couldn't keep hitting him, felt her wrist twisting to get free of his grasp, felt her hair dance on his nose and chin as she swung her head from side to side in a show of anger. He felt it for another moment, and then released her suddenly, letting her tickle and hit him with her lovely, broad hands on his chest, which was about to burst.

20

A SHORT TIME after Nofar had begun visiting the alley, her parents began to complain about not seeing her in the evenings. In truth, the days had become an annoyance that Nofar had to endure in order to finally reach the evening, when she went out into the alley. Only the embarrassment cast a shadow on the sweetness of the meetings: every time Nofar came into the ice-cream parlor, where she still worked after school, her body concealed another obstacle. There was the day she couldn't stop trembling. The suspense and the excitement tortured her poor limbs, causing them to move constantly as one thought tormented her—how strange she must appear to him. She was so preoccupied with that strangeness that she didn't notice that Lavi himself was trembling.

It's amazing how two people can meet without really seeing each other at all, and if geometry does not recognize that two parallel lines can intersect, it's only because mathematicians do not visit enough alleys. When her limbs finally stopped shaking, her underarms began perspiring. No matter how much she sprayed them at home, the moment she saw him, two semicircles began smiling on her sleeves, and it was so embarrassing that she didn't dare move her arms, afraid he might see the humiliating stains. But worst of all was that dampness between her legs. She was terrified that she had wet herself. When she returned home, she bent over to smell her underwear. She didn't smell anything, and, despite her relief, she was only more confused. She didn't want to ask her mother; she wanted to ask Maya but didn't dare. She typed "dampness on underwear" on her computer and with a single click was bombarded by such terrifying pictures that she didn't touch her computer for two days. The answer was hidden there, she had no doubt about it, but the thought of searching for it again depressed her. She kept thinking about the only line she had managed to read: "Touching yourself in order to know what feels good." But she didn't entirely know where to touch—she was too embarrassed, and perhaps that was why no time seemed right, because during the day the house was filled with activity and noise, and in the evening someone in the family might open her door at any moment, and, yes, she could lock it, but she might as well hang out a sign that said "Something is going on here!"

Until one evening, on an impulse, she went up to the roof. A few years had passed since she and Maya used to go up there together at night with camping mattresses and, lying on their backs, look at the moon and talk about things she no longer remembered, but which at the time were the most important things in the world. Now Maya did her important things with her girlfriends. Nofar put her camping mattress on the dark roof. From that hidden corner you couldn't see the neighbors' apartments or the glow of the streetlights. Here there was only one glowing moon, dripping silver milk. She lay on her back, her body stretched out on the mattress as her hands wandered over the rough sheets of tar paper. She lifted her nightgown, the one that had oranges printed on it. After a moment's hesitation, she took off the high-waisted cotton briefs her mother bought in packages of ten at the supermarket.

A gust of cold wind reminded her that summer was over, but she didn't give up on her moon tan, and abandoned her body to the blind eyes of a million stars. She closed her eyes because, though no one was there, it was embarrassing. She breathed deeply. The night air was fresh and good. And as she breathed, Lavi came to her. His smell, his lovely breath on her neck. Now her hands left the sheets of tar paper and moved between her thighs, wandering, probing. She searched for a long time, first awkwardly, a sad, restrained groping, the thought of returning home constantly in her mind, and then she let herself go. She moved her fingers rhythmically and what had been a groping question became an answer, became I know, I know me, and the moon smiled its approval as her cheeks reddened and blood flooded her lips and the lips between her thighs. The scene was so beautiful that two clouds hurried to conceal it, covering the eyes of the moon so it could no longer see the girl pleasuring herself, to keep it from being tempted to leave its place and descend to the roof right then and there.

On the roof, the autumn breeze blew down from the clouds. Nofar felt a slight chill, gave a slight smile, stood up, and went home.

21

DETECTIVE DORIT CAME to her office every morning at exactly 8:25. She was never late—law and order do not abide lateness. She was never early—law and order are not served by hastiness. In the city where crimes pile up, sweaty and damp, where the sun itself incites you to sin, there is nothing like the restrained coolness of the clock to restore a bit of order. Detective Dorit had the bad luck to be born in a Mediterranean country: her exemplary preciseness, which would certainly have been highly valued in a more Northern European climate, earned her the ridicule of her colleagues. Dorit noticed it—as a police detective, she had a good eye for detail—but continued to come to the office at precisely 8:25. The second hand on her wrist was as indifferent as the wheels of justice themselves, attentive to the facts and only the facts.

When she reached the office at 8:25, Detective Dorit had already spent two hours with her children. She woke them at six every morning and delivered them to three different schools, reminding each one what was expected of them. She warned her son, in elementary school, against being tempted into Internet bullying. She warned her middle-school son about the long-term damage of all drugs. She described to her daughter, a high school student, the horrors of the delivery room. And so her children stepped out of the car terrified to the depths of their tender souls, and it was no wonder that they sought immediate relief—the first by bullying children in the schoolyard, the second by smoking aromatic cigarettes near the middle-school fence, and the third with a quick bit of lovemaking with the boy who lived across the street from the high school.

Sometimes the trip to the city center took less time than expected. Detective Dorit had ten full minutes before she had to be in her office, so she decided to take a short walk down the street, to look at people and wonder which of them were likely to arrive at the police station as criminals and which as victims. On the corner, a beggar had taken his post and was muttering incomprehensible things to himself. None of the passersby seemed to notice the contradiction between the emotional muttering and his "I Am a Deaf-Mute" sign, but Dorit wasn't just a passerby, she was a detective, and that contradiction caught her attention.

"It didn't happen! It didn't happen!" The words burst rapidly out of the deaf-mute's mouth as they do from the mouths of criminals confessing after a grueling interrogation. If she had been in her office, Dorit would certainly have asked, "What didn't happen?" and would have relentlessly demanded names, times, and places. But it was 8:21, and she only had four minutes before she had to begin work, so she didn't ask and didn't investigate. The deaf-mute looked at the detective in her crisp uniform. All the words he hadn't spoken leaped around in his stomach like an army of frogs. "It didn't happen," he said, and, looking her right in the eye, repeated, "It didn't happen!" The sentence hopped around his mouth, and Detective Dorit glanced calmly at him, because what business did people have with frogs? What business did a detective hurrying off to work have with a beggar standing on the corner? And so, at 8:24, Detective Dorit turned back to the police station on the main street, and the deaf-mute remained standing on the corner, croaking "It didn't happen!" to all the passersby.

Days passed. The deaf-mute kept coming almost daily and kept croaking, even though the new habit decreased his income significantly. People walked more quickly as they passed him. No one listened. Nonetheless, the deaf-mute's words continued to echo in Detective Dorit's mind. Whenever she came to the office early, she went to the street corner to watch him. Sometimes he didn't say anything, maintaining his muteness, but other times he muttered constantly, swaying where he stood like that blind soothsayer: "It didn't happen! It didn't happen!" And even added in a whisper, "She's lying!" Dorit the Detective watched him with concern. One day, contrary to her usual behavior, she took five shekels out of her purse. She was sure that now he would say more, but the deaf-mute muttered, "Little pigs on the beach!" Then he closed his mouth. If that blue-uniformed bitch thought she could buy the truth from him for the ridiculous price of five shekels, she was absolutely wrong. He too had self-respect.

But it was the deaf-mute's renewed silence that disturbed Dorit even more. At 8:25 she went to her office, and this time the thoughts accompanied her over the threshold. Those words, "It didn't happen!" and "She's lying!" sat down on the interrogation table and waited for her to examine them.

22

THE DAYS ACCUMULATED, as did the gifts at Lavi's door. A fleece shirt. Thermal gloves. A tactical flashlight. A green balaclava. His father's I-have-a-secret expression, which at first had thrilled him, now became tormenting and oppressive. Lavi was careful not to say anything to add fuel to the combat-unit story, hoping it would dissipate on its own. He didn't add to it—nor did he refute it—and that was enough to cause Arieh Maimon's chest to swell with pride. He considered his son's silence to be honorable and evidence of his ability to keep a secret, two qualities he valued in himself as well. Nor did the arrogance of that silence escape his notice—since the boy didn't know whether he would pass the tests, he told no one about it so that there would be no witness if he should fail. In his youth, Arieh Maimon had not talked about his screening for entrance into the elite combat unit either, and for precisely the same reason. He didn't want to be the recipient of sympathy steeped in gloating if he, heaven forbid, failed. That similarity between him and his son moved him, and Lavi, well aware of his father's emotional reaction, began to worry. He pinned his hopes on the time that would pass and erode the story. He did not yet understand that the longer he kept silent, the more he nourished his father's dreams.

And so the internal clock of the lie continued to mark time in Lavi. The hands showed the minutes, which turned into hours, which turned into days. He wondered whether the hands would move that way forever, whether the time to speak the truth would never come. After all, more lies remain undiscovered than are revealed, harmless little lies absorbed into the fabric of everyday life until they are indistinguishable from the truth. Time kneads all of them into a single lump of dough, and does it matter what really happened and what didn't?

One morning, as he was sadly chewing the protein omelet, his father offered to drive him the following Sunday.

"And if you need a note for school, just say the word. Or does the army send you one?"

Lavi sipped his chocolate milk, but the omelet stuck in his esophagus and wouldn't go down. After a long moment, when he saw that his father was waiting for an answer, he cleared his throat and mumbled, "The army is sending it."

"I don't understand why they don't do that screening during the summer vacation," his mother said, "instead of taking you out of school." Her voice came from the kitchen where she was laboring over the wheatgrass juice.

"This is also a learning experience," his father said in a satisfied voice, "and if Amos's son is going, despite his exam results, then our Lavi definitely can."

That's what he said—"our Lavi." For a moment he lowered the financial pages and smiled at him, actually smiled. And at that moment Lavi knew that he had to go, even if he hadn't been called up. Even if it was five days in the field. Even if Eitan, Amos's son, was a head taller and four times broader than he was, and had been preparing for the tests since he was five years old.

When the day came, he packed his fleece shirt, his thermal gloves, the waterproof watch with the compass, five pairs of boxers, special woolen socks, and a copper brush he had no idea what to do with, but his father told him he needed.

He also packed some energy bars, a sleeping bag, and anti-mosquito spray. On the morning of the big day, his mother hugged him with both arms and his father got up long before he did and made him sandwiches, which he wrapped in cling wrap. Apart from the protein omelet, there were tahini, hummus, and salami sandwiches, and one with chocolate. In the car Arieh Maimon talked about his own tests for the elite combat unit, about the eggs he stole from the kibbutz, and about the kibbutz boys he met later in the unit who became his best friends, and to this day didn't know about the eggs. They drove and drove, and Lavi hoped they would never arrive, not only because he had never heard his father talk so much, but also because he didn't know what he would do when they reached their destination.

When they saw the sign with the name of the base on it, Lavi told his father he would rather go the rest of the way alone. Arieh Maimon didn't argue. It was more than a mile to the base itself, but he realized that Lavi wanted to arrive alone, like a grown man, not like a boy whose father has driven him. Lavi took the waterproof bag with the state-of-the-art back-straps and stepped out of the car. Arieh Maimon watched him as he began to walk.

After a mile, Lavi looked back and saw that the road was empty. He walked back to the intersection and tried to thumb a ride. Three cars passed without slowing down. He took out an energy bar and sat down on the side of the road. He had five days to get through. He was in no rush.

Nofar had waited for him in the alley and looked with awe at the backpack he was carrying. "Wow." He showed her the fleece shirt, the flashlight, and the gloves, and she brought a jug of water from the ice-cream parlor so he could put the watch in it and see whether it would keep working. "I found you a beach with a campsite, and there's a bus every hour on the hour." Once again he had wanted to ask her to go with him, and once again he hadn't.

The first night on the beach he didn't sleep at all. He was afraid that someone or something... The following nights were better, and he no longer jumped at the slightest sound. The people on the beach were nice. Maybe they thought he really was eighteen, or maybe they didn't care. In the tent next to his was a large Russian whom everyone called the Landlord, because he'd been on the beach long before the others. On the second day Lavi asked the Landlord where he was from before the beach and what he did, and the looks of the people around them made him realize that the question was not such a good one. Then someone with dreadlocks told him that you don't ask people on the beach where they were before the beach. But the Landlord didn't care. He told Lavi that he'd had a start-up company, made millions, and then decided to leave everything. Then he laughed a huge Russian laugh that made his mustache vibrate, and Lavi thought that if bears could laugh, they would laugh like that.

On the third day Lavi woke up and found the Landlord sitting on the beach. He sat down beside him and saw that he had a large tattoo on the back of his hand. The Landlord saw him looking and said, "It's the sun." When he showed Lavi the tattoo close up, it really did look a little bit like the sun. The Landlord's hand was very large, and three prominent veins crossed it like three huge rivers.

"I did it myself when the army stuck me in the Ural Mountains so I would remember that there is such a thing as the sun. Because in the Urals, there is no sun."

Lavi tried unsuccessfully to imagine himself in a place that had no sun. He knew where the Ural Mountains were because a map of the world hung right in front of him in class and he always remembered such things by heart. But he hadn't known that there was no sun there, only that they were purple and stretched from Kazakhstan, which was green, to the Arctic Ocean, which was turquoise. The Landlord rubbed his tattooed hand with his other hand, and the sun was crumpled for a moment, then returned to itself. "Now I have lots of sun," the Landlord said. "Now it's coming out of my ass."

"And what's that?" Lavi asked, pointing to the letters under the sun in a language he couldn't read.

"My name: Vladimir."

"But you said your name is Zev."

"Yes, but there they called me Vladimir."

On the fourth day Lavi had no more energy bars left and he went to the shopping center on the promenade to buy something. He was about to order himself a pizza when he suddenly saw a grocery store. Surreptitiously, he went inside and looked at the shelves. The eggs were in the back, next to the milk and bread.

Five days and three stolen-egg omelets later, Lavi boarded a bus in one beach city and took it to another beach city. His skin was scorched from the sun because on the last day he hadn't applied sunblock. And so he appeared at the door to his house sunburned from marches, exhausted from night navigations, and saturated with sand and sweat. His father looked at him questioningly. Lavi shook his head. The embrace was a total and utter surprise. "Never mind, boy, at least you tried."

23

THEY SAY THAT with a car, it hurts the least. He didn't want it to hurt. From what he understood, if you do it with a car it doesn't distort your face too much. He didn't want to look bad afterward. He googled pictures of people who had died that way, but what he saw didn't satisfy him. He didn't understand whether those dead people looked bad because of the carbon monoxide or because they'd been ugly when they were alive. In the end, it didn't really matter very much, the picture they'd put on the news was the one he'd left with his PR guy anyway. That was the most accessible one, and there were no copyrights to worry about. He looked wonderful in it: mischievous green eyes, a mysterious half-smile, even his hair was perfect. He felt a thrill of excitement whenever he imagined hundreds of thousands of people seeing that picture in the newspaper, with the caption that would be printed in mourning black: "Avishai Milner's suicide note: 'I'm innocent!'"

He didn't know exactly when he stopped planning her death and began planning his own. After all, he had been a vegan for sixteen years. He continued practicing yoga even in jail. He couldn't destroy sixteen years of living right only because of a lying bitch. And there was also the matter of TV: every time he imagined her death, it ended with those sympathetic reports, with sad music that would be played when her face appeared on the screen. But that sad music was his. And the face that looked out at everyone from the screen, noble and tragic, was his face. That death was his death—he wouldn't let her take it away from him.

He worked on that note for almost two weeks, from the moment he was released on bail. "Sometimes the best way to kill a rumor is to kill yourself"—that was his opening sentence. He wasn't sure about how to continue. Every morning he woke up filled with energy and sat down to work. He wrote, erased, rewrote, polished. He hadn't felt such joy of creation since he'd worked on his first album. Even when he got stuck, he didn't give up. With the humility of a sales clerk, he appeared at his post every morning to begin his day's work. Finally, the note was so beautiful that Avishai Milner was sorry that he couldn't print up thousands of copies. He wanted all the birds in the city to hear his swan song. One sleepless night, he even sat down and set the final verse to music. When he finished, there were tears in his eyes. He knew: he had never before written anything so beautiful.

Now he had no choice but to turn to more practical matters: when and how. The afternoon was preferable because the news editors would have time to prepare a long enough report for the evening broadcast. The place had to be meaningful: first he chose the ice-cream parlor where the blood libel had been fabricated. Then he considered the amphitheater where he had been crowned the winner in that wonderful finale. There was no parking near the ice-cream parlor. The amphitheater had a huge parking area and it would be a picturesque place in which to die. But a brief Internet search showed that Eliran Vaknin would be performing three shows there that week, and just the name of his singing rival was enough to eliminate the place once and for all. He decided to do it outside the ice-cream parlor.

The only thing left was to choose what he would wear.

Black was flattering, but if his face looked grayish, the general effect might be too gloomy. Blue was better. There's something aristocratic about blue. After a long shower he locked the front door and set off on his way. He laughed joylessly at the parking ticket resting on his car. On the way, he felt his hands shaking on the wheel and remembered the note in his blue shirt pocket. The thought of the note calmed him. He tried to think about his parents and his sister. He spoke to himself in the second person, as he always did when he was excited, "Avishai, are you sure?"

I'm sure.

If it had been a game, he was no longer playing. If it had been a story he wanted to tell everyone, a hoax, well, that story was on its way to becoming reality. He had good reason to say that. He wasn't pretending. It was really true—Avishai Milner was found dead at the entrance to the ice-cream parlor where he had been unjustly accused.

"Avishai Milner was found unconscious at the entrance to the ice-cream parlor where he was accused."

An anonymous caller alerted the police. He gave them the exact address. Perhaps it was a passerby. Or a shrewd agent who had recognized the potential for a comeback. And perhaps it was Avishai Milner himself.

24

THE INTERNATIONAL DAY for the Elimination of
Violence Against Women was a windfall for the catering companies in the capital city. Various government offices held a
variety of events to celebrate the day, and apart from speeches
and speakers, each event had napkins, refreshments, and soft
drinks. The president's residence, for example, ordered thirteen
trays of feta-filled pastry. The previous year they had forgotten
to mark the day, and the public outcry was enormous. The
social secretary was fired and replaced by a determined young
woman who had arranged for two battered women and one
female professor to be present. The day before, in a moment of
brilliance, she decided to invite a fourth guest, a sort of national
hero, the brave girl who had fought back in the alley.

Lying in bed, drifting between wakefulness and sleep, the
social secretary suddenly had another idea—she sat up and
texted her assistant.

> We need a large poster saying "WE ARE PUTTING AN END
> TO IT!"—with an exclamation mark!

And on the morning of the event, everything was in
place—the poster, the battered women, the refreshments, the
female professor, and the young girl, a bit shy, who stood in
the corner with her sister and her parents. While waiting for
the president to appear, Nofar's father eyed the feta pastries.

But his wife whispered in his ear that it wasn't respectful—the president hadn't arrived yet. And so, silenced, reprimanded, and, most important, hungry, the father remained standing beside the spotless white tablecloth, hoping the president would make an appearance soon.

Nofar's father didn't know it, but at that precise moment, as the president stood at the door to the hall, straightened the knot of his tie, and peered at the loaded trays, he too was experiencing the sharp pinch of hunger pangs. He hadn't eaten anything since morning. To take his mind off the pain in his stomach, the distinguished president focused on his speech: a piercing condemnation of any form of violence against women. "We are all mobilized in the struggle against it..." His fingers, the fingers of a good grandfather, moved along the words printed on the page. Thirty years previously those fingers had moved in the same relaxed manner along the backside of the head clerk at military command headquarters—Ruthie or Rachel, something with an *R*, he couldn't remember exactly—but the backside he remembered quite well. She made and served him coffee—back then, he still drank it with three sugars—and when she turned around, she seemed to be offering him her backside as well, so he reached out and partook. She froze, began to cry, and fled to the outer office. He followed her and found her beside her desk, sobbing. As she stood there, trembling with fear, she seemed the picture of enchanting helplessness. How she wept when he pawed her in the outer office, on the desk, which he would later take with him to his next post—a mahogany desk he had confiscated from the home of the most notorious murderer in the West Bank. A genuine antique. And today, an hour earlier, on that very desk, he had finished writing the draft of his speech for the

International Day for the Elimination of Violence Against Women.

"Let's get started," he said in a thundering voice to the social secretary, and she told her assistant to announce to everyone that the president would be there in another minute.

But where was Nofar? The battered women were sitting in their places on the small stage. At the polite distance of two seats away from them sat the distinguished female professor. The slide show revealing the horrifying statistics had already begun behind them. The photographers and journalists were in their assigned places like obedient dogs. Only the girl had vanished as if the earth had swallowed her up. Her embarrassed parents were still standing there, but she was gone. The social secretary went over to investigate, first with a smile, then with increasing anxiety. The event had to begin, and soon. Eyes searched everywhere, but they found not even the smallest trace of the girl to fasten on to. Phones were pulled out—the father and mother called her at the same time—to no avail. Her phone was switched off. She had switched it off in a panic twenty minutes earlier when she learned from a quick look at social media that Avishai Milner had tried to kill himself. Because of her.

She fled to the bathroom. Where else could she run to? But instead of escaping to the one adjoining the hall, which had been searched half a dozen times already, she had run off to a bathroom that was farther away. She turned right in the marble corridor, through a small courtyard filled with well-trimmed roses, straight into a spacious hall where a large photograph of the signing of the Declaration of the State hung on the wall. In the presence of those formidable people, Nofar felt particularly vile. A wave of tears flooded her. Avishai Milner had tried to kill himself. Because of her. Miraculously, someone had found him in his car. She pictured the face familiar to her from her nightmares, now lifeless. How could she shake the honorable president's hand when her own hand was covered with the blood of Avishai Milner?

She would leave and confess. Right now. They would definitely put her in jail. Her body began to shake. She had to go back to the hall and ask her parents quietly to drive her to the police station. But before she did that, she had to call Lavi and say goodbye. With trembling fingers she turned on her phone, ignored the twenty unanswered calls from her parents, and punched in his number. When he answered, instead of speaking she burst into tears. He was frightened. Asked her what happened. Asked again, and when she couldn't reply he said, "Where are you? I'm coming." In the end, choking on her tears, she told him she was at the president's residence, that Avishai Milner had tried to kill himself, and that she was going to the police now.

"You're not going anywhere." His voice was remarkably authoritative, which surprised her and, even more, surprised him. "But," she sobbed, "but—"

Instead of the rest of the sentence, a series of small, un-controllable sobs escaped her lips. It was too much. Someone could die. Every such thought evoked additional sobs. Her face was wet and red from so much crying, and she didn't know whether he was still on the line.

He was on the line. Of course he was. And he seemed totally unmoved by the entire business. "Don't you see that he's only trying to break you? A stunt for the media. You really think that someone so in love with himself would be willing to say goodbye to himself and die?"

"But how . . . how do you know? How can you be sure?"

From his room on the fourth floor, Lavi took a deep breath. He wasn't used to lying, and now, like a child learning to ride a bike, he had to focus completely on maintaining his balance. "I know because I was there when it happened. I saw everything: he did it in front of the ice-cream parlor, and he himself called the police. If that's what attempted suicide looks like, then I'm steamed broccoli." When Nofar didn't reply, he added quickly, in a nervous whisper, "We'll talk about it tomorrow in the alley, okay?" And then, once again in the most authoritative voice he could muster, he said, "Don't do anything before we talk about it tomorrow."

He hung up and crossed his fingers in the hope that it had worked. In the bathroom of the northern wing of the president's residence, Nofar sat on a toilet and tried to calm down. It's all right that you cried. You already know that they love to photograph you with red eyes. Take a deep breath and go back to the hall. Come on, open the door.

But when she opened the door, her breath caught in her throat. Not because of the face that looked out at her from the mirror, swollen from crying and the color of eggplant, and not because her hair was unkempt and unattractive. What horrified her was not the Nofar in the mirror, but the face beside hers, almost identical but prettier. Maya.

Her younger sister had opened the door to the farthest stall. She herself had been hiding there for more than an hour, long before her older sister arrived. The moment they had reached the president's residence, Maya realized that she had made a terrible mistake by going there with the family. True, the social secretary had explained to their mother that "the entire family is invited." And true, her mother had urged Maya to come because "It's not every day you receive an invitation to the president's residence," and "Don't tell me you'd rather go to school." But in retrospect, she really would rather have gone to school. The president's residence turned out to be incredibly boring, and, as in other places, everyone was busy with her older sister and treating Maya as if she were a vase.

It would be the same thing in school tomorrow: during free periods Nofar would be surrounded by a crowd of boys who'd want to hear about the president. Maya knew that crowd of boys—after all, until a few weeks ago it had been her crowd. Why couldn't there be two suns in the sky? Why did the rise of one large orb of light necessitate the setting of another? But the laws of astronomy were binding—a circle of boys surrounding Nofar meant that it did not surround Maya. And perhaps even worse than school and the president's residence was their home. To be a sister means that part of you is always comparing. Even if the words *Why can't you be more like her?* are never spoken, the question still hangs in the air: *Which one is loved more?* The answer changes from parent to parent, from one time of life to another. The agreed-upon lie of all parents—*both of you! in equal measure!*—might still be preferable to the truth.

On her way to the bathroom, Maya had also passed the photograph of the signing of the Declaration of the State. And no matter how thrilled everyone looked to finally have a country, Maya was sure that the man in the left-hand corner was thinking only about how much he wanted to be in the middle. She entered the bathroom and knew: no one would come looking for her. That knowledge made her body limp. Her features remained: the large eyes, the sculpted lips, but now each feature was separate, making a set of discrete notes that did not come together in a melody. The substance that organized Maya's face, that bound all her features together harmoniously, the elusive quality that was charm—that quality had abandoned its post. She glanced in the mirror and was horrified. She hurried to hide in the farthest stall. Despite everything, she still hoped that one of her parents would come looking for her. As the minutes passed and no one came, silent tears welled up in her eyes.

Suddenly she heard the sound of feet running in the corridor, then the bathroom door opening. She knew immediately that it was Nofar. She would have recognized the sound of her sister's steps anywhere. She understood from the noises coming from the other side of the door that her sister was crying, and wondered what exactly she had to cry about. But then came the conversation. Nofar spoke to a boy Maya didn't know but whose existence she had already guessed. She cried. Told him about Avishai Milner. Cried some more. Mumbled something about the police. Maya didn't understand everything, but one thing was clear—something was wrong. Suddenly she heard the door to the stall next to hers opening. She too decided to go out. And at that moment, their eyes met in the mirror.

For a moment it seemed to Maya that Nofar was about to fall. She didn't realize that she herself was the cause of Nofar's horror. At first she looked around, wondering who had so upset her sister. But no, only the two of them were there. And if Nofar was so appalled at the sight of her, that meant there had been something in the conversation that she was not supposed to hear. Maya went over what she had just heard: Nofar crying to the boy she didn't know about Avishai Milner, who tried to commit suicide. Nofar was considering going to the police and withdrawing her complaint. If Nofar were to ask Maya, she would reply that Nofar shouldn't dare do it. If he wanted to kill himself, that's his problem—he should think twice before harassing young girls in alleys, really. (Really?)

Suddenly a new thought slithered into Maya's mind, twisting

and turning so much that at first she could barely hold on to it. Then the thought flicked out a forked tongue and began moving on its belly: maybe it wasn't true. Maybe none of it was true. Was that why Nofar was so frightened? Was that why she looked at you with such apprehension? Maya had already opened her mouth to ask, but stopped herself. What kind of sister are you? If positions were reversed, Nofar would have gone to Avishai Milner for you and killed him herself. Like when you were on that family vacation and you went out to walk on the promenade, and suddenly that disgusting drunk pinched your ass. You were so scared and you started to cry, and then Nofar, of all people, who is always so quiet, ran after him almost the whole length of the promenade so she could spit at him. When she came back, she hugged you and said, "We won't tell Mom and Dad if you don't want to." How dare you even suspect her? And so Maya smashed the slithering thought and hurried over to her sister with open arms. "Come on, we'll go to the ceremony. I'm sure you'll be wonderful."

They stood there for a long minute, hugging in the bath-room of the president's residence. When they finally stepped apart, Nofar's breathing was calmer, and the charm seemed to have made its way back to Maya's face. But not for very long: the moment they reached the hall, everyone gathered around the older sister. "Were you crying?" "Poor thing." "Never mind, sweetie, you are a very brave girl." A sea of people surrounded Nofar, and Maya was left like a beached jellyfish. The pretty-but-ordinary sister of the heroine from the alley.

The ceremony began. The president's speech was strong and resolute. "We are all together in this struggle." Maya understood very little of the female professor's words, but they definitely sounded erudite. The battered women moved her to tears. She was sure the same would be true when Nofar spoke onstage, but to her surprise she noticed that her big sister was avoiding her, looking at everything but her. Like an acrobat on a tightrope, careful to avoid gazing down into the abyss.

25

"SO?" OF ALL the things she thought he might say, that was the most unexpected. She had been sure he would be at least slightly shocked by the suicide attempt that was described in greater detail in the morning papers, but Lavi simply looked at her with eyes that were as black and stimulating as the espresso she served in the ice-cream parlor and asked, "So?"

Bewildered, Nofar said nothing. His totally unruffled reaction to her words angered her. But it also calmed her somehow. Because if he reacted that way, maybe it really wasn't such a big deal. She picked up a small stick and drew lines on the ground with it. "So maybe it's time I say something."

Lavi was terrified. What they had together was based entirely on her lie, as if a beehive had taken up residence in a carcass and the honey was sweet. Since their conversation the day before, he had been afraid she would suggest something like that. Actually, even before she said a word, Lavi knew that the girl who had returned to him in the alley was not the same one who had left him before going to the president's residence. In the time he'd spent with Nofar, he had learned to read every movement of her face. He worked as hard at that as he did at his studies. His parents, who placed great importance on the boy's scholastic achievements, would not have liked it. How would his knowledge of any girl's facial features help him be accepted to a university? It would be more practical to devote his time to trying to understand Newton's third law.

But on that day, the knowledge Lavi had accumulated proved useful—as soon as he saw Nofar in the alley, he understood that the situation was grave.

"You can't back down now. Maybe you could have then, the night it happened, but now it's too late."

That night, when there were only twenty witnesses, seemed so far away to Nofar now. She had thought it was a lot then, but now that group felt remarkably small. A pretty girl soldier. Her lover, the officer. A few customers. Could it be that she had fabricated the story because of them, to avoid being the object of ridicule after she had brought them all there with her screams? She could also have told the truth at the police station: *I'm sorry, a mistake, a misunderstanding.* Instead, she stuck to the story from the alley. Kneaded and leavened it, then kneaded and leavened it again until she put it in the oven and it turned so crispy and golden and beautiful that it was a shame to destroy it.

"But he tried to kill himself!"

"And didn't succeed."

"He'll go to prison! Because of me!"

"Prison is no fun, but it'll be over in a year. But if you talk now, no one will ever forgive you. Not even in another ten years."

She was silent. She nodded and said that maybe she should think about how to compensate Avishai Milner. Start saving her allowance. When he got out of prison, a large envelope filled with her savings would be waiting for him. Maybe she would devote her life to helping the exploited. She'd be a lawyer, let's say, or maybe a doctor would be better. She'd work to save lives to make up for the one she destroyed. Lavi watched her as she spoke. He saw clearly that her eyes were pleading with him to reveal the secret, to save her from herself. But if there were no secret, he wasn't sure what would be left for them.

Never mind if she felt guilty, he'd help her. Together, they would train her guilt until it became a domestic dog. You feed it, take it out for walks, and then you both forget it was once a wolf. The longer the lie remained a burden to Nofar, the more Lavi feared that, God forbid, the truth would come and stand between them.

26

THE EVENT AT the president's residence was all over the TV news. Pictures of Nofar at the speakers' podium broke hearts. How innocent she looked, standing there, shy and reserved, her hands hugging her body with such endearing embarrassment. She was as fragile as a kitten—everyone wanted to pet her. She was as brave as a lioness—everyone wanted to sing her praises. Fashion companies that saw her as a trendsetter sent clothing and gifts to her home, and she, stunned by her good fortune, wore them in amazement: flared dresses that suited her figure, earrings that brought out the color of her eyes. The pathetic ice-cream server looked in the mirror she had always avoided and was astonished to see the change in herself. Whenever she left the house, her expression seemed to ask, "Is this really me?" And that astonishment, that humble embarrassment, enhanced her magic so much that the entire world hurried to nod at her, "Yes, that's really you."

Yet she still did not believe it. She shared the clothes she received with her schoolmates and her little sister, her expression almost apologetic. Perhaps she should have been more careful. Her generosity saved her from the other girls' resentment, but it also deepened it, because it underscored the gap between what she had and what they had. Not sensing that, she walked around with feet that barely touched the ground. For the first time in her life, Nofar felt lucky simply to be who she was.

Then came the yellow days. The haze, like a ruined sunny-side-up egg, stained the sky. People closed their shutters. People bolted their windows. But sand knows how to get in. Every morning Nofar's mother swept the house, but the dust continued to pile up even as she swept, and Ronit could just as easily have tried to soak up the sea with a rag. The withered sky demoralized people. Many lost their temper about the most minor things: who had first dibs on the magazine section in the café, who had the right to pull into the empty parking spot. Even those who made love did it half-heartedly, just going through the motions. When the yellow days passed, colder days came. The city, which had been bubbling-hot on the yellow days, now cooled like a pot of cooked food left on the counter.

And so the school ceremony in honor of the assassinated prime minister grew closer. Two months earlier, it would never have occurred to Nofar that she could sing onstage during the ceremony. The girls who participated in those events were a breed unto themselves. They wore their self-confidence with the same aplomb with which they wore their white blouses. But now she decided to try, to fight the other girls for the role. In history class she wrote a note to Shir saying that she planned to audition, and cringed to see the shock on her friend's face. The history teacher kept talking, and Shir wrote on the desk that it didn't seem like a good idea. But as Shir wrote and the teacher spoke, Nofar could feel the second Nofar, the secret one, knocking inside her, demanding that the door be opened.

On the morning of the auditions, wardrobe doors opened with a roar, hurrying hands pushed aside one blouse after another in the search for the appropriate white one. Sleeves were rolled up. Buttons were undone. All the way to school, girls sang the song they would perform at the audition. If their enthusiasm might seem somewhat exaggerated in relation to a matter as serious as the murder of a prime minister, that's only because certain people are naïve. After all, the official ceremony was no different from any other event where a stage is the major focus, and it doesn't matter if it's a stage adorned with neon lights and balloons or memorial candles and bouquets. But in fact, the auditions ended even before they began: the moment the teacher saw the ice-cream server she cried, "Nofar Shalev!" as if she had unearthed a treasure. The evening before, the teacher had learned that the schools chancellor would be visiting on the day of the ceremony. She could already picture the famous young girl singing against the backdrop of the poster, "WE SHALL NEVER FORGET," a sight that would certainly make a huge impression on him.

The biblical Joseph wore a coat of many colors, and Nofar wore a white blouse and tight jeans, so it was no wonder that Maya once again did not sleep at night, her lids swollen, her expression nasty. Because she too had gone to try out for the ceremony but had left empty-handed. Because the white blouse suited Nofar more than any coat of many colors. Because Nofar's voice echoed from the amplifiers whenever there were rehearsals, and it seemed to Maya that they were always rehearsing because never once did she go out during break without coming across her sister, standing on the high stage and waving to her. The more Nofar blossomed, the stronger the suspicion in Maya's mind grew, no longer slithering along the ground but standing upright: Really, sister? Really?

The day of the ceremony in memory of the assassinated prime minister finally arrived. A black velvet curtain had been hung on the stage, the words "WE SHALL NEVER FORGET" woven into it with silver thread. True, the curtain had become worn out over the years from so many memorial days for the fallen, and on the previous Holocaust Day a spark from the eternal flame had almost destroyed it completely. Nonetheless, it lent the school a festive air. On the black stage, Nofar pulled back her hair. She had invited her parents to the ceremony, and, after some thought, also the boy who was blackmailing her. She undid the top button of her blouse especially for him. It was only a shame, she thought, that, given the nature of the event, her loved ones could not applaud for her.

The ceremony began. A blue-haired boy played the opening chords on his bass guitar. Liron Kahanoff, a seasoned veteran of school ceremonies, adjusted the microphone and began to speak. She read the eulogy written by the national eulogist—a devoted teacher and popular poet: *A black-hearted villain with a gun / Slew him one night in November / All Jewish hearts cried out as one / We shall always, always remember.* Nofar heard through her earbuds, but the words blurred because she was too excited to listen.

Lavi stood in a corner of the schoolyard and surveyed the audience. He could not be suspected of looking at other girls. If his glance happened to fall on the girl standing in the first row of students, it was only because the others were looking that way. He had watched the movements of the boys' heads, and a few moments later saw that they were all facing the same direction, as sunflowers face the sun. Out of pure curiosity, he too moved his gaze. What he saw astonished him to his core. She had never told him she had a sister.

Maya was standing in the first row, her hair loose, her lips parted. Within her, sisterly affection warred with sisterly envy, and in that sort of war blood is miraculously not shed, but rather water: salty tears that beguiled those who saw them. (Indeed, the national eulogist was thrilled to see how much

the little verse he had written touched the girl in the first row.)
Maya hoped her sister would succeed and that she would fail,
and those contradictory hopes made her nostrils flare and her
lips tremble, made her blood boil and her cheeks flush. The
struggle going on inside her did for her face what no cosmetic
wizardry could do: it highlighted her features and deepened
them. If Maya's face was round and beautiful to begin with,
now it was truly perfect. There was a good reason everyone
was looking at her.

Lavi shifted his gaze back and forth between the girl standing onstage and the one in the first row. The resemblance was
amazing, but the difference was no less so. He could easily
recognize the unique shape of the eyes, the same yet different
elegant curve. And there was the jawline, slightly more chiseled
on the face of the girl in the front row, somewhat coarser on
the face of the girl onstage. As if someone had amused himself
by playing the same musical notes in two different styles.

Now Lavi wondered if the younger sister had the same
fingers as Nofar, too long and large for a girl. He had noticed
the first night that she had the hands of a boy, and somehow
that had both repelled and attracted him. He stared at the spot
where the younger sister was standing and wondered what
sort of hands were hidden under the arms folded on her chest.
And the moment he fixed his gaze on her breasts, he could not
look away, studying them carefully and stopping only when an
insistent voice inside him shouted: traitor, traitor, traitor.

Lavi had almost summoned the willpower to look away,
when Maya stared right at him. Once again, he was warmed
by the resemblance between Nofar and her sister. And once
again, the difference confused him. Like those deceptive
dreams when, in the fog of sleep, a familiar person materializes
with a different appearance. As if he were dreaming about

Nofar, but had made her more beautiful. Lavi and Nofar had already told each other many things as they sat in the alley, but she had never mentioned her sister. It was the silence that told Lavi more than anything she might have said.

The rhymed eulogy had already ended. Now the girls on the stage sang a sad song in two-part harmony. Liron Kahanoff threw back her shoulders and pushed out her breasts, exactly as she had seen it done on a talent show. Nofar wanted to search for Lavi in the audience but forced herself to look at the horizon and think about sad things, just as Liron had told her she should. As the music rose from the stage, Lavi was surprised to see that the sister in the audience was looking at him as intently as he was looking at her. While he was still stealing glances at her, Maya's eyes scanned his face. One sad song was followed by another sad song, but Lavi and Maya were totally unaware of that. Maya's eyes examined Lavi's face in minute detail, slowly, deliberately, making no effort to hide what she was doing. She saw immediately that he was not from their school, and the way he was looking at her and at the same time staring at the girl onstage gave rise to a strong suspicion in her mind.

Many boys pursued Maya. Handsome, robust boys. Lavi Maimon couldn't compare to even the most pathetic among them. He was scrawny. His face was gaunt. His appearance totally lacked the charisma that can endow even the skinniest boys with some measure of attractiveness. Nonetheless, Lavi Maimon had something that made him remarkably appealing. Unbearably appealing, in fact. He held the beating heart of her big sister in his charmless hands.

But right now, the national anthem. Everyone stood waiting for the blue-haired boy onstage to tune his guitar. Nofar looked around at the faces in the audience. There was her father, studying his mobile phone. There was her mother. As the first guitar notes rang out, Nofar broke into a charming, off-key version of the well-known words.

As she sang, she searched for Lavi's face. For a moment she was afraid he hadn't come, but then she saw him, at the far end of the schoolyard. He was facing in her direction, but she couldn't catch his eye. He was entirely focused on a different spot, close to where she stood. She tried to understand what had drawn his attention so strongly. She scanned the area close to the stage.

Liron Kahanoff, who was standing under the picture of the assassinated prime minister, looked at her in surprise. In the first row, the teacher suddenly tensed. And Nofar did not even notice herself ceasing to sing. The anthem, which had frozen in her mouth, was the last thing she cared about at the moment. She saw him looking at Maya. She saw Maya looking at him. With the utmost clarity, she saw what was going to happen. He was being added to her sister's league of admirers. The battle was lost even before it had begun. Her defeated body shook. Her chest shriveled. Like a birthday candle stuck indifferently into a cake by a waiter, catching fire for a moment and immediately going out.

From where he stood, Lavi could sense the change in Nofar and railed against himself. You idiot, you asshole, you moron. Nofar was onstage and her sister was in the audience, yet everyone was looking at her sister. Damn it, even you are looking at her sister. Did you think Nofar wouldn't notice? He had to hide his eyes from her. It would be futile to tell her later that everything was fine, because the image of her younger sister still danced in his eyes.

People often prefer to deny what is right before their eyes, especially if they can continue to hold on to what is in their hearts. Nofar wanted to believe that everything was all right, and such a desire can bend reality. As they reached the second verse of the national anthem, she pulled herself together and joined the singer beside her, her voice clear and confident, so clear and confident that everyone assumed it had all been planned in advance. Lavi forced himself to look away from the younger sister and look only at the sister onstage. Nofar sang the anthem with sad eyes and trembling lips. A brief thought about that terrible moment when she looked at Lavi and Maya was enough to bring tears to her eyes. The teacher nodded in satisfaction—the schools chancellor had received his due portion of tears. The ceremony had been a success.

Moving lithely, Maya made her way through the audience in the schoolyard. The closer she came to Lavi, the less distorted, the more impressive the boy looked. Lavi was so intent on trying to correct the injustice he had done to Nofar that he didn't sense Maya approaching him. Nofar now disappeared into the wings with the rest of the performers, and he wanted to hurry over to her and tell her how beautifully she had sung. At first, he didn't feel the hand touching his arm. Then he straightened up all at once, as if he had been struck by lightning.

"You're Nofar's boyfriend." She didn't ask him. She told him. Her entire bearing in the schoolyard seemed to be saying *I am here. Look at me.* Lavi glanced at the kindly-grandfather face of the assassinated prime minister. What would he do in this situation? On the stage, the teacher turned off the eternal flame. In another minute Nofar would come out of the wings.

"I have to go."

"I heard the two of you talking on the phone when we were in the president's residence."

"I really have to go." Before Maya could respond, he took off almost in a run, and it wasn't clear whether he was hurrying to reach the sister in the wings or hurrying to flee the sister in the schoolyard.

He arrived at the same moment Nofar emerged and immediately told her how wonderful she had been, and she thanked him excitedly. Wordlessly, they agreed not to mention the existence of her little sister. And since Maya wasn't mentioned, Nofar could tell herself that the look she had seen was nothing more than a random meeting of eyes. She insisted on attributing the shadow darkening Lavi's eyes to the change in the weather.

27

ON THE MORNING of the memorial day for the assassinated prime minister, Avishai Milner sat on the bank of the polluted river and prayed to the river gods to capsize a kayak for him. Preferably with a young female kayaker, but in his situation he was ready to compromise. He'd even take a senior citizen. He'd leap bravely into the polluted sludge and give mouth-to-mouth resuscitation to even the filthiest mouth.

Since his discharge from the hospital after a very brief stay, people had been looking at him strangely. Repulsion mixed with pity. Avishai Milner found it unpleasant. Also unpleasant were the endless phone calls from his parents. He knew: he had to find himself a new plan, a way to tilt the scales in his favor. He decided to head for the river.

On weekdays the river was deserted, except for serious rowers hefting their oars with the utmost concentration. Only people sitting on the toilet or rowing strenuously have that sort of totally self-involved expression. Several years earlier, people had been shocked when a canoe capsized and no one leaped into the water to rescue the canoeist. On land, people are allowed to abandon each other to their hearts' content. A person can drown in his sorrow in the middle of the street and no one is expected to offer assistance. But on the river, it's another story. The man who finally jumped in was crowned a hero. His name was on everyone's lips for several days.

Avishai Milner waited a long time for a kayak to capsize. To no avail. They all sailed smoothly past him. No female kayaker thrashed around in the water. The totally focused expression on the faces of the rowers seemed to ridicule him. Since being released on bail, Avishai Milner saw ridicule everywhere, even in the posters of the little lost dogs displayed on trees around the city.

A group of children made its way to the dock, and Avishai Milner tensed. A tired teacher, her voice hoarse, reminded the students to board the boats carefully in groups of four. None of them looked in his direction, none of them recognized Avishai Milner, and, under the present circumstances, he was forced to admit that it was for the best. While the children were snapping pictures of each other on the riverbank, Avishai Milner studied them carefully. He picked one out easily: he hung back, the other children hit him on the head in an unmistakable way, not with affection, and so unobtrusively that a too-busy or too-indifferent teacher would not notice. Surreptitiously, Avishai Milner walked toward the boy. Two other boys now snatched his hat from his head, giving Avishai Milner the opportunity to study him well: thin, short, runny nose. Any one of those things alone was reason enough. Because he was too thin, too short, and his nose ran too much. Because something in his existence grated on the other boys' nerves, and they were already twitchy from the constant agitation of childhood.

There were other short, skinny children there, yet only that boy's hat flew into the river to the sound of his feeble protest. The boy who had chucked the hat into the water shouted, "Oops!" He looked over at the teacher and, seeing that she had no intention of getting involved, allowed himself to laugh out loud. The hat landed in the middle of the polluted river. All the children watched it to see whether it would sink or continue to float. For several seconds the hat was carried along on the current, and then sank. The children looked back at the dock, curious to see if the boy would cry. He didn't. He only looked at the river. After all the others had turned away, he remained focused intently on the water, as if the power of his gaze could split the river in two and expose the muddy bottom where his hat lay among the fluttering fish, green ferns, and snack wrappers.

Slowly, Avishai Milner approached the group of children crowded together on the dock. The sun was high in the sky. No one paid attention to him. Life preservers were being handed out in the middle of the group, and the teacher begged the students to put them on quickly. That boy still wasn't wearing his. If that rejected child fell into the water now and was rescued by a courageous passerby, would he not receive all the accolades that sort of near-tragedy called for?

"Sir! Watch out for the children!"

The teacher's voice was shrill and frightened as she pulled him back quickly. "You almost knocked over Noam!"

He stammered, "Sorry." Saw her shocked expression as she looked at him. She knew him from somewhere. He could feel her eyes on him as he turned around and walked away. He began to run.

28

LAVI MAIMON HAS a girlfriend. The rumor spread through the class slowly—he wasn't important enough for them to hurry to tell each other. The ones who mentioned it did so with a raised eyebrow, somewhat surprised: "Did you hear, even Lavi Maimon has a girlfriend already." And so the rumor spread from one to the other, slowly, like a local train, dawdling at every station. Until one morning Ido Tal stood at his desk and said, "So let's have a look at her." As Lavi was still wondering who he was talking about, Ido Tal added, "Your girlfriend. A babe? A pig?"

They had been in the same class since the first grade. Teachers call that being classmates, even though they clearly weren't mates. But they weren't enemies either. Ido never hit or cursed Lavi. He had never taken an interest in him. Until now. Lavi knew that Ido was interested because he rubbed his stubble in the same way that Lieutenant Colonel Arieh Maimon did when he was concentrating on what an analyst on TV was saying. The sort of thing that men with stubble do that Lavi, with his almost completely smooth chin, could only dream about. Ido kept rubbing his stubble with one hand, then put the other hand on Lavi's shoulder and said, "So? Babe or pig?"

Lavi didn't know how to reply. He didn't want to think about Nofar as a babe or a pig. Nofar was Nofar. But the boy in front of him stared at him with hungry eyes. They'd already had twelve years of school together, and Ido Tal had never looked at him that way: as if Lavi had something that Ido did not. So he said yes, he had a girlfriend. And when Ido said, "Show me a picture," he said he didn't have one, even though he did. He had snapped a candid photo of Nofar at work a short time after they met. He had come to the ice-cream parlor when she was busy with customers and he decided to wait outside. He watched her through the glass door as she plowed the fields of chocolate and vanilla. How pretty she looked then, bending over the counter, skillfully balancing three scoops of different flavors on a single cone. Impulsively, he had pulled out his phone and taken her picture. He had planned to show it to her later, but was embarrassed. At night, as she hurried to catch the last bus home from the alley, he watched from his room. Sometimes he sneaked a glance at the picture during particularly boring classes. Perhaps that was how the rumor that ended with Ido Tal had begun. One way or the other, he was sure he wouldn't show the picture. He had no desire to hear whether Ido Tal thought Nofar was a babe or a pig.

But he knew what Ido Tal would say if he saw the picture, and that knowledge began to poison his thoughts, as if the boys in his class were sitting in his head, constantly saying things about her, rating every part of her body. He was offended for her, he offended himself, and maybe that was why, the following day, when Ido Tal sat down beside him and said, "Bro, at least describe her," Lavi said, "She's beautiful. Really beautiful."

The number of eyes looking at him increased because it was one thing if Lavi Maimon had a girlfriend, and something else if he had a really beautiful girlfriend. His heart hammering with cowardly fear, he repeated to himself that, for him, she really was beautiful, but the more the boys demanded to hear what she looked like, the more stressed he became, until he blurted out a remarkably accurate but totally incredible description. It was precise and painfully faithful to a certain face. But not Nofar's face. And not Nofar's body. There were, of course, similarities—after all, as children they were almost identical. The color of their eyes. The shape of their lips. But where their bodies were concerned, Lavi abandoned his girl-friend and described another. Even if his listeners had no way of knowing, Lavi himself knew quite well: instead of singing the praises of his girlfriend, he was describing her sister.

Over the next few days he kept telling himself that, in fact, nothing had happened. After all, Ido Tal and Nofar would never meet. The only place they came across each other was in his head, every such encounter ending with Ido's sneer and Nofar's wounded look, in an endless circle that made his head spin. And when your head is spinning, your body becomes clumsy. After two days he barged into a teacher, causing a Coke to spill on her blouse. She was still reprimanding him loudly when Ido Tal came to his aid: "It's not his fault that he bumps into things—he's in love." A raucous cry from the back of the room. Giggling from the first row. Lavi felt the warmth rise to his cheeks. He knew he was blushing, and as usual, that knowledge caused him to blush more.

He didn't miss the teacher's surprised look. She never would have guessed that someone like him could have a girlfriend. The commotion in the classroom had already begun to sub-side when Ido Tal leaned forward, smiling that mischievous smile of his that even teachers fell victim to, and demanded, "Maybe you should ask him for a picture? He won't show us one!" Cries of agreement from the class. They all wanted to see. Better-looking, more impressive boys than Lavi were suddenly staring at him because how could he have a girl-friend when they didn't? Even those who, on a normal day, wouldn't talk to Lavi except to ask for a shekel for the cafeteria were curious now. The teacher glanced at her watch, saw that several precious minutes had been lost, and although she had less patience for II Kings than for the students themselves, she was still a teacher, the responsible adult, so *ya'allah, sit down, he'll show it to you at lunch.*

He hoped they'd forget all about it by lunch, but the Bible lesson fanned the flame of their baser instincts. The bell had only just rung, but he already felt Ido Tal's hand on his shoulder. "So?"

"She ... she doesn't like to have her picture taken." The skepticism in Ido Tal's green eyes glittered like a dagger drawn from its sheath. These days, you won't find a teenager who doesn't like to be photographed. Unless we're talking about awfully unattractive people, and the girl—so they were promised!—was super-attractive. Lavi felt a toad hopping up his throat, hop after hop, one more and it would hop right out, smooth and green, another fabricated story about the beauty who refused to be photographed.

He hated himself more with every word, and with every word he knew there was no going back, he could never tell them the truth now. He thought about the way she laughed. Her laugh was round and orange, like apricots. And if you listened carefully and cut it in half, you'd really find a hard pit there. He wanted to leave the classroom now and text her to come to the alley right away, and when she did finally arrive and offer to bring them both ice cream, he would say, "No ice cream, I want the apricots of your laugh." Anything but to be here in the classroom facing Ido, still dubious, still demanding, until he put an end to the discussion: "So tell her that the guys in your class won't take no for an answer. Tell her that without a selfie of you two, we don't believe she exists."

That evening, Ido Tal made him a member of the group. Not the WhatsApp group for class, the one their teacher had started at the beginning of the year that included everyone. The second group, the one no one talked about but everyone knew existed. Even those who weren't members heard the sniggers that suddenly rose from nowhere in the middle of the lesson, saw how the members of that group hurried to put their hands in their pockets. Lavi wasn't sure whether it was Ido who had founded the group, but it became clear when Ido added him. It was also clear why. And what would happen if he didn't deliver.

The next day, his heart pounding, he told her he'd like to visit her at home. Nofar looked at him in surprise. Until then she had been sure that he, like her, didn't want a reason to leave the alley and venture into the outside world. There, with the laundry dripping on them and the bugs racing around under them, they had known moments of pure joy. The alley was a dump, there was no doubting that, but it was their dump.

Still, he persisted. He wanted to see her room.

The thought of him in her room made Nofar shudder. She pictured the cubicle where she had lived her entire life, a beloved room, familiar and comfortable, which now, as she tried to see it through Lavi's eyes, suddenly seemed terribly ordinary. The flowered bedspread that she had chosen herself a year ago to be her holiday gift now seemed too childish. And the walls, where she had not hung a single poster because she liked the white, the way the shade and sun danced on them at different times of day, those walls suddenly seemed naked and pathetic. She was ashamed of her desk, which had once been her cousin's and still bore the marks where various stickers had been pulled off. She was ashamed of her bedside-table drawers, filled with her childhood dolls.

So the dolls were thrown out, not even one left as a memento. The flowered bedspread was folded carelessly and shoved into the closet, and the only reason it wasn't thrown away was that it had been outrageously expensive. The desk was moved from one corner of the room to another, and after much thought and many sighs, Nofar moved it to a third corner until, finally, after tears and a brief stop in a fourth corner, she angrily returned it to its original place. No one but Maya understood what was happening. She watched her father struggle to drag the desk in its wanderings from corner to corner, watched her mother valiantly defend the bedspread, and asked, "So when is he coming?"

"None of your business."

But, in fact, it was her business. Very much so. And also her parents' business as soon as they understood what was going on. They had a long conversation that night: should they allow him to sleep over? Should they allow her to sleep at his place in the future? Should they talk about contraception, or would that only be an unnecessary embarrassment, and could they welcome him with a smile without being too heavy-handed? They spoke about a thousand other things that became totally redundant when it turned out that Nofar had carefully planned his arrival at a time when they were both at work. Only she and Maya would be home, and Maya, thank heavens, had more important things to occupy her.

29

TEN TIMES HE took his phone out of his pocket to text her that he couldn't come, and ten times he looked instead at the messages from the group. There were funny videos and nasty comments and pictures of girls who put stuff in and out of their bodies, even a snake. The first two days after Ido Tal had brought him into the group, Lavi didn't write or send anything, trying to be as quiet as possible so they wouldn't notice him or throw him out. On the third day, Ido wrote, "So, Maimon?" Lavi had been expecting that, and a moment later he sent the grossest picture he could find, something really disgusting but funny too. They all wrote "Wow" and "Woweeee," and for a moment he hoped that offering would be enough for them. When Ido texted, "The one in the middle is Shkedi's mother, right?" he was overjoyed. But a minute later Ido wrote again, "*Ya'allah,* time to be serious: tomorrow night a picture of the lucky girl." And Lavi knew he was still in trouble.

There was a sign on the Shalev front door that said, "WELCOME TO OUR HAPPY HOME," along with a brightly colored drawing of a smiling family, and it angered Lavi to see that even there, on the sign, one of the girls was drawn a bit prettier than the other. He knocked hesitantly, and then a bit harder. But there was no need to knock again: a dancing heart waited on the other side of the door and leaped to open it. How pretty she looked to him, with her hair pulled back and the blue dress he knew. Embarrassed, they stood facing each other for a moment, then he kissed her on the cheek the way he had seen the boys in his class kiss their girlfriends at the entrance to school. In the alley he had never kissed her cheek. Of all the places in the world, he thought the cheek an especially boring one to kiss, but here, at the door to her home, it seemed appropriate. She took his hand and glided quickly through the neatest-it-had-ever-been living room, straight to her room, and closed the door, breathing a sigh of relief.

They talked about TV. About the series they liked and the ones they didn't like, and about series they had once liked and then stopped liking. They spoke quickly, with nervous excitement that the words wanted to hide but their speed exposed. Silence lay in wait at the end of every sentence like a frightening dog at the end of the street. That might be why, when they heard a knock on the door and Maya came in, they both greeted her happily. Not only Lavi, but even Nofar was momentarily glad to see her little sister.

Maya came into the room to ask whether anyone wanted a Coke, and also to have a look, to investigate, to take in a bit of the thing that existed between her big sister and that boy. She didn't miss an iota of the relief that showed on their faces. She had been sure she would be sent away unceremoniously, that Nofar wouldn't let her even open the door. She had thought the boy would look away from her, as he had during the never-mentioned conversation at school. Instead, the two of them said yes to the Coke. Maya left, returning a moment later with a bottle and some glasses, and that moment was all Nofar needed to regret having let her sister come into the room. One time, the only time someone comes to see her, is sitting in her room—it's Maya's laughter ringing out in the hallway again. It's Maya telling them, with her infectious enthusiasm, about a teacher in some school who had been caught growing marijuana.

Nofar remembered the article—she too had seen it in the morning paper, but it hadn't seemed interesting enough to mention. Now, as Maya spoke about the article, it suddenly seemed like the most interesting thing in the world, as if Maya had actually been there when they caught the teacher. She showed them how a math teacher smokes a bong, and did it so well that they almost spilled their Cokes from laughing so hard. Lavi asked Maya whether she had ever smoked, because if not, how did she know those things. "Of course not," Maya said as she nodded "yes," so that neither Lavi nor Nofar could know whether she had smoked or not, which made it even more intriguing.

And so it continued, Maya spoke and they laughed, and Nofar made a great effort to tell herself that it was actually okay, that it was fine. After all, days had passed since that moment at the ceremony when she saw Lavi and Maya looking at each other. And even if a large sign saying *"DANGER"* had been hung in her mind then, an endless number of other signs had been hung there since, one on top of the other, so who remembered what had been there first? But now she did remember. All at once she remembered, perhaps because she had never really forgotten, but had only wanted to forget. She stood up suddenly, surprising Maya and Lavi, and said, "Okay. Thanks for the Coke," went to the door, and opened it.

The small cloud that passed over Maya's face vanished immediately. She took the Coke bottle and her own and Nofar's empty glasses, saying, "But Lavi, you didn't drink anything."

That wasn't true. He had drunk a little. But he stopped when he felt the nausea in his stomach, though he knew that it had nothing to do with the Coke, but rather with what he had to do. The moment Maya came into the room, he had begun thinking about how to take her picture without her noticing it. But you can't take someone's picture without their noticing it. Maybe if you work for the Mossad. Maybe Arieh Maimon could. Or Ido Tal. But Lavi couldn't.

He had no choice. He'd have to forget it. And the moment he realized that, conversation became suddenly easier, even fun. Maya put down the glasses, did imitations of some pot-head teacher, and he laughed and hoped she'd leave the room soon so that he and Nofar could finally be alone together. Now, knowing he wasn't going to do it, he was sure they'd manage to talk to each other normally. But then, just as Maya took the glasses and walked past Nofar on her way out, every-thing was destroyed. They stood beside each other, and he knew exactly what he had to do to remain in the group and extinguish the doubt in Ido's eyes. His stomach suddenly felt like it did when the air-raid sirens had blared in the summer: you're walking down the street and everything is normal. All of a sudden everyone starts running, and you tell yourself it's just a siren, but there's a thin layer of ice on all your organs, like a chicken when you take it out of the freezer. That's how his stomach was now, and he wondered whether, in that condition, he could speak normally. But he did so really well: Maya was about to leave the room when he said in the most natural voice in the world, "How about we take a selfie together?"

They agreed. Why wouldn't they? Maya with the enthusi-asm of someone used to being photographed, Nofar with the awkwardness of someone who had never been photographed. True, she had been on television and radio and in the papers, and of course her parents had photographed her, but a boy had never asked her to take a picture with him, and, certainly, no boy had ever said to her, "I want to have a picture of you." Perhaps Maya was sensitive enough to understand that, because she moved away from Nofar and said, "But why with me? Just the two of you should be in the picture," as if she didn't want to steal the moment. A wave of affection for her younger sister rose in Nofar, making her feel somewhat guilty for the rude way she had sent her out of the room earlier, so the older sister reached out to hug the younger sister's slender waist and said, "No, first the three of us together."

He looked at the pictures all the way home. In one of only him and Nofar, she looked both embarrassed and proud. Embarrassed because he was taking her picture and proud for the same reason. The embarrassment and the pride cancelled each other out, eliminating the arrogant glow that pride bestows upon certain portraits, as well as the shy charm that embarrassment confers on others. Even broken glass can glitter like a diamond if the sun treats it kindly, but there was no kindness in that picture. The sun touched Nofar's face exactly where her pimples had set up house, exposing reddish spots on her forehead and cheeks. Her smile, usually broad and generous, looked forced. Almost false. Her eyes retained the same alert, knowing look, but the photograph deprived them of their unique shade of pale blue. And still he loved her. And still she seemed beautiful to him. Just not enough.

Perhaps what pained him most was the hint of a question mark on her face. The eyebrows were raised slightly in surprise: "Me? You really want to take my picture?" The argument was written in every feature, as if the likeness did not belong to one girl but to two, struggling with each other: one reassuring, "Yes, he wants to take your picture," and the other refusing to believe it.

161

The second picture was even worse, which was surprising because Nofar was so beautiful in it. Everything that fate had kept from her in the first picture, it restored in this one. Her expression was open and lovely, her smile radiant, and playful blue fire danced in her eyes once again, as if the battle that had been raging in them earlier was over and now she could glow in comfort. Never, not in any photo, had Nofar looked so enchanting. For a moment, only for a moment, he thought it might be enough. But then his eye wandered to the sister hugging her. It's important to remember that Maya had tried. She had wanted to leave her sister what was hers. She wasn't to blame that Nofar had insisted they hug, and she wasn't to blame that Lavi had insisted on taking their picture. But from the moment they insisted, the moment Maya moved to Nofar's side, the same thing happened to Maya that happens to a girl when she is measured against another girl. Her back straightened. Her head was held higher. Her neck grew longer. Her breasts became rounder. And all the other changes well known to science occurred: silkier hair, clearer eyes, redder lips. In short, when Maya stood beside Nofar, the younger sister's beauty increased a hundredfold, proving once again that this planet has one and only one sun—there is no room for two.

But the choice was still his. When he began to edit the picture, cut it in half and design the file, the choice was still his. It still wasn't clear which of the two girls would soon be sent to oblivion and which would be saved and uploaded into the file. Because Nofar really did look beautiful there. Remarkably sweet and lovely. You could see in her eyes how smart she was. And special. The bus made its way back to the city and Lavi shifted his gaze from Maya to Nofar, from Nofar to Maya, and each time she looked more beautiful, more beloved, more possible.

"What a b-a-a-b-e."

"Bro, how did you hook one like that?"

"She must be some cousin who's a model. Nah, just kidding."

He didn't read those messages. Didn't even glance at them. As if, the minute he uploaded the picture, he lost all interest in the group.

She was on his phone. She existed close to him even when he didn't see her. Even if they weren't face to face, her face was in his pants pocket. That thought never ceased to excite him. Even when he was sad or nervous, the second Nofar, the smiling one, was still preserved on Lavi's phone. He kept her with him, and the knowledge of that second existence illuminated her actual existence, like a light reflector on the side of the road.

30

"SO," MAYA ASKED, "have you slept with him yet?"
Steam filled the bathroom and clouded the mirror. Nofar was
brushing her teeth in front of her misty reflection. Maya was
standing in the shower, shampooing her hair. She turned off
the water for a minute, and droplets rolled down the length
of her body. The beads of water became trapped in her pubic
hair, which had begun to grow when Maya was thirteen and
now looked as if it had always been there. Their parents
had bathed them together in that bathroom throughout their
childhood. They had shampooed each other's hair, pulled each
other's hair, floated boats and dolls.

First their father had been exiled from the bathroom: for
many years he had been forbidden from entering when they
were in there, even if the curtain was closed. Then their
mother was pushed out as well. *Come on, Mom, get out, please.*
But they continued to accept each other without hesitation,
one showered and the other sat on the toilet seat and brushed
her teeth, or examined the state of her eyebrows in front of
the large mirror. Over the many hours they spent together,
they learned to know each other's bodies by heart. A beauty
mark. An ingrown toenail. The precise fullness of each breast
and the small differences between them. No lover would ever
know either one of them the way they knew each other.
Morning breath. The position they usually slept in. The marks
their feet left in borrowed shoes. When one used the other's

hairbrush, which was taboo, the hair left on the brush gave her away. (Numerous arguments about those brushes: each always preferred the other's brush, even when their mother bought identical ones.) Such total knowledge, and yet, Nofar thought, tensing in front of the mirror, there's another kind of knowledge. Strange that they had never talked about it before. Strange that they were talking about it now.

She opened the two cabinet doors so they were facing each other, mirror facing mirror in an endless reflection, all the possible bathrooms visible, and inside them, all the possible conversations. Maya turned on the tap again. The drops of water that were entwined in her pubic hair were washed away all at once, the pink flesh behind them suddenly broke through, and Nofar looked at it, wondering whether Maya had already done it. Of course she had, she answered herself. With all those boyfriends of hers, she'd probably done it a long time ago. But who knows? Maya had never said anything, and Nofar had never asked. Now, her younger sister's direct question—"Have you slept with him yet?"

Like all the soap bubbles they had made together in the bath, counting the seconds until they disappeared, Nofar now counted the seconds until the silence would be broken. "You don't have to answer if you don't want to." Maya reached out for the towel, and Nofar handed it to her quickly, a substitute for her reply. While the younger sister was drying herself, Nofar undressed and stepped into the shower.

"Do you love him?"

She actually preferred the previous question. Maya didn't sense it, or perhaps she did, and that was why she went on. "He looks like a good fuck." The word burst forth from the depths—Maya had submerged her face and hair in the huge towel. When she removed it, her face was red with embarrassment. It had excited her to say those words. It had excited Nofar to hear them. Until then, only characters on the TV screen spoke that way, and now they were doing it. Nofar turned on the water to the maximum pressure, grateful for the deafening tumult that cut off their conversation. What exactly was a good fuck? Who does it depend on? She of course didn't know how to have a good fuck. And somehow, she had the feeling that Lavi didn't really know either.

She was right about that. The boy had read endlessly about fucking, had watched it at every opportunity, but the more he watched, the less he knew. The people he watched on his computer didn't look in the least like him or Nofar, and the things they did seemed far beyond his grasp. The thought of having sex with his girlfriend aroused in him equal measures of terror and interest.

Especially now. He lived in constant fear that she would find the picture. Without their wanting it, a certain distance grew between them. Nofar couldn't imagine why. She thought it was because they'd be apart when she went on the upcoming school trip to Poland. She'd be gone for only a week, but every day she didn't go to the alley was like an eternity.

PART TWO

31

AND RAYMONDE REALLY wanted to go. She didn't remember having ever been outside Israel. She barely remembered Morocco, where she was born. It was mostly the smell that remained, a combination she just couldn't put into words. It was indescribable, the way you can't describe the sound lentils make when you move your hand around in them—you have to be there to know. The clear memories were of the *ma'abarot,* the transit camps for North African Jews arriving in Israel: the sound of rain on the tin roof in the middle of the night, a constant, thunderous drumming, like rifle fire. It was no wonder Amsalem the *madroub* ("the crazy one") ran outside with his hands on his ears. Since the war, everything sounded like gunfire to him, as though the Jordanians were coming to finish what they started. They had taken the whole unit except for Crazy Amsalem, and even though he was discharged a year ago, he was still waiting for them to come for him, to finish the job.

First memories: a wool blanket her mother knitted for her and that she curled up in like a chick in a nest. Even now, she would recognize that blanket if she came across it on the street. She tried to knit one like it for her granddaughter, but her daughter-in-law said that wool itches. She'd rather buy something softer. "Don't be insulted." She wasn't insulted. *"El tmar dikelti ana la-abt bidmahoum,"* she said in Arabic, and when her daughter-in-law asked, "What did you say?" she translated, "I said that I played with the seeds of the dates you're eating now." For a minute she was afraid they'd have one hell of an argument, but her daughter-in-law said, "I really love those sayings of yours, you should write them down," and went off to buy a soft blanket that didn't itch.

She kept the blanket she knitted for her grandchildren in her closet and waited for them to grow up and come to sleep at her place. Then she would show them what a really warm blanket feels like. But they didn't come. Once she heard the *zrira,* the little one, whisper that Grandma smells old. The next day she put the blanket outside the seniors' home so at least the cats could curl up in it. And that was how she became friends with Rivka. When she stood up to go inside, she saw her on the bench, next to her walker, tossing supper leftovers to the cats, even though the home manager said they weren't allowed to. She liked Rivka already when she saw her holding the dry bourekas they'd served the night before. "I wet it with cottage cheese," Rivka told her as she sat down beside her on the bench, "but even so, I'm embarrassed to give it to them." The cats were spoiled. They ate the cottage cheese but left the pastry on the pavement, just as the residents of the home had left it on their plates the night before.

The next day Raymonde waited for her on the bench, with a piece of chicken and half a carrot she'd taken out of the soup and hidden in her kerchief. When Rivka saw what was in the kerchief, she smiled broadly, and Raymonde knew that she had made the right move to get her attention. She'd never had to work for men's attention—they always ran after her—but she really wanted Rivka to like her. That woman had the most beautiful smile she'd ever seen, a smile that went from her mouth to her cheeks, from there to her eyes, making them slant like a Chinese person's eyes, and from there to her hair. It was all puffed up because her hairdresser teased it every week, even though she didn't have anyone to tease it for—her husband had died a long time ago, the grandchildren hardly ever came, and the cats really didn't care. Rivka had a soft, pleasant voice and she spoke correct Hebrew, like the *kibbutznikim,* because as soon as she came from the Holocaust, they put her into a kibbutz, and she didn't leave until she had her second child.

After the first child, she decided she didn't want them to put her babies in a children's house—she wanted to hear them when they cried at night, she wanted to go and sing to them until they went back to sleep. So after her second child, she took her husband and they moved to Ramat Gan. From what Raymonde saw during visits, the children turned out a little screwy, the one from the children's house and also the one from Ramat Gan, which shows that maybe it doesn't make a difference, children's house or not. What makes a difference, Rivka told her, is if you have a mother who's afraid to love you the way she should because maybe they'll take you away someday, too. And if you have a father who's a big schmuck. Raymonde didn't know the father. He had died of a heart attack a week before the surprise party for his ninetieth birthday. For months they planned how to surprise him, and in the end, death came and surprised him better than any of them. But she knew Rivka and thought she had no problem loving. When she said that to Rivka, Rivka thought a little and said maybe that was the only muscle that didn't get ruined in old age, but got stronger. And maybe something falls out there, too, like the way your teeth and hair fall out, something that's been blocking it, so that, unlike the teeth and hair, it's for the better.

It took a lot of time for them to convince Rivka to go back

there. When she had come to Israel, she swore she would never set foot in that place again. With their washing machines, she had no problem. She liked shoving her dirty underwear into the open mouth of her German washing machine. But she didn't like the idea of visiting there. When people from all kinds of organizations came and talked to her about the educational value, she sent them to her survivor friends, who went and came back with endless stories about the camps and the children, and some Toblerone for her from the airport. While she shared the Toblerone with Raymonde on the bench—there was no point offering any to the cats—she talked about things she remembered from there. Raymonde sat and listened. She spread open her mind and collected the stories the way you spread large sheets of cloth under olive trees to collect the olives that fall. The time on the bench was Rivka's time, and the nighttime was Raymonde's. If sleep runs away from us, Rivka would say, then instead of trying to catch it and never succeeding, let's run away from it. So they had what their grandchildren called a pajama party, but without snacks that give you heartburn. Raymonde would go to Rivka's room and sit down on the couch, and Rivka would make tea and say, "Tell me, please." Sometimes Raymonde would talk until almost morning, and then they would watch the sunrise together. Rivka said that was the most romantic thing there was between a man and a woman, or between people in general.

She knew that people grow to look like their spouses, or their dogs, so it didn't really surprise her that they also start to look like their closest friends. When the residents of the home began to say that they looked like Siamese twins, it was half a joke, but a year later people really began to get them confused. Rivka took Raymonde to her hairdresser, where they teased her hair and dyed it exactly the same blond color that film stars have. Rivka's skin had become darker because of age spots, and Raymonde's had become yellower because a woman who's spent so much time on her feet is like paper that's been left in the sun for too long. Even their faces began to look alike—time had completely sanded them down. One day, when Raymonde came back from visiting her new great-grandchild in the nursery at the Barzilai hospital, she told Rivka that they were all the same, Ashkenazi and Sephardi babies, wrinkled and red with a little bit of hair. Rivka laughed and said that the people who came to visit here, at the old people's nursery, probably thought the same thing about them.

That's why Raymonde didn't go to Rivka's funeral. It would be like seeing yourself lying there, wrapped in shrouds, being lowered into the ground. For the first few weeks she went out to the bench alone to feed the cats for Rivka, but after a while she got tired of it. If Rivka had wanted to feed the cats so badly, she should have stayed around longer. She shouldn't have let something as small as the flu take her like that, in such a cowardly, old person's death. But though she didn't feel responsible for the cats, the schoolchildren were something else. She was the one who had talked Rivka into doing it, and it would be a shame to disappoint them.

This is how it happened that, after the funeral, Rivka's phone stayed with her. The night before Rivka passed away, when Raymonde visited her in her room, Rivka gave her the phone because she was tired of the constant calls from her children. They didn't have anything to say as it was, just asked how she felt, sounding like they were in a big hurry, and she was sick of answering "Everything's fine." For the first few days after the funeral, Raymonde didn't dare touch the phone. It lay in her bag like a dead black mouse, and the scariest thing was when it suddenly started to vibrate there—it almost gave her a heart attack. When she went to pay a condolence call, she tried to tell the children that she had their mother's phone, but none of them listened to her. They were too sad or too busy with the other visitors. She could tell they were taking time off from work and had to be there not just because of Rivka, but because it was the right thing to do.

Then there were no calls at all for a long time, but she still charged the phone just because it made her sad to see it blinking with that weak light phones have before they die. Until one night there was a call from the school. They wanted to ask what time they should pick her up tomorrow to take her to the airport. Suddenly she remembered Rivka's delegation, how she had encouraged her to go to Poland, but then was sorry, because what would she do without Rivka for eight days? And now she had a lot more than eight days to be without her. She had planned to say no, that something had happened, but the woman on the other end of the phone, exactly like Rivka's children, didn't really ask questions to get answers, but only so she could ask "Does tomorrow at seven sound okay?"—the words she had planned to say from the beginning. She'd only asked "What's convenient for you?" to be polite. Suddenly Raymonde heard herself reply, "Seven thirty. I have t'ai chi before that," which wasn't true at all, she didn't do t'ai chi. Rivka had done it, and look at how much that helped her. Those Chinese are good at public relations, but everything else is rubbish. The woman on the other end thought for a minute, then said, "Okay." Raymonde could tell from her voice that she wasn't happy, but she felt uncomfortable arguing with a Holocaust survivor.

Raymonde ended the call and went over to the suitcase with Rivka's things in it. The same day Rivka died, the home took her things out of her room for the new resident with the purple hair. Ten days earlier, Rivka's children had promised to come and take the suitcase, but they'd hurried off into their lives again, the way cockroaches scurry around after being sprayed, and it had been in Raymonde's room ever since. Rivka's passport was there, along with her identity card and credit cards. Her socks were still neatly folded, and that made Raymonde laugh. It made her laugh twice, once because Rivka folded socks—who folds socks?—and the second time because the socks stayed folded after the feet were gone. If she'd known earlier, she would have had a good laugh at Rivka's expense. They had always laughed at each other, but with a smile, like sisters. Now she couldn't laugh at her anymore, and anyway she didn't have time to laugh. She had to pack.

The first time abroad requires organization. She tried on the socks and saw that they were exactly her size. Siamese twins. And everything had that wonderful smell of Rivka, which made her tear up a little. She packed her things in the suitcase with Rivka's, thinking that she was the only one who knew there were two women in it, one living, the other dead. She told the home that she was going on vacation with her family and left them Eli's phone number in case of an emergency. By the time her youngest son bothered to call them back, she would manage to go halfway around the world. When she finished packing everything, she looked at the passport again. Rivka smiled at her. She smiled back.

At night she couldn't sleep and knew it was from excitement. She thought of what it would be like on the plane, and what it would be like to set foot in another country. She would have loved to talk to Rivka about it, but that was impossible. Maybe she'd leave a letter for the manager of the home, just so she'd have a fit.

On the way to the airport Raymonde wasn't frightened at all. That was one of the few advantages of her age: you're not afraid of anything but the one thing that no one dares to mention in your company, and if you yourself mention it, people say don't be silly, as if you were talking about something completely imaginary, a demon from a fairy tale, and not about something as logical and expected as death. At the airport she met the children, who were very nice and polite, especially with all their parents standing around and taking pictures, as though they'd never seen a plane in their lives.

She walked around the duty-free shop and saw that everything was very expensive, but she put so much perfume and so many creams on her hands that they smelled like a bordello. She put on eyeliner and lipstick that cost thirty dollars, and when the salesgirl asked whether she wanted to buy anything, she said she would never buy anything for that price. As a matter of principle. Then she applied blush, and when she heard the loudspeaker call her name, that is, Rivka's name, she hurried out. On the plane, her hands shook with fear of flying, and the guide, who thought she was emotional about going back there, held her hands and tried to calm her down. It helped a little, and the whisky the flight attendant brought also calmed her down a bit. Fifteen minutes later she felt well enough to look out the window and see clouds from above for the first time in her life. They looked the same as they did from below, but completely different.

When they landed in Poland, her fear returned. Israelis bend the rules, but in Europe it's no laughing matter. Who knows what they'd do to her here if they found out? They didn't find out. With those sour faces of theirs they stamped her passport, and she said "Thank you" in English, even though she was really saying, "Damn you all to hell."

32

MEANWHILE, IN THE seaside city, Lavi was learning the slow pleasure of anticipating Nofar's return. Anticipation is an acquired taste. At first it's sour and bitter, but later, as you get used to it, it becomes difficult to stop savoring it. He had left his computer games almost entirely. Missing Nofar was now his major hobby. She had become increasingly beautiful in his mind. Every day she was gone added another quarter inch to her height and the size of her breasts, deepened her smile and the blue of her eyes. In his memory, he kept replaying their meetings in the alley, and every time they seemed to be more thrilling, more passionate, funnier. It was true that those meetings had been wonderful, but there was no way they could compare to those he re-created in his imagination, and even more so, the ones he was planning for them when she returned from her trip.

In order to meet the girl who returned from Poland, he first of all had to give up the one he carried around in his mind. Unintentionally, he had a mistress, the perfect one of his fantasies. But now she was 2,500 miles away, if the computer was right. Every morning he asked his father what the weather was like in Poland. Arieh Maimon was moved to the depths of his soul by the way his son shared his affection for weather maps. He also told him what was happening in Berlin. He didn't know that it wasn't Warsaw his son was interested in, but the girl who was walking around on its streets. But he did notice a new spark in the boy's eyes, as if someone had finally turned on a streetlight that had been broken for too many years. And so, while touring the ghettos and the camps, Nofar unknowingly contributed to their father-son bonding, which was no small thing.

On the flight there she dreamed about Lavi and woke up with dampness between her legs. The flight attendant walked through the plane, offering drinks, and their teacher, Lilach, said, "God help anyone who asks for liquor, even as a joke." Everyone giggled, and although Nofar knew for sure that they were giggling at what Lilach said, and that no one could read on her face what she had dreamed, she still felt they were laughing at her. She pressed her nose against the window of the airplane and looked out. The clouds under her were white and fat. The day before the flight, she and Lavi had sat in the alley and looked up. There was a cloud in the sky that Nofar thought had the shape of a peacock, and when she asked Lavi if he saw a peacock there too, he said of course he did. Then Lavi had pointed to a different cloud and said it looked like a hammer, and when he asked her if she saw a hammer too, she said of course she did, even though she wasn't sure about it.

They both knew she was flying the next day, and that gave their meeting a special and slightly strange feeling. Every few minutes a plane flew above them, and Lavi said it was because the ice-cream parlor was on the flight path for takeoffs and landings. They looked at the sky and tried to guess where each plane was going and where each plane was coming from. Then they tried to guess who was sitting inside and if they'd had fun on their trips or if they'd fought the whole time, the way Lavi said his parents had fought on the last trip he'd taken with them.

When Lavi was silent for a bit, Nofar knew it was because of what he'd said about his parents, and when the next plane passed above them, she said that maybe there's a couple doing it right now up there, in the airplane bathroom, and they both laughed. On her flight she dreamed that they were the couple, and when she woke up, she was mortified. Her face remained red long after the flight attendant had gone and the kids had stopped giggling. Maybe when she got back to Israel they should just do it. Maybe she wanted to. But the best thing would be if he blackmailed her.

How does it feel when someone's inside you? And how strange it is that she has that kind of hole in her body, a space that someone else is supposed to enter. Whatever she does in the world, when she moves and walks and speaks, her body holds that possibility. Waits for it in some way. She turned her head from the window to look at the other girls on the plane, peeking at them from under her almost closed lids. She knew that most of them had already been there. Most of them already knew how it felt when someone entered you. Your body could take someone else into it if you wanted to, and although she knew it didn't change anything, maybe it actually changed everything.

33

THE FIRST THING Raymonde encountered when she walked out of the airport was the cold. It hit her like a slap in the face. It was unbelievable that people lived in such a cold place. And it was even more unbelievable that Rivka, who wrapped herself in shawls even in August, had lived in this cold for years. Or maybe that's why she had all those shawls, because if you're born in such a frozen place, the cold gets inside you and never comes out—eighty khamsins can't rip it out of you.

The guide put them on a bus and started counting them. She counted them four times because she got a different number every time. Raymonde was a champion counter from her days in the grocery store, but she didn't feel like helping, not after the guide had called her in the middle of the night and asked if she could give up her t'ai chi because they wanted to get to the airport early. Then she saw her buy 200 euros' worth of perfume and makeup in the duty-free shop and thought that asking an old lady to give up her Chinese exercise so some idiot could go shopping was really chutzpah. So Raymonde sat there and let her count, and in the meantime she looked at the children. How young and beautiful they were. Not all of them, of course, some were young and ugly. But even ugliness, when it's young, is a little less ugly, as though there's still hope for improvement.

She saw right away who the king and queen of the class

were. She had a real sense for things like that. Even in the retirement home, as soon as she arrived she knew right away whom to get friendly with and whom not to. Rivka always said that the home was like a high school for elderly people, and Raymonde agreed with her, although she didn't really know what it meant because she had never gone to high school. Now, as the Holocaust survivor of a high school class, she understood how right Rivka had been. It was exactly the same thing, only noisier. The intrigues, the fights, the games. Before they reached Auschwitz, she already knew exactly who was against whom and who wanted whom. Like when she watched *The Young and the Restless,* she could predict the romances even before the characters knew they were about to fall in love.

At the hotel they gave her a very nice, large room, much nicer than her room in the home. The blankets were folded neatly, and you could see that whoever ironed them took her work seriously. In the bathroom she found one pubic hair, but instead of repulsing her, it actually made her laugh a little, and it made her a little curious too, because she'd never seen a blond goy's pubic hair before. She opened the small fridge and took out a chocolate bar with an unfamiliar wrapping and decided she liked the taste of the chocolate in Israel better. Then she stood at the foot of the bed and tried to decide which side she would take. Victor always used to sleep on the right side; even when he was sleeping, he wouldn't let anyone be farther right than him. And after he was gone, she left him that side out of respect. But this trip was hers and Rivka's, and she wanted to let Rivka choose first.

After a few minutes of indecision, she decided to leave her the left side. She lay on the right side, planning to take a little nap, when the guide called to remind her that the survivor's testimony would be at five o'clock in the lobby. Raymonde said fine. She covered herself with the Poles' feather blanket, damn them to hell, which really was wonderful, and closed her eyes. She just had to remember to get up in time, so the survivor wouldn't have to wait. But what survivor were we talking about here? She hadn't seen any survivor on the bus, and she'd been the only old woman on the plane. (In the home they called her "elderly," but that only annoyed her. She wasn't elderly. She was old.) Suddenly, doubt began to gnaw at her. When Rivka talked about the trip, she didn't say anything about testimonies. You visit the camps, talk a little bit about the cold and the snow, make a stop at the shopping center in Warsaw, and fly back home. It's one thing to improvise a few memories standing in front of the barracks, but it's something else to give a complete testimony.

There went her afternoon nap. Raymonde paced the room. If she were younger, she would have sneaked out through the window, like she did when her father locked her in so she wouldn't see Victor. But when you're eighty-eight, running away like that doesn't look good, and it wouldn't be fair to Rivka either. Now she was sorry she hadn't gone to the Internet course they opened in the home. They say you can find everything on the Internet. You type in *Auschwitz* and you get all the information. But when everyone else went to the course, she and Rivka were busy with their conversations. Computers are for people who have no one to talk to, Rivka would say, and now Raymonde wanted to scream at her that computers are also for people who are supposed to talk about something they don't know anything about. But there was no one to scream at.

Her small suitcase, with the folded socks and passport, lay on the left side of the bed, which she was saving for Rivka, and she opened them—both the passport and the socks. Maybe there was something in them she could use. The socks had the same light fragrance she loved, and the passport had Rivka's smile, but this time it didn't look so pleasant. Maybe a little mean. It wasn't nice to think about Rivka like that. She isn't the one who sent you here. You were the one who decided. But for the first time since they met, she sensed a little bit of gloating in her friend. It was like, for example, when you finished eating and only then realized that there was some aniseed in your food. She saw it when she thought back to the time they were sitting on the bench and one of the residents walked past them and slipped. Raymonde stood up to help him and Rivka stayed where she was and watched. She always watched when other people fell. Didn't get up to help and didn't put a hand on her mouth in shock and didn't shout "Oy!" like the others. Raymonde always thought it was the walker that held her back, but maybe it wasn't only that. Maybe there was some curiosity there—seeing if the person who fell would get up.

She closed the passport. The picture made her feel bad, as if Rivka was watching her now to see if she would stay standing. Ten to five. She went into the bathroom and penciled in her eyebrows. Once she had had the most beautiful eyebrows in the country. Two half-moons, Victor used to say, a moon split in two. He was nice with words, her husband—with earning a living, less. When she finished her eyebrows, she moved to her lips. Painted them brightly, like the female Indian warriors when they paint themselves before a battle, and then she went out to the hotel lobby to do battle with the guide and the Nazis and the Holocaust.

When she reached the lobby, everyone was already seated. She could smell the boys' aftershave, strong and controlling, sending out the message they would shout out if they could, *Hey! I shave!* And she saw the sad look in all the girls' eyes. Even before she said a word, they were ready to cry. What they call a supportive audience.

"Come, Rivka," the guide said, putting a compassionate hand on her. "I know how hard it must be for you to begin, and I promise you that all of us here are with you." She had to gain time. Maybe she'd ask the guide to get her something to drink. But she, damn her, had already brought her a glass that was full to the brim. She said, "Begin when you want," but what she meant was "Start now." Raymonde remembered a show Victor once took her to see, but the performers were really late, and at first the audience clapped good-naturedly, then angrily, and then they started to bang on the tables. It would be interesting to see how long it would take for the people here to start banging.

"Today," she said in a shaky voice, "I unpacked my suitcase in my room and looked at my socks. And I thought about how I didn't have socks then, and how cold it was." Someone at the side of the room started to cry. Raymonde looked at her suspiciously. It seemed too soon. Even though what she said, with the socks, was completely true. She really didn't have socks, or shoes, and that had really hurt terribly. Not because of the cold. Because of the heat. In the summer months, the tin shacks in the transit camp got hotter and hotter, the nights weren't enough to cool them off, and before you knew it, another scorching day had started. The children who were tempted to go outside to play screamed in pain. An old memory, the memory of painful feet, suddenly came into her mind. She didn't even know she remembered, and now it came back all at once. Attias's sweet little girl who died of heatstroke, and her mother ran back and forth with her in her arms until, of all people, Amsalem the *madroub,* the crazy one, managed to stop her. She didn't know what he said to her, but she remembered that, from far away, she saw his lips move and the mother listened, then gave him the little girl—as small as a rabbit—and started wailing to high heaven.

She told them that, changing some details. She told them about the hunger, how it eats your stomach from the inside and you try not to think about it but you can't think about anything else. In the middle of her speech she felt it wasn't nice not to give Rivka more room, but she couldn't stop. Suddenly all the memories of the transit camp came and stood in line, like when they stood in line for food and people shouted and pushed, then apologized and were ashamed for suddenly turning into animals, but a day later they pushed again. That's what hunger is like, it makes saliva fill your mouth and meanness fill your soul. Raymonde knew that Rivka would have wanted someone to tell her story. The way an olive tree wants you to take all the fallen olives and make oil from them. So she took those olives from Rivka, added them to her own and pressed them together really well. What came out was so bitter—but so pure—that it would be a shame not to give it to the children.

She didn't know how long she spoke, she only knew that she kept drinking. The guide handed her glass after glass, and she drank and spoke. For every story she took out, she put a glass of water in. Because the thirst had been the worst then. That's what she told them. Worse than the hunger and the disease and the people outside who treated them like shit. Going entire days without drinking enough because the trough was far away and also half empty, and the headache pounding between your temples was making you crazy. Until they finally hooked them up to the water system, which she didn't tell them, there was nothing worse than the thirst. When Raymonde finally stopped to breathe, she saw everyone looking at her with red eyes.

After that evening, the children kept following her around. They fought about who would sit next to her on the bus and about who would hold her hand at the camps. After a whole day on her feet, when all Raymonde wanted was to lay her head down on the right side of the bed and rest a little, they would knock on her door and ask if they could come in. At first, she thought they were pestering her because the hotel didn't have any TV in Hebrew. They were bored, poor things. How long can you watch *The Young and the Restless* dubbed in Polish (even though she understood what was going on, even in Polish)? But after a while she realized that it was something else. Some who came wanted to hear emotional stories and cry a little, too. But there were others who came because they missed home, though they would never admit it, and they wanted a grown-up to put a hand on their shoulders and remind them not to go to sleep too late. Others had lost a grandparent, and she recognized them from the way their eyes searched her face trying to extract from her old age the image of a different old lady. And there were some who came for her, to ask if everything was all right. It moved her that they cared so much. Even if she knew that part of it was just for themselves, so they could feel like angels. No one had ever showed her so much love. No one had ever listened to her so intently.

From one camp to another, she got better at it. She improved. Every evening she would prepare the next day's story. She told them both Rivka's stories and her own, and also stories they put on TV on Holocaust Day instead of *Big Brother*. At first she was afraid the guide would figure it out, but after the second day, when she finished speaking and everyone was standing in front of the showers, handing each other tissues like they were popcorn at the movie theater, the guide was already completely hers. She even asked if Raymonde was available to join other schools this year. "Sometimes there are cancellations at the last minute," she told her, which was like saying that sometimes survivors went and died right before the flight so that she was really stuck. Raymonde had no problem being a substitute survivor. The hotels were nice and the children were wonderful, even if they were little pests sometimes, and she was even getting used to the cold. At the age of eighty-eight, it's fun finding out you're really good at something. Raymonde had already decided that, before the next time, she'd do what they called an investigation. First she'd talk to people in the home who had been in the camps and managed to put together an honest sentence. Then she'd sign up for the Internet course. Maybe she'd get some new material there.

After checking that she was prepared for the next day, she would take a long, hot shower, and then sit with Rivka. Since the first night, the smile on her passport picture had become pleasant again, and Raymonde was truly ashamed for the bad things she'd thought about her. She would lie in bed every night and tell her what she'd seen that day. The two children who kissed behind the barracks when they thought no one could see, and how their cheeks were so red, not only from the cold. The pile of clothes the guide took them to see that gave Raymonde such bad heartburn that she couldn't put anything in her mouth later. I thought something of yours might be there, she told Rivka, and wondered if maybe they'd been the same size then, too.

She told her about how the rain smelled different here, and laughed with her about the Poles who sometimes spoke to her in their language, but she answered them in Hebrew, and she told the children that speaking that foreign language was more than she was willing to do. She also laughed about every time the children called her Rivka and she forgot to turn around, but instead of suspecting anything they just called louder—*Rivka!*—and then she remembered, turned around, and apologized for her bad hearing. Maybe that's why they insisted that she sit in the first row at every ceremony they had in the camps, so she could hear. They didn't let her have a little nap in the back.

She already knew by heart all the words to *Yizkor,* the memorial prayer they read every time. The other texts changed from camp to camp, and the songs too, even though they all sounded the same. The one who played them was Ori, a handsome boy with a guitar, whom Raymonde saw kissing three different girls on the very first day. The only reason she forgave him was that she could tell he was a homosexual. Otherwise she would have told someone. When she had something in her heart, she couldn't hide it. That's why it was still working so well after eighty-eight years. Not like Victor, with all his cute jokes and smiles and songs and stories, then boom, he drops dead in the middle of the grocery store because all the debts he was hiding sat on his heart like the big sacks of rice, twenty pounds a sack.

At every ceremony, a few girls sang along with the boy who played the guitar. They always wore shirts so thin that you felt like running over and putting coats on them. And there were also the girls who were studying dancing, wearing black bodysuits that made their nipples stick out so much from the cold that they looked like they might fall off any minute, and those black tights that were stuck in their slits, which didn't look very healthy to Raymonde. They all had sad faces, because the Holocaust is very sad, and also because they were freezing their bottoms off. If they at least had a little flesh on them to keep them warm. They stood in the middle of the camp like scarecrows, dancing and singing in memory of the ones who died, while they themselves appeared as if they had just arrived on the death march.

Only one of them looked as if her mother still remembered how to cook a pot of food. A nice ass, round as an apple. Pink, healthy flesh on her hands and hips. Raymonde liked her from the start. She wanted to ask the girl to sit next to her, but the main singer, Liron was her name, always took the seat. Day after day, that Liron sat down next to Raymonde. Even if one of the other children was there first, she would tell them to move, and they obeyed her. Raymonde knew people like that from the home. That Liron had scooped her up the way the women in the home scooped up the lonely widowers who sometimes came to live there and still had control of their sphincters. She didn't like it, but she didn't want to say anything. She just waited to grab that sweet girl for a minute and tell her that she sang very nicely. It was in Majdanek that she finally managed to talk to her, and the girl was so moved that she almost tripped on the railway tracks.

That only made Raymonde like her more. And what she liked the most was when she saw her at dinner in the hotel, putting some food aside for the cats. She immediately thought of Rivka. Even though she wasn't sure that Rivka would want to help Polish cats, who had done nothing to stop the horrors. But on the other hand, why were the cats to blame, it happened even before their parents were born, and Raymonde decided to pile food on another plate just for them. The guide stared but didn't say anything—after all, she was a survivor—and later Raymonde took the plate over to the girl. They went out together to feed the cats, and the girl—in the meantime Raymonde had found out that her name was Nofar—ran to her room and brought back another shawl for Raymonde so she wouldn't be cold. Raymonde was sure the girl would ask her more about the Holocaust. That day she had told them about the ghetto, and it was so sad and terrible that Raymonde was afraid she would have nightmares from her own stories. But the girl didn't ask about the Holocaust. And she didn't talk about herself either, the way many of the children there did. First they asked about the Holocaust and then, when they got tired of it, they told her whom they loved and whom they hated, and didn't even ask her to keep it a secret. An old lady—whom did she have to tell it to anyway? Her husband had died a long time ago, and all she had left of her twin sister, her soul sister, was a suitcase, a passport, and socks. Instead, the girl looked at her and asked what it was like to be old.

Not elderly, old.

Raymonde didn't know what to say. She hadn't closed her mouth since she set out on this trip, and now she was silent. The girl didn't fill the silence. She let it be. She listened to it the way others listen to the words people say. At the end of that silence, Raymonde told her that being old is being completely alone. So alone that sometimes you make up things just to be less alone. Now it was the girl's turn to be silent. Or rather, both of them were silent, but this time the silence was the girl's. Her cheeks were pink from the cold and there were tears in her eyes, and Raymonde had no idea whether they were because of what she'd said. Nofar wanted to tell her that if being old meant making up things so you wouldn't be alone, then it really wasn't very different from being seventeen. Instead, she said *psss-psss-psss* to the cats and tossed them another piece of salami.

34

MAYA STOOD AT the door to Nofar's room and looked inside. A fiery red spot blazed in her chest: you're not supposed to be here. It was early afternoon, and the house was deserted. Her father was at work. Her mother was at work. Her older sister had just been picked up and taken to yet another TV panel.

While Nofar had been in Poland, Maya enjoyed the silence at home. For an entire week she was like an only daughter. When they drove to the airport to pick up the older daughter, their mother said that Maya wouldn't be bored now, and wasn't it wonderful that the house wouldn't be empty anymore. And it was true: the moment Nofar came back, the turmoil began again. At a high school in the northern part of the city, two boys were accused of taking part in a gang rape, and since the victim was unwilling to speak publicly, everyone turned to Nofar for her opinion. During the three weeks she'd been back in Israel, the older sister had been going from studio to studio. The younger sister was left at home, which was once again unbearably crowded, even though there were no people in it. She stood in that empty house now, in the doorway to the room that was not hers.

You shouldn't be here, Maya.

She opened the wardrobe and looked inside: blouses, pants, dresses. Various items of clothing that fashion shops had sent Nofar in the hope that she would be photographed wearing them and then post the pictures on the Internet. "Your daughter is a trendsetter," a messenger told their mother, who was shocked by the parade of clothes that streamed into the house. Maya remembered that the messenger hadn't mentioned Nofar's name. He simply said, "Your daughter," and it was clear to everyone which daughter he meant. Gently, Maya moved the tower of folded pants in the wardrobe. She looked behind the shirts. She unfolded the tank tops. It wasn't there.

Maya closed the wardrobe door and sat down on the bed. The smell of her sister's sleep rose from the sheets. She decided to search the drawers. In the first one she found the jewelry box each of them had received from their parents for their bat mitzvah. There were two necklaces in it, one with a heart pendant and the other with a teddy-bear pendant, and they both looked outrageously childish to Maya. Also in the box was a bottle of pale-pink nail polish that Maya had never seen on Nofar's nails and a half-bottle of nail polish remover. There was no time for that now. She had to close that drawer and open the one under it. A smile of surprise spread over her face when she found a packet of condoms, as yet unopened. She checked twice to make sure—the wrapper said a package of eight, and there were eight inside. Four interesting stones lay next to the condoms. Maya recognized one of them from the family trip they took years ago—a vague memory of a fight between her and Nofar about who the crystal belonged to, and in the end their father decided: "It's mine." Nofar must have asked him for the stone again when they reached home. And although Maya hadn't remembered the crystal, the fight, and their father's intervention until that moment, she was suddenly hurt, as if it had happened yesterday. Perhaps she needed that hurt in order to open the third drawer. She found two cigarettes hidden in a box of perfumes and wondered whether Nofar had bought them or stolen them from their hiding place in Maya's room. Next to the box of perfumes was a wrinkled ticket from a performance by a singer they loved in Yarkon Park. They had sung together there until their voices were gone. Their mother sat behind them and pretended to be enjoying herself, but they both knew she was suffering, and that only made them love her even more that night.

Maya closed the bottom drawer. She had to get out of there. She wouldn't go back to school today. She would go into her room, cover herself with her blanket, and go to sleep. No one would notice she had disappeared. But instead of leaving the room, Maya lay down on Nofar's bed and pulled the blanket over her head. This is where Nofar sleeps every night. This is where her body rests. If she closed her eyes, maybe she could feel what it was like to be Nofar. She breathed in her smell. Ran her hand over the cotton sheets. A pleasant sleepiness began to caress her, and she abandoned herself to it. Daylight entered through the half-open shutters, and Maya turned her back to that light and pressed up against the cool, dark space between the mattress and the wall. In another moment, sleep would come. And just then, as her hand landed heavily in the narrow space between the wall and the mattress, at that precise moment, she felt the notebook.

Now she was wide-awake. The room was the same room: the gentle afternoon light coming through the window, the cool cotton sheets with the smell of Nofar rising from them. Maya's body was curled up on the mattress in exactly the same position, her fingers resting in the space between the mattress and the wall. But sleep spurted away from her like sparks. Her fingers were no longer heavy with tiredness. The notebook under them was shooting small electrical currents into them.

You can still leave. Get up and go.

But you can't. That notebook owns you. Even before you look at it, it is already looking at you. Showing you the real Maya.

It took her less than ten minutes to read everything, and less than a minute to understand what had happened. On the first few pages her big sister still had the same handwriting she knew, more beautiful and rounder than her own, but after some empty pages Nofar's handwriting reappeared, looking suddenly different. The letters had become angled and small, and they pushed right up against the edge of every line on the page, as if someone were chasing them. And there were tears too—those places where the purple ink had smeared, then dried again. "It's not true. Everything I said. I made it all up. And he's the one paying the price."

Maya put the notebook back. There was an entire orchestra playing in her mind: it didn't happen it didn't happen it didn't happen. The suspicion that had flickered inside her at the president's residence had now become a proven fact: he hadn't touched her. He hadn't even tried. Avishai Milner had never attacked Nofar. The fame, the embrace of the entire country, the boys who at this very moment were certainly encircling her sister—all that for something that never happened.

Maya's head was spinning. She had to sit down. She thought she would be able to get to her room, but the weakness over-whelmed her in the hallway. She flopped down on the floor. It had to be stopped. They couldn't allow that man to go to jail for no reason. It wasn't right. It wasn't fair. She began to write the words in her mind: "The accuser's sister reveals the truth—Avishai Milner was unjustly accused." Such courage.

Such honesty. Such profound moral obligation to everything that is just and worthy. She would cry on morning TV. She would cry on the evening news. She would cry on the cover of the latest gossip magazine. She knew she had to overcome her mental block and act immediately.

Nevertheless, she continued to sit on the cool floor tiles for a few long minutes. Unconsciously, her fingers stroked her ankles in a repetitive, soothing movement. Their fingers were different—Maya's were delicate and Nofar's were coarser. Nofar had once tried to take her ring but couldn't get it on. But their ankles were identical. Maya had noticed it when their mother took them to buy shoes. She didn't know why it mattered now, but still she thought about it, making a precise list in her mind of the similar and different parts of their bodies, from toenails to eyelashes.

She was so deep in thought that she didn't hear the sound of the door opening. How frightened she was when Nofar and her mother bent over her with worry in their eyes: "Maya? Is everything okay? Why are you on the floor?" Hands reached out to help her up, and they sat her on the couch. Her big sister brought her a cup of tea, and as their mother touched her forehead to see if she had a fever, Nofar put her arms around her in genuine concern, asked her whether she wanted another cup of tea. And perhaps that would have been enough if Nofar hadn't spiced the tea with the events of the day: the people she met on the panel, the invitations she received to which programs, and even the possibility that she would be the spokesperson for a chain of fitness clubs that offers a kickboxing course for young girls. "Isn't that amazing?"

"Amazing," Maya said.

But if it's so amazing, why are your eyes so dark, Maya?

Why are you sitting on the couch and not speaking—so silent that later that evening their parents asked if everything was all right. Why are your eyes so dark, Maya, and what shapes are your fingers drawing as they wander around your ankles during the entire evening news?

35

NOFAR'S MEETING WITH Detective Dorit was set for
two thirty the next day, but by the time they left the house
it was already two o'clock, and it was clear to both her and
her father that they were going to be late. The air outside was
cold and wet, and her father turned on the heater as soon as
they got into the car. He lowered the heat a bit and asked
twice, "Okay for you?" as if he were an attentive hostess in a
gourmet restaurant and not her father, the eternal chatterbox.
Since the business in the alley had exploded, they had barely
spoken. Until now, Nofar had been sure it was because of her.
After all, she came home late almost every night, and in the
morning she was too tired to communicate. But now, when
she saw him so totally immersed in changing the radio station,
she suddenly realized that her father was embarrassed around
her. And she was right, because her father truly did not know
how he was supposed to act after what had happened to his
older daughter.

Damn it, he didn't even know exactly how it had happened.
One morning Ami sent his daughter off to her summer job in
the ice-cream parlor, and she came back surrounded by police
and cameras. His head was bursting from all the appalling
possibilities. All the stories he had ever read in the newspaper
or seen on TV seemed absolutely possible now. It terrified
him. It filled him with guilt. Why hadn't he been there? Why
hadn't he given her the tools to keep herself safe? What tools?

It didn't matter. Somewhere in this world there was a set of tools, and he hadn't given them to his daughter. If men could be fired from being fathers, he would have been out of a job a long time ago.

There were things Ami wanted to ask her, but he didn't know how. What happened? Where exactly did he touch you? All the questions racing around in his head caused his feet to freeze, a layer of cold that climbed up his body, sending his fingers to turn up the heat. Nofar, on the other hand, felt as if she was about to suffocate, but she didn't dare open the window. Neither of them said anything, and it was unbelievable now that he was the man who had taken her in his arms when she emerged from the womb. That man, now sitting beside a teenage girl and unable to summon the courage to look at her, once knew every small wrinkle of her skin. Why, despite all that, or perhaps because of it, because he had known her so completely, the way a father knows his daughter, couldn't he just come out and ask her what happened? Police investigators, TV reporters, the kids at school could ask that question, but not him.

Her father's father had died five years earlier, putting an end to the in-between period when a man can be both a child to his parents and a parent to his children. Since Ami's father's death, his mother had become a rebellious child, refusing to take her medication, taking offense at the most trivial things. Ami was no longer somebody's child, but only a father to his daughters. In his sleep, he sometimes imagined someone running a familiar hand through his hair. Then he woke up and saw that he had forgotten to turn off the fan.

In the car, Nofar listened to the bubbly voice on the radio announcing incredible discounts on electrical appliances. In another minute it would be two thirty, and they would be officially late. Her father called the station to say there was a traffic jam on the highway because of the rain. That wasn't true. They wouldn't reach the highway for another fifteen minutes. But he was always like that, reporting the facts with a slight deviation that would suit his needs. The person on the other end replied that there was no problem. They should take their time. Now that there was no longer any danger of being late, the silence in the car grew more oppressive. At first they had supposedly been allied by their battle against the clock, angry at the slow driver in front of them, cursing a sleepy traffic light. But now that there was no longer any reason to fight the battle, each of them was on their own again.

A small chair in the police station. Black tea in Styrofoam cups. A keyboard with letters faded from use and accumulated dust in the narrow slits between the keys. Detective Dorit was much less attentive than the last time. She answered the phone three times and sent texts almost nonstop. Nonetheless, she said once again that Nofar was a very brave girl. She said it twice, once to Nofar at the beginning of the conversation, and the second time to her father toward the end of their meeting. "You can be proud of your daughter, she's a very brave girl," she said in a formal, serious voice, like a teacher summarizing at parent–teacher day.

The prosecutor from the district attorney's office joined them and promised to demand severe punishment at the trial, no less than the maximum prescribed by the law. Normally there is greater leniency in such cases, but this one is high-profile and they would make an example of the perpetrator. The prosecutor said that, according to the law, the punishment for rape is up to sixteen years, for sodomy five years, and for indecent assault three. Those explicit words—rape, sodomy,

indecent assault—were like fists pounding Nofar's head. Her
father sat beside her, his face gray. The prosecutor continued
speaking, and though the words rolled lightly off her tongue,
they were actually as heavy as iron weights shackled around
Avishai Milner's feet. Nofar found it difficult to follow, and
the prosecutor, who noticed, spoke more slowly. Since this
was an attempted felony, it would likely end with a four-year
sentence. Perhaps five. Not enough, but that's the situation.

Detective Dorit walked them to the elevator. As the door
closed in front of them, Nofar's father asked if she wanted to
stop for a hamburger on the way back. Like they used to when
she was a little girl and he would take her to the doctor when
she was sick. Her mother would complain mildly—*the child
has pneumonia, what good will a hamburger do?* But her father
insisted that it had healing powers. And he was right. When
she had sat down beside him in the middle of the day, a hill of
french fries in front of her, and behind her was the knowledge
that all the other kids were at school now, she had truly
felt better. Who knows, maybe that would happen this time
as well. They drove to the shopping center. They sat down.
They ate. But there was no happiness in the conversation,
only the sour sweat of effort. She hated him for his hollow
laugh, and he hated her for her evasive look, and their hatred
frightened them so much that after the hamburgers, they ate
ice cream. All the way home in the car Nofar wanted to
throw up. Until then, Avishai Milner's trial had seemed like
a distant spot somewhere on the horizon, so abstract that it
was difficult to know whether it moved or was stationary and
perhaps would never come. But now it was here, almost right
here, and suddenly she realized that it was really happening,
she was really accusing that man of attempted rape.

Nofar leaned her head on the window. Inside the suffocating

car the glass was pleasantly cool, covered with vapor. The cars and the rain outside were invisible, and she could see only headlights. She pressed her nose against the fogged-up glass and drew shapes and letters on it with her fingers. She wrote "Dad, it didn't happen." If her father had turned his head to the window at one of the intersections, he would certainly have seen the words written on it. But he looked straight ahead for ten traffic lights and four turns, and when he finally turned to her and said, "Ready to go?" it was too late—the letters had lost their shape and were dripping down the glass.

36

LUCKILY FOR RAYMONDE, she took pity on the cats that
day. She hadn't gone outside to feed them since coming back
from Poland, but on that day she felt bad about it because of
Rivka. She collected bones from the soup at lunch, sat with
a small plastic bag on her lap, and put them inside without
anyone seeing. She could have asked Areh'le to buy her one
of those bags of cat food—he always asked if she needed
anything—but she felt awkward about asking something from
a man who didn't know her real name.

They had met two weeks before at a get-together of survivors from Theresienstadt. He went to get some soda water for
his heartburn and poured for her first and then for himself,
then said he didn't remember that there had been so many
Filipina prisoners in Theresienstadt. His joke about all the
foreign health aides in the room made her laugh so hard that
she spilled her soda water. A nice Filipina standing nearby left
the old woman in her care and came to help, but Areh'le told
her in Yiddish that they were fine, and that made Raymonde
laugh even harder. Since Victor, no one had ever made her
laugh like that.

It frightened her, laughing so much. Too much good all
at once. Like polishing off a whole bag of cookies in half
an hour. Piggishness. And to laugh like that at a meeting of
Theresienstadt survivors. So she told Areh'le she was going
to the ladies' room—Rivka's words—and stayed there long

enough to give him a chance to leave. And also to give him a chance to stay. She straightened her hair, applied more pencil to the most beautiful eyebrows in the country, and the nice, cheap lipstick her daughter-in-law the bitch had brought her. She heard the master of ceremonies outside say that they were about to begin, but suddenly she felt pressure in her bladder. She'd been so busy making herself beautiful that she'd forgotten to pee, and by the time she came out everyone was sitting and it was very embarrassing. The emcee stopped talking while he waited for her to sit down, and her heels made the loudest racket in the world, clacking on the floor while everyone else was sitting and waiting. But the worst thing was that she couldn't find a seat no matter where she looked. There were only serious faces staring at her, thinking she had some nerve coming in so late and wondering who she was. No one there knew her. In a minute someone would call out and there would be one hell of a commotion. Raymonde felt her legs getting heavy, like just before the time she fainted during Feldenkrais. What if she fainted now and they took her to the hospital and found out that Rivka Kanzenpold had died a few months ago? The room started spinning, and suddenly, in the sea of serious faces, she saw a hand waving in the air. His hand was delicate, like a woman's.

Later, he told her that those hands were the only reason he survived. He knew how to carve so well with them that the Germans lined up with blocks of wood for him to make toys for their children. Most of all, he loved to carve rocking horses. To imagine the *kinderlach* riding them. He didn't care that they were Nazi babies. Children are children. On the stomach of each horse he carved the initials of someone who had been taken. Until one of the officers discovered it and smashed his thumb with a hammer. Luckily, it happened right at the end of the war. The German children stayed on the home front, rocking on their horses, and he was sent to Theresienstadt.

After the war they actually tried to find him, and one Holocaust Day there was a newspaper article about his horses. That's how he found out that they still talked about them after the war. The German officers used him as an example of their humaneness. After all, they had looked after him, and a museum collected his work and tried to decipher the message in the initials. But he didn't tell anyone that it was him, and when Raymonde asked why, he said he didn't want anything at all to do with those horses. And anyway, why should anyone believe it, because after that hammer blow he never carved anything else again. (Except for avocado pits—she would find out about them later. He extricated them from the soft flesh and turned them into expressive faces, a different one every time. Raymonde wanted to ask who they were but didn't. All she did was keep her avocado pits on the windowsill and got excited when, one day, a tiny stalk sprouted from one of them.) But at that moment, in the hall, she still didn't know about avocado pits or rocking horses. She didn't even know his name. All she knew was that his raised hand rescued her from that sea of faces, and, as if it were a lighthouse, she navigated her way to it until she dropped down into the seat beside him, the one he'd saved for her, and the emcee of the Theresienstadt survivors' meeting resumed speaking.

At intermission, they went to the table with the sweet pastries. People passed them and asked, "How are you both?" and the "both" made it clear that everyone thought they were together, married. It didn't surprise her. She remembered that lone hand raised in the middle of the hall, how he kept it in the air until she was beside him so she wouldn't make a mistake at the last minute. She felt uncomfortable for feeling so comfortable with his attention, and she decided she would leave early. As it was, she would have enough information for the next trip from her Internet class and the Yiddish class she had signed up for. She was surprised when he said he would join her. He didn't have the strength to listen to the government representative make his speech. And definitely not the organization director's speech either. He'd been a schmuck in Theresienstadt, and he'd only gotten worse since then.

When they went outside, she thought he would offer to walk her to the bus stop, but instead he raised a hand and a driver pulled up. He opened the door of the shiny black car for her, and she smelled genuine leather upholstery, the strong scent of a car well taken care of and not often used. He took her downtown to eat at a Polish restaurant that had white napkins and fat, pretty waitresses. There were a lot of crumbs around his plate, but he told her it wasn't because he was ninety. Even when he was nine, he ate like a degenerate, but before his parents could argue with him about eating like a mensch, they were gone. She told him about her parents and he listened the way he ate, so totally engrossed in what was in front of him that he didn't mind if a few crumbs fell—what counted was the thing itself. He didn't notice her vagueness, because he wasn't interested in the small details. What interested him was her parents, and when he listened to her that way, she could actually hear them talking, after years when their voices had been dimmed in her mind. She asked him about his family, and as he told her, more and more people who once existed crowded around their small table with its white tablecloth, and somehow there was room for all of them. In the end, he told her he hadn't spoken that way for years. Since his wife. Maybe it was easy to talk to her like that because they were both from Theresienstadt. She could have told him right then, but she thought she would never see him again and the time with him was so beautiful that she decided not to say anything.

Since then, he had come to visit her almost every evening. To keep him from bumping into any of the residents, she asked him always to come after ten. He agreed happily—he couldn't sleep at night anyway. When she was young, she had been warned about men who only wanted one thing, and with Areh'le she remembered that warning with a smile. Not because of her body. It wasn't her body he wanted to enter. It was her soul. The way he constantly undressed her. Hurriedly, like her hasty lovers and like Victor in the grocery storeroom, not even stopping to take off their clothes, just anxious to join together as quickly as possible. He asked her things no man had ever asked. Bluntly. With no gentle probing. What did she regret the most? If she woke tomorrow morning with the body of a twenty-year-old, what would she do? (Would she marry Victor again? Raise her children the way she had?) What trait did she have that she wanted to pass on to her grandchildren? Who did she miss the most? At first, those questions embarrassed her. Embarrassed her the way it had embarrassed her when Victor asked her to undress in the light, the day after they were married, no shutters and no sheet. She had almost refused then, self-conscious about her breasts, which looked too small, and he hugged her and said there was nothing more beautiful than a man and a woman naked together in the light, and to show her, he undressed himself. She already knew his body, but it suddenly looked larger—it filled the entire room. Look, he told her, all this is yours.

She wondered what Victor would think of Areh'le. They were different in almost every way. Apart from that insistence: a man and a woman naked together in the light. And after a while, she dared to extend a probing hand with Areh'le as well. On their fourth night together, she told him that she had questions of her own. He listened gravely, answered to the best of his ability. Until the night reached its deepest moment, and the darkness began to fade away. They would boil water for tea—like Rivka, she left the teabag in the water for a long time—and together, in silence, they would watch the sun rise. Those silences were no less precious than their conversations. Perhaps more. There are many people you can talk to, but people you can be silent with are a rare commodity. In those silences, she tried to tell him that she was not from Theresienstadt. That her name was Raymonde. That she had never thought it was still possible at their age.

He would look pensively through the window, then smile at her—even at ninety, he had a lovely smile—and say, "Good morning, Rivka." Then he would leave her room and slip away quietly to the driver waiting for him in the street. She didn't want anyone to see him go out, and he agreed with her because he thought that the worst thing about being old is that everything is allowed and there's nothing to hide, and without things to hide there's no suspense or passion. He thought it was a game, thought she was acting like a teenager who might be thrown out of a girls' school, while in reality no one throws you out of a retirement home except the burial society. He didn't have the slightest suspicion that it wasn't the house manager she was afraid of, but him, of the moment one of the residents met him and asked him to give regards to Raymonde. (You mean Rivka? No, Raymonde. Raymonde Azoulai.)

At night she was with him, and in the morning she was in the classes she had signed up for, Yiddish and Internet and t'ai chi, which she had begun to like, and in the afternoon she slept. But on that day, instead of going up to her room to rest, she decided to go downstairs and feed the cats. And so it happened that she was there on the bench when the girl suddenly appeared at the entrance to the home. When Raymonde saw her, her heart almost dropped into her briefs. It was frightening just to think what would have happened if the girl had gone over to reception and asked where Rivka Kanzenpold was. They would tell her she's been dead for months, and the girl would tell them it couldn't be, she was with them on their trip to Poland. Raymonde looked around to see whether any of the residents were there now. This visit could cost her dearly. On the flight back from Poland all the children promised to come and visit her, but that hadn't worried Raymonde. She knew they really meant it on the plane, in the air, but they would forget about it when they landed on the ground. She hadn't heard from them for three weeks, and suddenly that girl was here the way people used to visit in the old days, before there were phones, when they just knocked on your door and came inside.

"Do you remember me?" the girl stood in front of the bench and asked. "My name's Nofar."

"Of course I remember," Rivka replied, adding in her kibbutznik Hebrew, "it's so nice of you to come and see me."

Two residents that Raymonde could never stand came out of the main entrance, looked briefly at the girl, and continued on their way. They must have thought she was her granddaughter. Raymonde swallowed her fear the way you swallow a blood pressure pill: first it sticks in your throat, and a minute later it's on the way down—just breathe deeply and take a sip of water. "Come here, *maydele*," she said to the girl. "Sit down next to me."

As soon as the girl sat down, Raymonde sensed something was wrong. She said she'd come to ask how she was, but one look was enough for Raymonde to know she'd come to tell her something you can't tell other people. She'd crossed the entire city to see a familiar stranger. Her eyes were red, and her sweet face was completely swollen, as if she were holding a whole doughnut in her mouth without swallowing it. Raymonde knew how to get secrets out of people with the same skill she had squeezed out blackheads on her children's backs when they were young and still let her do it, or the way she took almonds out of their green shells. You just had to press in the right place.

But here, she didn't even have to make an effort. It was the only reason the girl had come. And really, a few minutes later she told her everything. How that singer had insulted her in the ice-cream parlor. The girl still remembered exactly what he had said to her, as if it was written on her hand and she just had to read: "You pie-faced moron! You stupid cow! You should tweeze your eyebrows before going out in public. And those pimples, didn't anyone ever tell you not to squeeze them? You just need a few olives on your face and they can sell it as a pizza. But forget the face, what's with that stomach of yours? Didn't the owner of this place tell you that if you eat too much, you'll look like a hippo? Who would ever want to fuck you, huh? I'll take one scoop of cookie dough." And then the money he thrust at her, a piece of paper that made it clear who was the customer here and who had to serve him. Raymonde listened in silence and the girl told her how he ran after her, and she swore that when she screamed in the alley, she didn't know things would go so far. She just wanted him to leave her alone. But then everyone came and he humiliated her again, this time in front of everyone, and when they asked her if he'd touched her, a kind of "Yes" came out of her—not intentionally, the "Yes" of hysteria—and then it continued with the police and, later, on TV. The girl kept talking and

Raymonde remembered that she had heard the story at the time. Rivka had been sick and Raymonde had had no desire to read the papers, but even so, the scandal had trickled down to her from the other residents. It seemed that the whole country had known all about it except for Raymonde, though she did now.

The girl began to cry, saying that the trial was coming soon, and that she'd been at the police station today. They told her he would be sentenced to five years in prison. Raymonde reached into her pocket and took out a handkerchief, slightly used, but the girl wouldn't care at all, she was too busy with her sobbing: *how can I tell them now, they'll punish me, they'll yell at me.* Raymonde waited for her to calm down a little and then said that, with all due respect, there's a little more to this world than what people say about you. There are things you must not do, and you did them. The girl cried more quietly now, without words, and Raymonde was afraid she might have gone too far, been too harsh on her. But it was clear that the girl had come all the way there just for that, for someone to slap her bottom and tell her what to do. People always come to old folks to tell them what the right thing to do is. But why would they know what the right thing is? The only difference between them and young people is a few dozen years more of mistakes and terrible decisions.

The girl looked at her with enormous respect. The way you look at a wise and kind Holocaust survivor who has just given you a wise and kind bit of advice. Suddenly it frightened Raymonde, the power the girl had put in her hands. And even before she realized what she was doing, she opened her mouth and told her about Rivka. The phone that had remained with her after the funeral. The calls that came. The suitcase. The passport. The folded socks. She told her about the Yiddish lessons and her Internet research. She told her about Areh'le and felt her face suddenly grow hot. Until that moment she had been cold, and now her cheeks were flushed. She wondered if the girl noticed.

Nofar didn't notice. She was staring down at the ground. "So it doesn't pass with age."

"It's not the same thing," Raymonde said quickly, slightly insulted. "With me, no one gets hurt, everyone wins. With you, it's different."

"But someone who can talk like that to an ice-cream server—who knows what else he could do? Think about it, a person like him, he definitely must have hurt some woman in the past!" All the way over there Nofar had wanted to confess, but now, when that woman criticized her, she suddenly found she was defending herself. "And even if he never hurt anyone," she added, "at least this will teach others a lesson."

That annoyed Raymonde, how hard the girl was trying to justify herself. "This is not a public-education mission. Someone will go to prison because of your stories. You have to stop this as quickly as you can."

The girl looked at her with a bitter smile on her face that hurt Raymonde, who kept on saying that she had to tell the truth. But the longer she spoke about the evils of lying, the deeper the bitterness grew on the girl's face, until she finally said, "I don't think you have the right to preach to me."

Nofar looked at her. She was no Holocaust survivor, she was a Holocaust conniver, pretending to be a victim to gain things. It was no wonder she was like that, and it was no wonder that Nofar was like that, too, since it paid off so well for both of them.

37

SHE DIDN'T SLEEP that night. All the way back from the home, she couldn't wait for the moment she would finally lie down in her bed. She had fallen asleep on the bus and almost missed her stop. It wasn't normal tiredness, it was almost like fainting. But when she finally reached her room and climbed into bed, sleep refused to come. Lying on her back, she was more wide-awake than ever. She tossed and turned until she realized it wouldn't work. She reached out into the space between the wall and the mattress and was horrified.

It was a handbreadth away from the corner of the room. Back in primary school, when she had first begun to write in the notebook, she had set that distance—one hand with fingers spread—so she would know whether the hiding place had been desecrated. She'd been twelve when she started writing, deeply immersed in teen detective books, and she greatly admired secret hiding places and secret codes of all sorts. Over the years, she realized that no one would be spying on her for the simple reason that she wasn't interesting enough, but she nonetheless continued to keep her notebook in the same place. Force of habit. Five years had passed since then, notebooks had come and gone, but the place was the same: a handbreadth away from the corner of the room. She had a precise physical memory of that place, and so, long before her mind understood, her fingers already knew with certainty: the notebook was not in its place.

It was there, but not exactly. It was three handbreadths from the corner. Nofar sat up in bed, told herself it had to be a mistake. She hadn't touched the notebook for weeks. She hadn't even stroked its cover the way she always did before going to sleep, as if the confession on its pages might burn her fingers if she touched it. Yet she knew where she'd put the notebook the last time she wrote in it. And she knew that wasn't where she found it. Suddenly, it occurred to her that Maya had been looking at her strangely since last night. Her eyes were red, as if she had an infection, and those infected eyes had followed her around from room to room.

"Maya?"

She called loudly, in the most normal voice she could muster. A moment later the door opened. The tension was visible in the way Maya stood. A spark of guilt was in her glance.

"Did you come into my room when I wasn't here?"

"Yes, yesterday. I came in to take a dress."

And why shouldn't she come in to take a dress? They took each other's clothes every day. They had always gone into each other's rooms, covering the distance between them without hesitation, and even if they sometimes became angry with each other—*get out of my room! don't come in without permission!*—the complaint was for show, like the borders in the European Union that existed only to be crossed.

But the air in Nofar's room grew suddenly thick. Because if Maya had come in yesterday only for a dress, why was she standing that way now, flushing and sweating slightly? The little sister was talking about a piece of clothing she wanted to borrow, but while her mouth spoke about the dress in the wardrobe, her eyes were looking at the narrow space between the wall and the mattress. If it were possible to follow looks the way we follow footprints, then all the footprints led to Nofar's mattress, of that she was almost positive.

"Which dress did you take?"

"In the end I didn't take one."

When Maya left the room, Nofar sat down on her bed. That was why her sister was acting so strangely. But if Maya hadn't said anything until now, maybe she wasn't planning to do anything about it. On the other hand, even if she didn't say anything today, what guarantee did Nofar have that Maya wouldn't tell it all tomorrow, or in another minute? Maybe she was only trying to find the courage.

Once again, Nofar reached out to the space between the mattress and the wall, and this time she wasn't completely sure that the notebook had been moved from its regular place. Maybe she had pushed it by accident in her sleep. Maybe Maya's look of alarm was only in her mind. And even if Maya had read the notebook, you can trust a sister. She wouldn't say anything. She wouldn't turn her in. So the girl tossed and turned in doubt all night, reassuring herself one minute, frightening herself the next, until she finally got out of bed and picked up a pen. For the first time in a very long while, Nofar filled the notebook with feverish, desperate writing.

38

WHEN THEY WENT to bed she said to Ami, I'll bet you
Maya has a fever tomorrow morning. Ronit had a sense for
such things, could detect an illness while it was still in the in-
cubation period. Ami said he really hoped not. He'd left work
early that day to drive Nofar to the meeting with the police,
and he was hoping to make up the time tomorrow. Ronit
asked again how it went with the police, and he replied again
that it had been fine, repeating exactly the same details he'd
told her earlier in the kitchen. His voice was very matter-of-
fact, and that's how she knew he was upset. The more upset
he was, the more matter-of-fact his voice became, and Ronit
knew that if he ever planned to leave her, he would tell her in
that TV-weatherman tone. They were silent for a bit, until his
breathing whispered to her that he had fallen asleep. Ronit lay
in bed listening to Ami's breathing and the soothing sounds of
the house. The humming of the refrigerator. The whooshing
of the dishwasher. She had almost drifted off to sleep when
she thought she heard Maya's door opening. In a minute, she'd
hear a faint knocking at their door and Maya would tell her
she didn't feel well. But although the footsteps stopped right
outside their door, the knock didn't come. Silence. She kept
straining to hear what was happening in the hallway, but there
was no sound, and in the end she fell asleep.

The next morning, as Ami was preparing to take his
daughters to school, Maya said she didn't feel well. Ronit

was just about to call the doctor for an appointment when Maya looked at the car pulling away and said, "Mom, I have something to tell you."

There were three lawyers among their friends, but Ronit didn't plan to consult any of them. She was happy to call Noa to ask about a clause in their lease, but she wouldn't call to ask her about the attempted rape story her daughter had fabricated. Of course, Noa would be there for her, she'd drop everything, come to take her out for coffee, and give her good legal advice as she patted her shoulder. But the thought of Noa's fingers touching her shoulder gently was precisely the reason she didn't call. Noa had that half-nod when you told her something bad, a sort of tilt of the head apparently meant to show that she was totally listening to you, but the gesture made Ronit feel like a frog being dissected in a biology class. And since their daughters were small, Noa had habitually reacted to all of Ronit's stories with "If that happened to my Ofri..."—for example, "If Ofri refused to straighten her room the way Maya does, I think I'd..." Or "If Ofri had problems getting along with other kids like Nofar, I imagine I'd..." Or "If Ofri accused someone of attempted rape for no reason, I'd..."—statements that made it clear to the listener that Ofri never refused to straighten her room, had absolutely no problems getting along with other kids, and definitely wouldn't accuse anyone of attempted rape for no reason.

Sometimes, a small part of Ronit wished that something would finally happen with Ofri, not hard drugs but a joint in the drawer, not bulimia but some unhealthy diet, not an abortion but, let's say, a late period, something that would enable Ronit to place a sympathetic hand on Noa's shoulder and say, "If that happened to Nofar, I think I'd..." But Ofri was an outstanding student and a very sociable girl, and she had a steady boyfriend who was madly in love with her. The only thing that bothered Noa was that, although she had been asked to join the Intelligence Corps, Ofri preferred the pilots' course. That was why Ronit would never consult with Noa, even though it was free advice and her friend was an excellent lawyer. She was prepared to pay for the advice of a lawyer who would not put a hand on her shoulder or say a single word about his daughter, but would only explain how to persuade Nofar to confess in such a way that would cause minimum damage.

She found one on the Internet. She searched for names of lawyers who handled the worst criminals and found one who seemed especially good. "You're in luck," the secretary told her on the phone. "His morning meeting was just cancelled." She called school to say she would be late, drove to a skyscraper downtown, took the elevator all the way up to the sixteenth floor, and stood at the receptionist's desk.

"I have an appointment at eleven."

"Talia Shavit?"

It took a moment for Ronit to nod. When making the appointment on the phone, she'd been suddenly afraid that, despite confidentiality, the story might be leaked. Nofar was at the heart of a media frenzy, so it was better to be extra careful. Now she stood before the name she'd chosen, surprised.

"You're Talia Shavit?"

"Yes."

She had never used an alias before, and she was visibly tense as the secretary verified the details of the meeting on the computer. She thought that, at any moment, the woman would look up from the screen and reprimand her loudly, "Ronit Shalev! You should be ashamed of yourself!"

But the secretary merely smiled and offered her an espresso from the machine. The language teacher wasn't used to such treats—there was only instant coffee and UHT milk in the teachers' lounge. Ronit thanked the secretary and sank into a black leather armchair. She had noticed quite a while ago that lawyers' armchairs in TV series were always black, perhaps because clients' sins could be absorbed into the upholstery and remain unnoticed. Ronit went over the list of the lawyer's clients in her mind. She had read about them on the Internet, and though they seemed quite guilty to her, all of them, amazingly enough, were acquitted. They too had sat in this armchair, which was so black that nothing could stain it. They too had sipped espresso across from the abstract painting that apparently had been very expensive. But their legs hadn't trembled the way Talia Shavit's did.

I wonder where she is now, Talia Shavit. The last time Ronit saw her, she was giving a speech at the graduation ceremony of the education faculty. Talia Shavit had been a wonderful student, a wonderful dancer, and a wonderful friend, and Ronit couldn't wait for college to end so she wouldn't have to see her anymore. Her wonderfulness was so comprehensive that it made her absolutely awful. With Noa, for example, only Ofri was totally wonderful. Everything else was deficient to some degree or other—her job paid well but was boring, her husband was sweet but not sexy—and it was those things that made it possible to love her. Perhaps that was why Ronit had chosen Talia's name, so that once in her life, when the lawyer's door opened, someone would call out "Talia Shavit?" and she could say "Yes."

She had already drunk three cups of coffee when the door finally opened, and as she sat across from the lawyer her leg jumped like a hyperactive grasshopper. She told him about her daughter—Nofar Shavit—a very lovely girl, an excellent student who helped at home, was kind to the elderly, didn't leave a single kitten in the neighborhood hungry. Only, she was a bit confused, had accused someone of an attempted assault that didn't exactly, well, happen.

The lawyer asked several questions and then promised her that she had no cause to worry. Nofar Shavit would recant her false accusation, and the case would be closed quickly. As a minor, her daughter did not bear criminal responsibility. Even a suit for damages, if there were one, could be easily dismissed—no one had heard of the case, so the damage caused to the accused was definitely minimal. "Not like that Avishai Milner. If it were him, it would be another story entirely...."

"Another story?"

Ronit's voice shook slightly, but the lawyer didn't notice. "The whole country is talking about Avishai Milner's case. If it turns out that the girl is lying, he can ask for millions in a libel suit." Ronit shrank in her chair as the lawyer added, "And just think about the media scandal. All the papers that bought the story will stand in line to crucify the liar who sold it to them. In short, Talia, you can thank God that isn't the situation with your daughter."

When Ronit returned to the shady street, her wallet was 2,000 shekels lighter and her heart even heavier than before. She sat down on a wooden bench and took a used tissue out of her bag.

You carry a child inside your body, and after she comes out you still carry her in your heart. And your daughter doesn't know that she was once inside your body. She knows, of course, but not really. She will never know exactly what it was like when she was inside, and what it was like when she emerged, because when it comes to those things, people are as stupid as goats. You know her body better than she does because you nursed it and diapered it and stroked it when it hurt, and when she grew up you watched over her even when she already needed a bra. You know her body better than she does, but you don't know her. You ask, "How are you?" and she replies, "Fine," and every "fine" is another small door slammed in your face. You sit and wait like a beggar at the door—maybe your daughter will be kind enough to open it and toss out a coin. And gradually, you understand: your daughter is a stranger.

The used tissue began to shred in her hand. Passersby looked at her red eyes, slowed down a bit, then continued walking. She had to tell Ami. She should have told him in the morning right after Maya spoke to her, but she had decided not to, for Nofar's sake. It would be better if Nofar knew that Ami had no part in it. That way, when her older daughter refused to speak to her anymore after Ronit forced her to go to the police, she would still have her father to speak to.

Instead of going to work, she went home and found Maya in bed. She hugged her younger daughter and said, "Everything's fine, Maya'le," and felt her daughter's young body shake with sobs. "You did the right thing," Ronit told her, and was surprised to discover that she felt more than an iota of resentment for the girl she was embracing. When Maya finally calmed down, she gave her a hundred shekels and sent her to the shopping center to spend it. When Nofar returned, Ronit would sit her down for a very serious talk. You're still my daughter, she would tell her, but you have to take responsibility. And now we're going to the police together. It will be terrible, but it will pass. Like a root canal. If Nofar refused to go, she would drag her by force, the way she had dragged her when she was two years old and ran into the road. Get over here, because I say so, because I'm the mother and you're the child, and I know.

But what do you know? Do you know how long it will take until the story passes? Nofar would change schools, that was clear, but even in the new school everyone would know who she is. The entire country knew her. The mere thought of Nofar going into the army, beginning university, while everyone around her was looking and whispering, "Is that the girl who...?" "Yes, that's her." "Maniac!" If being a parent means protecting your child in every way you can, Ronit still needed to know what she was protecting her daughter from—from the outside world? From the damage Nofar was doing to her own soul?

Ronit suddenly had the comforting thought that Maya was making up that whole story of the notebook. Maybe her younger daughter was simply jealous of the attention her big sister was getting. Ronit gave herself over completely to that pleasant idea. She hid inside it the way she had hidden in her parents' wardrobe when she was a child, until her mother reached inside and pulled her out. Her mother had died four years ago, a combination of bad genes and cartons of L&M Lights, but her voice was exactly the same as ever when she said to Ronit, "You should be ashamed of yourself! Distracting yourself with futile daydreams while your home is rotting from so many lies! The roof is about to fall in on all of you!" Her mother had been a Bible teacher. Her favorite part of the curriculum had been the prophecies.

"Aren't you going to answer your mother?"

"You're dead. I'm not talking to you."

"Everyone talks to their dead parents. It's completely normal."

Ronit grew silent. Her mother sighed. "So don't talk to me, talk to your daughter. Tell her she has to go to the police and confess. Or you'll do it instead."

"And if the humiliation crushes her? If she..."

"People aren't so quick to commit suicide."

Ronit made herself a cup of coffee with a lot of sugar, even though she knew exactly what her mother thought about women who drank it with a lot of sugar. "Ronit'i, I know it's difficult. But the fact that something is difficult doesn't mean you can just not do it."

"But think about it, Mom, if it were me, Ronit, at seventeen, could you do it?"

"Without thinking twice."

Ronit took a big sip of her coffee, even though it was much too sweet. "So maybe that's why, Mom. Maybe that's why I am actually thinking twice."

Her mother was silent. From the window overlooking the street came the mewling of a peevish cat. Ronit poured her coffee into the sink and asked, almost in a whisper, "What sort of mother turns in her own daughter?" And her mother's voice was calm and confident as it gave the reply she knew it would give: "What sort of mother allows her daughter to imprison an innocent man?"

Suddenly, she was upset about all the hours she had already wasted. The very fact of the delay seemed offensive to her now, as if every additional minute of waiting sullied Nofar even more. There was only one option. Ronit rediscovered inside herself the same firm decision that had taken shape when Maya first told her. And although the lawyer's words had shaken her resolve slightly, now it was as solid as concrete.

39

LATE THAT NIGHT, she sat in the dark living room and waited for her daughter to come home. On Thursdays Nofar worked at the ice-cream parlor until closing time. She wouldn't be home until midnight. Nonetheless, Ronit sat on the couch and waited. She didn't turn on the TV, didn't open a book, just sat on the couch even though the sink was full of dishes and there was a pile of laundry to fold. The dishes would wait. The laundry would wait. At nine thirty Ami came out of the study, asked why she was sitting in the dark and was she coming to bed. She said she was dozing, even though her eyes were as wide open as they could be. Ami shrugged and said, "So, good night, Rontchi," adding apologetically that he had a long day tomorrow. You have no idea how long, Ronit thought, and knew that tomorrow morning he would hate her when she woke him up and told him they were going to the police now. *Why didn't you tell me?* he would say. *Why did you face her alone?* And she would tell him he was right, because he really was right, but in her heart she would know he was slightly wrong as well.

On the other side of the wall, the neighbor's grandfather clock rang out twelve times. Ronit counted silently. She knew Nofar had arrived a split second before she heard the sound of the key in the lock because she recognized the sound the elevator made when it stopped on their floor. That's how it was, everything familiar and nothing known. The door opened. The sound of her older daughter's footsteps in the hallway stopped suddenly when she saw her mother sitting in the living room. "Mom? Why are you still up?"

Nofar turned on the lamp and the living room was instantly illuminated by bright light, blinding them both. Here was the carpet, the couch, the armchair. Here was the mother. Here was the daughter.

"Nofar, I want to see your notebook."

The sudden tension in her daughter's body did not escape Ronit's attention. Nor did the mild shudder that ran through her at the mention of the notebook.

"My notebook? Why do you want my notebook?" Nofar's voice was shriller than usual, and it slipped under the couch in an attempt to hide.

Ronit's voice sounded metallic to her when she said, "I asked you to bring it to me."

Nofar didn't move. "But why do you want my notebook?"

Ronit, without answering the question, said, "Now."

"But it's personal!"

"Now."

"But Mom..."

"Nofar!"

She didn't shout—she didn't want to wake Ami—but her whisper echoed through the house as if someone had broken all the dishes in the sink. Nofar was crying quietly now, but Ronit had no intention of taking pity on her. It didn't occur to her to use force, just as it didn't occur to her to search Nofar's room herself when she wasn't home. Twenty years in high school corridors had taught the language teacher to get what she wanted by speaking in an authoritative tone. And it worked now, too, because a moment later her daughter broke. With tears in her eyes, she went to her room.

When she came back, she handed Ronit the notebook in defeat. In a complaining tone she said, "I wanted to give it to you when it was finished. I didn't want you to snatch it from me," and dropped onto the couch.

Ronit opened the notebook, scanned the pages with the same speed-reading technique she used when marking language exam papers. Her astonishment grew from paragraph to paragraph. She didn't realize that her mouth was wide open. It had never entered her mind that such a young girl was capable of doing something like this. Although the style was quite immature, it was distinct. In crowded handwriting, the entire story was spread out before her. She called her heroine Jennifer. Ronit vaguely remembered the name from a TV series Nofar had loved—and when Jennifer was thrown off the cheerleading squad, she decided to accuse the team captain of getting her pregnant. Ronit read the descriptions that filled the notebook and came to the confession Jennifer made to her friend Amy, the same first-person confession that had upset Maya so much. "It's not true. Everything I said. I made it all up. And he's the one paying the price."

But it was clear that Maya had not read the pages that preceded that confession, how the captain slept with Jennifer and then left her for his ex, the bitch, and how Jennifer decided to hold on to him by faking a pregnancy. If Maya had read it, she would have understood that it was an immature draft of a fiction plot. In the pages following the confession, the fake pregnancy was abandoned for a description of the love developing between Jennifer and Josh—a story filled with pathos written by an adolescent girl, no different from the stories the language teacher had written herself at the same age.

Nofar looked tensely at her mother holding the notebook, her eyes following the movement of Ronit's eyes as she read. If only she believed it and didn't ask any more questions. She never thought she would dare to lie to her mother like this, but seeing Maya's eyes searching the mattress last night, she realized she had no choice. At first she thought she would simply destroy the incriminating pages, but immediately rejected the idea. Maybe Maya had photocopied them. So instead of destroying the words Maya had discovered, she surrounded them with additional words. They had surged from her pen with the speed of an escaping prisoner. She had scribbled quickly for long hours without stopping, the minutes nipping at her heels, her fingers hurting from holding the pen for so long. At any moment the door might open and her mother would demand the notebook. She had spun the ins and outs of the plot all night, until the first rays of dawn appeared. She collapsed on the bed in exhaustion and put the notebook back in its burglarized hiding place.

Now, in the living room, Ronit read her daughter's notebook and Nofar tried to read her mother's face. Again and again she repeated a silent prayer: Let her believe me. And yet, when her mother looked up from the notebook and hugged her, Nofar felt something inside her crack. Her mother's arms encircled her, and she burst into tears. Ronit stroked Nofar's head and said, "Enough, sweetie. I'm sorry I made you show it to me," and apologized for invading her privacy. Then she praised the writing and the style, and all the while Nofar was enclosed in the familiar embrace, which on the one hand was pleasant and on the other scratched like steel wool. Distressed, she wanted to break out of the comforting arms, but in the end she only burrowed more deeply into her mother's neck, crying so hard that Ronit suddenly froze, wondering why. She drew back, held Nofar by the shoulders, and asked, "Nofar, is it really just a story?" And although the girl had felt suffocated in that embrace only a moment before, now that her mother had backed away from her, she felt suffocated without it, and she gathered all her strength to say in a steady voice, her eyes wide with innocence, "Of course, it's just a story. What else could it be?"

40

"START VOLUNTEERING," THE lawyer told him. "You have to start volunteering." They were sitting on indescribably soft and comfortable black armchairs in the lawyer's office, and Avishai Milner thought about all the rape and murder cases that had paid for them. He ran admiring hands over the Italian-made leather and considered how many of the clients who had upholstered them were people like him, who had done nothing, and how many had actually done a lot. He thought of asking the lawyer, but decided not to, not only because it wasn't polite, but also because every minute there cost him twenty shekels. And yet it annoyed him that the best advice one of the leading defense lawyers in the country could give him was to start volunteering.

The lawyer sensed that. Nonetheless, he didn't get those armchairs only because of his knowledge of the law. He also had to have a good knowledge of people. He knew he had just told Avishai Milner the last thing he wanted to hear, but he also knew it was the thing that would make Avishai Milner hire him. People value someone who tells them what they don't want to hear. The defense attorney decided to say that out loud. "You know, Avishai, I understand that the last thing you want to hear now is 'Go out and volunteer.' But as a defense attorney, my job is to tell you the things you don't want to hear. That's the only way we have a chance to get you out of this."

For the first time since their meeting had begun, Avishai Milner didn't wonder whether the last sentence was worth its weight in legal fees. The lawyer leaned forward with a movement that caused his lower back to hurt, but was an inseparable part of the courtship dance required to attract a new client. "Judges place a high value on such things. Retirement homes. Children with cancer. Find something you can connect with. And if, God forbid, you're convicted, it can help reduce your sentence." The lawyer saw the fear that the word *convicted* ignited in his client's eyes and leaned forward a bit more. Now he felt real pain in that spot on his back. "I'm not saying it will happen. But we have to cover you for every possible situation."

In the pediatric oncology department, they thanked him politely and told him they didn't need any more volunteers. He suspected that they dismissed him because of the negative publicity he'd received and tried again, using a different name. The secretary called two days later with a similar response. Apart from their regular staff of volunteers, they were getting a nonstop flow of TV stars, actors on children's programs, unknown singers, well-known singers, and formerly well-known singers. They all wanted to come, sing, dance, make the children laugh, be photographed—especially be photographed. The children, she hated to say, were really exhausted, mostly because those volunteers brought candy with them, and there was now so much candy in the department that, in addition to cancer, they'd soon have diabetes too. "I can give you the number of the regular oncology department," the secretary said. "They really need volunteers there." Avishai Milner wrote down the number and then threw it in the trash.

In the end, he appeared at the door of a preschool for autistic children. Before that there had been a disastrous attempt at an old-age home. In his imagination he filled the place with song and restored the minds of the demented with the help of his voice and his guitar. But the old folks, though they could barely move and some were mentally disabled, were able to recognize "that one from the news." They drove him away with shouts and canes. In the preschool for autistic children he was blessedly anonymous. None of the kids knew him. Neither did the teachers. They had too much on their minds to wonder from where they knew the face of the guy who played the guitar. And the assistant, a sweet eighteen-year-old doing her national service, blushed as she showed him her engagement ring, and during the break she knitted a skullcap for her fiancé.

Avishai Milner looked at the children and was repelled, but after scolding himself for his reaction, he forced himself to approach them. How difficult it was to look at them. How much he wanted to leave. Those children appeared in his dreams at night, and he was afraid he would catch that thing they had. He knew that the faceless woman in the dream was his wife, he knew she was carrying his child, and maybe the baby would have it, too. Hesitantly, he told his dream to the national-service girl, who nodded and said she'd also had dreams like that at the beginning, even worse ones, but really, you get used to it. He observed her in astonishment as, with endless patience, she played with the kids. One day, when he had come to play the guitar for them, she greeted him with tears of happiness in her eyes—for a moment he thought it might be her wedding day—and told him that one of the children had spoken his first sentence that morning. There were many terrible days in the preschool, days when he almost got up and left. But since he didn't leave, he saw how even the terrible days passed, and on the day that followed a small miracle happened. Or the opposite: he came in and could tell from the tired eyes of the teachers that today was even worse. One way or the other, the hours he played his guitar in the school were separate and apart from his regular life. He navigated them as if they were an ocean in which he sometimes drowned, sometimes floated. When the national-service girl signaled to him, he put down his guitar and hurried after her to see: a girl was eating by herself. A boy was organizing his toys. And he knew that the national-service girl was a hundred times better than he was. He was ashamed for being what he was, for being ready to leave that place the moment he could, and even if that shame was the only thing he took away with him, he did not leave the preschool empty-handed.

41

IT WAS ALMOST by accident that Nofar finally found out about the picture Lavi had taken, although even accidents are directed by an unknown hand. Otherwise, how can we explain that the last bus arrived a full three minutes early that night? Was it the driver speeding through the city streets in his rush to return to the arms of his sleeping wife? Perhaps it was, perhaps it wasn't, but either way, Nofar and Lavi had to run as fast as they could to the bus stop. A moment earlier they had been sitting together in the closed ice-cream parlor. Lavi helped Nofar pick up the last chair, then treated himself to a double scoop. They were sure they had several minutes before the last bus arrived when Nofar suddenly saw it on the other side of the window. Without a word, she leaped out of her chair, grabbed her bag and phone, and began to run. Lavi hurried after her, waving his arms like a windmill. Yes, the hurrying driver couldn't miss the skinny boy waving desperately at him to stop, and yes, the driver was hurrying home to his bed, but he too had a heart. And so he stopped and waited for the panting girl to catch up and board, and he even waited another second for the boy to arrive and kiss her goodnight, because many years ago he too had been a teenager dashing to catch the last bus.

Lavi was so happy Nofar had managed to get on the bus that it took a few minutes for him to realize that she had taken his phone with her. When she ran out of the ice-cream parlor, she hadn't differentiated between the two black phones that were identical in size and shape. But their contents were very different. Nofar would discover that during her ride home. At first she was alarmed at her mistake, and then, after calming down a bit, she thought it was funny. She quickly texted her own phone from the one she had in her hand: "I took your phone hostage. Prisoner exchange tomorrow," and added a smiley. She waited for him to reply, and as she wondered why it was taking him so long, she wandered through his phone.

That was when she saw it, and at first she didn't realize whom she was seeing. The face was there—the blue eyes, the delicate shape of the nose, the teasing smile on the lips—and yet it took a few seconds for her to understand that she knew that beautiful face quite well. She knew the girl standing there, straight and confident, and she knew the empty space beside her, the place where Nofar herself had stood before she had been cut out by the computer program.

They say that experienced birdwatchers can identify a bird in the undergrowth by only a single cry, so well do they know the sounds. City people are also well practiced: with closed eyes, they can distinguish between the individual parts of the urban cacophony—the hum of a garbage truck, the music coming from a convenience store, the *wah-wah-wah* of a baby crying, the *ah-ah-ah* of a woman moaning, the *scrinch* of autumn leaves underfoot, the *bloop* of beer bottles being opened. But amid this endless mixture, it is difficult to hear the *tak!* of a young heart as it breaks. And so the bus kept moving. Soon the driver would wrap himself in his sleeping wife's arms. He can't be blamed for not noticing that the girl who had skipped onto the bus with the light steps of a doe was leaving it now as heavy and pale as a corpse.

★   ★   ★

The next day, Lavi Maimon went to the alley and found it empty. The guy working in the ice-cream parlor handed him his phone and said that Nofar had been there earlier and asked for Lavi to leave her phone. There were questions in the guy's eyes, but Lavi ignored them. She didn't want to see him. She'd found out. The dread that had been born in his stomach the moment he posted the picture to the group now shot up to his chest. And there it settled, heavy as an elephant. There was no way of knowing how Lavi managed to climb the four floors to his apartment. He called her landline over and over again all that day, with no success. He thought of emailing her, but didn't know what to say. When it was time for the evening shift, he looked out his window at the ice-cream parlor but didn't have the courage to go down.

In the days that followed, Nofar made a frightening discovery: a person could walk around with a broken heart and no one would notice. True, she tried to conceal it: she didn't cry in public, pretended to be fine. And yet. Every time his name flickered on the screen, she thought of Maya. How beautiful her little sister was. The sort of beauty that causes sparrows to fly backward. That causes turtles to race forward. And causes boys to lie. Since finding out about the notebook, Nofar hadn't exchanged a single word with Maya, and if at first the silence between them had been oppressive, now it was truly toxic. Lavi wrote dozens of messages to Nofar, but she didn't open any of them. Even if she had the fleeting thought that she might be able to forgive him, that picture bit into her flesh once again like a hungry dog.

The passing days joined together. Nofar replied to her parents' cautious questions about Lavi with unintelligible mumbling. It embarrassed her that they knew they were no longer seeing each other. As if what he had done reflected not only on him, but also on her. She wasn't beautiful enough. Good enough. Accomplished enough. As soon as Maya entered the house, Nofar hurried to leave. She stood on the street and watched the bus stop fill with people, and she kept watching even after the bus arrived and the stop emptied out. Like a beating heart, the bus stop filled up and emptied out, filled up and emptied out. She spent most of her time in her room, and she spent her time at school staring mournfully into space. Her teachers thought she was just beginning to process the trauma. The girls in her class competed for the role of supportive friend, the one whose shoulder would absorb the precious tears and whose ears would hear the whispered not-yet-published details of the incident.

But Nofar maintained her silence. After school, she hurried to work. The motorized whale carried her for fifty minutes before vomiting her up on the main street, and she went into the ice-cream parlor, her face expressionless, and scooped ice cream into customers' cones. She didn't go into the alley again. At the end of her shift she headed home, looking straight ahead. A pair of dark eyes watched her come and go, following her from above. At his window on the fourth floor, Lavi prayed she would look up and see him. But Nofar did not raise her eyes even once.

42

LONG WEEKS HAD passed since the deaf-mute had cried out, "She's lying!" in front of the police station on the main street. The suspicion his words had aroused in Detective Dorit had almost faded. Nonetheless, if she happened to reach the precinct early, she still took the trouble to stand in front of him and listen. But as the days went by, his words became background noise. Her ear became used to them just as people who spend their days in the city are so used to the beeping of buses that they no longer hear it.

Every now and then, Dorit felt her primordial instinct of intuition reawaken, but there were always more pressing cases. There were also those annoying calls from lawyers trying to give advice about her investigations. Usually she hung up even before they began to speak, allowing only the most senior ones to have their say. Avishai Milner's lawyer was one of the most senior lawyers among them. Dorit knew very well how much money he charged, and it was clear to her that no one pays that much money unless he is really in trouble or really guilty. Avishai Milner's lawyer demanded that Dorit give the accuser a lie detector test.

"You do realize, don't you, that we're talking about a minor here?"

He did. Nonetheless, he insisted, "Today's girls have highly developed imaginations," and hinted that it would be better to administer the polygraph now, before they went to court, so that nothing would sully, heaven forbid, the police's handling of the case.

Such insinuations might work with less experienced detectives, but they merely irritated Dorit. Avishai Milner's lawyer was known to be very well connected, but she was the one heading up the investigation. She thanked him summarily and hung up. There was a large stack of files on her desk waiting to be reviewed.

Nevertheless, late that evening, when she was finally alone in the interrogation room, Dorit stretched her legs and took a deep breath. She exhaled slowly, tiredly, and thought that for too long now she had wanted to go to yoga class and never found time for it. In a high-pressure job like hers, you have to know how to keep healthy. She inhaled deeply again. And there, at the base of her diaphragm, the deaf-mute's words still waited: "She's lying!" Dorit exhaled the words slowly. She opened the computer file documenting her meetings with Nofar Shalev. There was the transcript of the first meeting, then the second. And there, at the end of the second meeting, were the girl's words of indecision. At the time, Dorit had been sure Nofar had suddenly gotten cold feet, afraid of the emotional price she would pay if the case came to court—after all, at Nofar's age Dorit herself had remained silent in exactly the same circumstances—but why, in fact, had she been so convinced? As Dorit read the transcript of their meeting again, and then once again, she became more certain: the girl was speaking the truth. And yet, a vague sense of discomfort grew stronger inside her.

She left work and drove home with the radio tuned to a music station. She made dinner for herself and the children, watched TV with them until late. She checked to see that they had really gone to bed, and set her alarm, although there was no need—she would wake up without it. In the shower, she washed her hair with the same shampoo she had used since she was twelve. She got into bed and closed her eyes. In the absolute silence of the empty double bed she could hear those words again. Sometimes she heard a catchy song on the car radio and just waited for some quiet time to replay it. That was how she now replayed the deaf-mute's words: "She's lying!" And if at first the words had hovered unattached to anything, kites without strings, they were now firmly connected to that girl from the ice-cream parlor. Today's girls have highly developed imaginations.

When the alarm rang at six in the morning, Dorit, who was already awake, reached out and turned it off. Two hours and twenty-five minutes later she entered her office. Waiting for her on her desk were additional messages from Avishai Milner's lawyer. Dorit tossed them in the trash bin. Sat down. Called Nofar Shalev. The ringing was cut off immediately. Either the girl was screening her or her phone was off. Dorit waited until evening and called again, with no success. Then she dialed the number of the house landline. A slightly hoarse male voice answered.

Even before she opened the door, Ronit smelled the eggplant and knew that something had happened. If Ami was making his lasagna, something was wrong. Her husband had his own way of dealing with upsetting news: the day he was told about his father's biopsy, he barricaded himself in the kitchen with six eggplants and made enough lasagna for a week. When the budget cuts began in his office, they ate eggplant lasagna for a month, until his boss called him in to inform him personally. Ronit hadn't argued with him then. She knew he had to do something with his hands during times of stress or he went

238

mad. The eggplant jiggled and shrank, pouring out its juices in the frying pan as Ami poured out his thoughts and fears, and God help anyone who interrupted him.

She walked quietly into the house, intending to slip into the study. She didn't have to speak to him this very moment. She had 200 exam papers to mark. She took them out and was heading for the hallway when she heard Ami's hoarse voice coming from behind her. "That detective called today."

The 200 exam papers were suddenly very heavy. Ronit put them down on the dining room table. She had never done that before—she was always afraid that something would be spilled on them.

"And? What did she want?"

"She wanted to set a date to give Nofar a lie detector test."

Ami came out of the kitchen into the dining room. Tomato sauce stains covered the apron he wore, and had also stained the checkered shirt under it. He wiped his hands on a towel and looked silently at the pile of exam papers lying on the dining room table. He had flour on his elbow and his eyebrows, which made his hair look whiter and his face look old.

"And? What did you tell her?"

"I told her it was scandalous to take a seventeen-year-old girl who went through something like that and hook her up to a polygraph machine. It would be a black mark against the police. Did they really decide to believe the word of that piece of shit?" His voice rose to a shout, as if he weren't speaking to her but to that detective. A spray of tomato sauce dotted his right sleeve.

"And what did she say after you refused the lie detector test?"

"She said they obviously can't force us, and it's entirely up to us. Then she babbled something about how she believed it would help shorten the trial, as if that was the reason."

"You think she has a different reason?"

He hesitated. Now she saw clearly that it wasn't only the flour on his eyebrows that made him look older.

"I have to turn the eggplant."

He went into the kitchen and flipped the eggplant in the frying pan. She waited a long moment for him to come back and continue the conversation. Finally she realized that he had no intention of coming back. She picked up the exam papers and felt the wetness that had spread through the bottom part of the pile. The table wasn't clean—maybe a coffee stain or spilled water. But whatever it was, the liquid had already seeped into the pages. She cursed quietly to herself, and whether he'd heard her or not, he looked up from the frying pan and said with his back to her, "They're just covering their asses. They want to come to court with all the support they can get their hands on and they're not thinking about Nofar at all. You know who they give lie detector tests to? Criminals, not my daughter."

It had been a coffee stain. The exam paper on the bottom of the pile was so wet that she couldn't read what was written there. She would have to apologize to the student, explain what had happened and hope he wouldn't complain to his parents. Or she could simply tell him he got a ninety, knowing that the mark would make him so happy that he would never ask to see the exam paper. She took a towel and tried to absorb the wetness. Her head began to pound.

43

LAVI DIDN'T THINK it was possible to regret something so much that your entire body hurt. He had a terrible taste in his mouth, which made him think that hopeless longing tastes like canned food that's gone moldy. That taste was the reason the boy almost stopped eating, and he quickly lost the little bit of flesh that covered his bones. Soon enough, his parents were going mad with worry. His father was sure it was because he'd been rejected by the elite combat unit. It never entered his mind that it was possible to be so sad because of a girl. His mother thought it was a crisis of adolescence and insisted that he go to a psychologist.

There were bags of green tea, white armchairs, and a Magritte print in the psychologist's office. His mother waited outside as he sat in one of the white armchairs and discovered that it was very comfortable, amazingly comfortable. He wondered whether all that whiteness caused the patients' thoughts to become brighter, or the opposite, whether it made the dirt of life more conspicuous. A few moments later, it was already clear to him that the psychologist's office made him uneasy. Everything was so clean and orderly, everything but him. He said nothing for five minutes, though he knew that every minute of his silence cost his mother ten whole shekels. On the way home she asked him how it had gone, and he said it was great.

During the day he sat and thought about Nofar, at night he lay in bed and thought about Nofar, and once a week his mother took him to the psychologist, where he was silent and thought about Nofar. On the way home his mother asked him how it had gone and he said it was great, and he continued to think about Nofar. Until, one day, his father took him to the psychologist. They had already reached the office, which was in a pricey neighborhood, when his father asked, "Are you sure you want to go in to see her?" Lieutenant Colonel Arieh Maimon had never spoken the word *psychologist* out loud. Lavi looked at his father, surprised, and Arieh Maimon said they could go to the beach and exercise there instead.

Lavi had never exercised on the beach. On the days before the combat-unit screening, whenever he left the house his father would say, "You're going to exercise on the beach?" and never waited for a reply. Since Lavi had come home from the screening, his father had never stopped asking him if he was going to exercise on the beach, but now he suddenly reached over to the back seat and picked up the special running shoes he had bought him as a gift. Lavi didn't want his father to see what a terrible runner he was, but he had even less desire to spend another fifty minutes in the psychologist's white armchair. So they drove to the beach and ran on the sand. More accurately, Arieh Maimon ran and Lavi straggled along behind him. When they finished running, Lavi's muscles hurt so much that, for a moment, the other pain about Nofar was pushed aside.

In the days that followed, his father took him to run almost every evening. He also taught him some hand-to-hand combat techniques. Whenever they practiced the moves, Lavi ended up lying facedown on the sand, with Arieh Maimon standing over him. Lavi didn't care about lying with his face in the sand. He only hoped that at some point the taste of sand would be able to cover the taste of canned food gone moldy.

44

BEFORE DAWN, RONIT felt it again: many years had passed since her pregnancies, but still, in that twilight moment between sleep and wakefulness, they sometimes returned suddenly—small movements in her stomach, elves tickling her from the inside. As if she once again had a baby girl there. If she remained in bed for another brief moment and breathed slowly, the feeling, that shadow of longing, disappeared. It hadn't really been there from the beginning, that shadow of longing. Ronit would get up to face her day, and although her body contained all the necessary parts, something was missing. Every now and then her underwear surprised her with thick red stains. And though they disturbed her daily routine, nonetheless having them was better than the day after which she'd never have them again. Perhaps that was why she still sometimes dreamed about that fullness: nine months during which you aren't alone for even a minute—you are more than the sum of everything you are. Perhaps it was a shame that she hadn't understood back then that, from the first moment, she had to begin to let go. First the girl in her womb would kick, then she would emerge, then crawl, walk, run, and in the end she would tear herself out of this house just as she had torn herself out of that womb.

She tossed and turned in bed, telling herself that everything was fine. But if everything was fine, why had that detective called to ask for a lie detector test? Maybe she should talk to Nofar. Since that night, she had been very careful around her daughter. She didn't want to hurt her again. As it was, Nofar hadn't spoken to Maya since that business with the notebook. Ronit was used to the stormy arguments between her daughters, the shouts and slammed doors, but this silence was new. She had never intervened in their fights, and now, as well, she waited for time to heal their relationship. But the silence only deepened, and Ronit began to miss the old fights. Nofar's shouts when she discovered that Maya had lost her purple fountain pen, for example. They screamed at each other until Ronit feared their eardrums would be damaged. Maya said Nofar was making too much of it, it was only a pen, and Nofar swore that she would never ever forgive her, and two hours later they were making grilled cheese sandwiches together.

Awake in bed, Ronit thought about the notebook that had started it all. Jennifer, Josh, Amy—those ridiculous names made her smile. With so many hours in front of those American shows, it was no wonder Nofar wrote about a football team and its cheerleaders. What a shame it was that, because of the notebook, her daughters weren't speaking now, and how fortunate that it was only a story, a harmless bit of fiction, a product of the imagination of a young girl who had a gift for writing.

She closed her eyes, determined to go back to sleep. The noise of a garbage truck came through the window. She would have to get up in an hour. She turned over on the mattress once again. Her muscles ached from sleeplessness and house-work. She hadn't stopped cleaning since the detective's call. As if she had a rottweiler in her head—every time she wanted to take a break and think, it barked and drove her to another chore. She had already folded all the laundry that needed folding, and all the laundry that didn't. If she watered the plants one more time, the poor things might drown. She had to stop for a moment, even if her mind demanded otherwise. But that was actually why she had to stop. To check carefully: who was barking here and why? But she kept on cleaning, and when she wasn't cleaning she marked exam papers, and when she finished marking exam papers she went to bed, where Ami was sleeping and she was awake. The garbage truck drove off, and in the ensuing silence Ronit's thoughts once again wandered to the notebook. It was only a story, she told herself, only a story. But on the other hand, she thought as she tossed and turned, a story can contain a kernel of reality as well. Sometimes fiction is written in the ink of truth.

Suddenly she stiffened. Under the large blanket her body was covered in a cold sweat. Beside her, Ami persisted in sleeping, not waking even when Ronit whispered in alarm, "The pen." Because she understood all at once what had been bothering her, what had caused her to toss and turn all night. Purple ink and black ink. The fountain pen and a regular pen. She closed her eyes and tried to re-create the sight of those pages. Had there been two different colors in the notebook? That night, she had read the pages in the weak light of the small living room lamp, and it had been difficult to see the differences. Yet she was almost convinced: the color of the confession was purple and all the rest was written in black ink. And if the purple fountain pen had been lost many weeks before, then the words written in purple ink—that emotional, first-person confession—had been written earlier. They stood alone. And the other words, the reassuring ones, the Jennifer-Josh-Amy story that came before and after the confession, were written only later. Her daughter had added them after the fact.

To her surprise, Ronit found that she wasn't really surprised.

The realization hadn't landed on her out of the blue, but had set down on shoulders that had been waiting for it for many days. It had been placed on her like a white veil after a long engagement, or the opposite, like a mourning veil after a fatal illness. It was remarkable how much a woman can know without knowing she knows it.

45

THE GIRLS' MOTHER arranged to meet with the police detective. Maya heard her talking on the phone. "Dorit?" she said. "This is Ronit Shalev. Nofar's mother." She was standing in the kitchen and Maya had just come home from school. The delicious smell of chicken schnitzel and the popping sound of hot oil filled the house, and their mother was standing between the frying pan and the counter, her back to Maya, saying into the phone, "Will you be at the station tomorrow morning? Can we meet? I need to show you something." A moment later she hung up, and Maya said to herself that maybe she'd been talking to a different Dorit altogether, but she knew: her mother's stance told her. She stood next to the frying pan hugging herself very tightly, as if she were trying to keep herself from falling.

Maya left the house quietly, stood on the street for ten minutes, and then went into the apartment again, saying loudly, "I'm back!" During those ten minutes on the street she hadn't texted, hadn't surfed the Internet, and hadn't sent any likes for anything. She had simply stood on the street as she had never stood there before. After going into the house and calling out, "I'm back!" she walked quickly to her room. Several minutes later her mother came to ask whether she wanted schnitzel, and Maya said she wasn't hungry. When her mother left, Maya tried to call Nofar. She sent text after text that Nofar didn't read. To keep herself from climbing the walls, she turned on the TV. She watched three cooking shows and six reruns. Five hours later, when the front door finally opened, she was in the middle of watching a talent show. An attractive transgender woman was trilling a familiar pop song. Maya hurried out to Nofar, but her older sister passed her on the way to her room without speaking.

"Mom found out."

Nofar froze in the hallway. Maya stood in front of her, speaking in an urgent whisper. After all, their mother might come in at any minute. The words flew out of Maya's mouth like a flock of pigeons. Maybe her sister would finally forgive her for what she'd done. When she finished speaking, she looked into her big sister's eyes. She was sure Nofar would cry, but her eyes were as dry as the pavements at the end of August.

"Thank you."

Before Maya could say anything else, Nofar had already gone into her room and closed the door. She stood inside and knew: it wasn't her lie that was being revealed now, it was her mother's. Her mother had pretended that love was an ocean, and Nofar had never guessed how small and enclosed that ocean was, a fish tank in a corner of the living room, and as long as Nofar kept swimming in circles of the right diameter, the water was calm and the love too deep to be fathomed.

As the younger sister stood in the hallway considering what to do now, Nofar's door opened again and she rushed out. Maya heard the front door open and close, and except for the applause of the audience at the talent show, the apartment was silent.

Nofar hurried to the roof, taking the steps at a run. The iron door squeaked slightly when she opened it. In the building next door, TV sets flickered like fireflies, and the only thing separating the two buildings was sixty feet of emptiness, an abyss five floors deep. A clamor of commercials came from the apartment across from her. It was evening, the air smelled of meatballs and omelets and pasta, and shouts of all sorts came from the apartments—*Come to the table! He took it from me!*—and with all that noise, no one heard the quiet steps moving across the roof.

Nofar stood close to the water tank and looked down. There were people everywhere. Watching TV, eating, showering. And no one in the buildings across from her had the slightest idea that there was a girl on the roof holding a lighter in one hand and a notebook in the other. Here, in the darkness, no one would see the fire. And if there were no notebook, her mother wouldn't have anything to show Detective Dorit tomorrow. There would be no hard evidence, as they called it on TV. She put the notebook down on the roof. She flicked on the lighter. Reddish light flickered on her fingertips as she moved the flame toward the pages, and in that reddish light she suddenly saw her mother's face.

The lighter dropped out of her hand. Nofar didn't dare pick it up. Despite the darkness, she felt her mother's eyes fasten onto the bound pages, and she cringed. Her mother knew what was written in that notebook. Her mother knew what she had done. In a moment she would come over and grab it. Maybe even slap her. She definitely looked capable of it, and Nofar knew she deserved it.

But her mother didn't move. She stood where she was and looked at her. In some way that was worse than a slap, standing there and waiting for her to say something. Innumerable stars glittered in the sky above them, and innumerable lights were turned on in the buildings around them, but nonetheless the roof was immersed in darkness that was its alone. Nofar felt her knees tremble and knew that if her mother didn't take the notebook now, she would give it up herself. To remain standing there, facing that expression, was more than she could bear. She began to walk forward when her mother suddenly said, in a voice that in no way resembled her normal one, "Pick it up."

It took a moment for Nofar to understand what she meant. The words floated above the building without joining together in a logical sentence. Then her mother pointed to where the lighter had fallen, and Nofar saw it at her feet, black and shiny. She bent down to pick it up, but when it was in her hand once again, she didn't stand. From that height, the roof looked much larger. From that height, her mother looked huge.

"Now light it."

With a trembling hand, Nofar lit it again. The flame was redder and hotter, illuminating and darkening the roof at one and the same time. Nofar looked at her mother. It might have been the interplay of flame and shadow that made her face seem so strange. Like someone else's mother. Ronit gazed at her daughter's tormented expression, at the notebook, at the roof of the five-story building, and said, "Now finish what you started."

The notebook in Nofar's hand was heavy. When the flame touched the first page, the spark that rose from it scorched her fingers. And yet she didn't move, remained bending on the roof, burning page after page, not only the incriminating ones but the entire notebook, and all her words curled up and melted in the heat. In the end, after the last of the pages had been burned to ash, Nofar looked up for the first time to meet her mother's eyes. She needed to see her to know that this moment existed, that the roof, the lighter, her burned fingertips, the small pile of ashes in front of her actually existed. But her mother was no longer there.

Nofar didn't know how long she remained on the roof. The TV sets in the apartments across the way were turned off one by one, until all the windows became dark. Then she went downstairs. The house was dark and quiet, as if everyone was asleep, even though her mother and Maya were obviously wide-awake. Nofar opened the cabinet and took out a box of cornflakes. She hadn't eaten since morning, and now she was suddenly very hungry. She chewed quickly, with her mouth open. Her thoughts returned over and over again to that moment, to the woman who, simultaneously, was and wasn't her mother. Her hair smelled of smoke, so she took a shower and shampooed it thoroughly. She cleaned under her nails until the bits of paper were gone and the charcoal stains were washed away. She scrubbed herself with soap twice, but the scorched smell seemed to rise through the foam. She turned off the water and dried herself. She ran her fingers through her hair, sprayed on deodorant, rubbed in cream, added perfume. She dropped the towel, turned on the water in the bathtub, and filled it to the brim. She stayed in the water for a full forty minutes, her skin wrinkled like an old lady's, but the smell of burned paper still clung to her.

46

"FOR THE LIFE of me, I don't understand why you're in-
sisting on this." Superintendent Alon looked very tired, even
more tired than usual. Dorit wondered whether it might have
been better to postpone the conversation to a day when he
was less tired, but since his wife, Miri, had given birth to the
twins, Superintendent Alon was tired all the time.

"I'm just saying that it's odd that on Thursday afternoon,
the mother called and asked when she could see me, and
on Friday morning she called to cancel. Her voice sounded
strange on the phone. And on top of that, the girl refused to
take a polygraph when—"

"It wasn't the girl who refused, it was her father."

"So why did her father refuse to let her take the polygraph?"

Superintendent Alon sighed. He spoke slowly, in a tone
that tried to be nice but actually wasn't nice at all. "Dorit,
you yourself are a mother, and if, God forbid, your daughter
was going through something, wouldn't you go crazy if the
police asked her to take a lie detector test?" Dorit said
nothing. She had the feeling that he didn't expect her to
answer his question. Superintendent Alon nodded. Clearly,
her silence was the correct response. "I don't understand why
you even suggested it to the father. Since when do we ask
teenagers to take lie detector tests? And especially in such a
clear-cut case—"

"I'm not sure this case is so clear-cut. I'm telling you, the mother's voice on the phone was strange." Superintendent Alon's eyes opened so wide that she could see the capillaries under his lids. "Are you crazy? The suspect confessed—confessed!—the first time we questioned him. And that girl, she gave the most convincing testimony I've ever heard in my life. Did you see her on the Friday night news? Miri cried in front of the TV set!"

"She speaks well, that's true."

Superintendent Alon gave her an admonishing look. He glanced through the window of his office at the bustling corridor, then lowered his voice even though the door was closed and no one could hear them. "Do you understand that you're talking about the victim of sexual assault here? Let me explain to you what sexual assault is—"

"I really don't need you to explain to me what sexual assault is."

"Listen, I'll explain it to you—sexual assault is something very serious. We have eyewitnesses who were on the scene right after it happened and heard it all live. We have the confession of the suspect himself. We have the detailed testimony of that brave girl you've turned against now, God knows why."

"I want to call Avishai Milner here again. And I want to see her again. No polygraph, just a talk."

"No talk," Superintendent Alon said and stood up. When he stood, you could see how broad and tall he was, and how much time had passed since he'd polished his shoes. Anger pulsed in Dorit's temples. This was her case, her investigation, and no one had ever told her what to do with her cases. She opened her mouth to protest, but Superintendent Alon spoke first, "Dore'le, I'm doing this for you. This is a high-profile case. You should be thankful the father didn't talk to any journalists about that lie detector test. Everyone would have hauled us over the coals, and when I say *us* I mean *you,* because I don't intend to end up being the shit from the police who harasses female victims."

And with that, as far as he was concerned, the conversation was over, because Superintendent Alon put his hand on his friend's shoulder and walked her to the door, giving her an amiable but decisive smile before he closed himself in his office again. Detective Dorit stood in the corridor for a long minute. She could still feel the touch of Superintendent Alon's heavy, bearish fingers on her shoulder. She turned and went back to her office, threw the summons she had already prepared for Avishai Milner into the trash, took her bag, and hurried downstairs.

The deaf-mute stood in his usual place on the busy street. Through the traffic noise Dorit could hear his never-ending muttering, "It didn't happen! She's lying!" Two taxis stopped with a squeal of brakes when she stepped resolutely off the pavement. She crossed the street in five determined steps and stood in front of the beggar. He stopped his muttering and looked at her hopefully.

"You stand here across from the police station one more time and I'll arrest you for vagrancy. Do you understand me?"

47

ON THE FIRST day of the week, the city wakes in alarm, leaps out of its weekend coma like a student who realizes she has woken up late on the morning of an exam. Bus drivers pull quickly away from the stop, close their hearts to the pleading of a running passerby. Deaf to the shouts of pedestrians, motorcyclists don't hesitate to drive onto the sidewalk in order to bypass a stubborn traffic light. At falafel stands, the oil grows increasingly hotter. Eggplants are slaughtered casually. Pita bread arrives hot from the bakers in packages of ten, swollen and sweaty. In cafés, the weekend newspapers that customers had fought over the night before are now thrown away. In government offices, clerks gather the courage to unlock the doors and announce "We're open"—it's the first day of the week and a throng of people is about to charge inside. No one stands still. The city, as if attacked by fleas, jiggles and scratches.

As the streets filled with people, Nofar stood and watched, running her fingers through her hair. It seemed to her that everyone was wondering why she stopped there. As if, somehow, even though she wasn't blocking anyone's path, her lack of movement was disrupting the traffic.

People looked at Nofar, but Nofar didn't look at them. It was shadows that preoccupied her. Everyone who walks on the street has a shadow attached at the heel. Noon will reduce it to a negligible narrow stripe, but as the day lengthens it too will lengthen until night comes and people blend together into one large darkness. To flee that darkness, they will hurry off to their illuminated homes. But for the moment, morning shadows. How many of the people passing her here had already lied today, between brushing their teeth and drinking their first cup of coffee? How many lasted until noon? Small tall thick thin lovely ugly white lies, always white.

Maybe she would go to the police station now. It was probably busy there, too, on Sunday morning. She'd wait patiently until Detective Dorit was free. It wasn't an emergency. She had time. The hours would pass, the shadows would grow longer, and when the detective called her in, she would tell her exactly that: the shadow wasn't attached to her foot now, she was attached to the shadow.

The minutes passed and she remained standing where she was. Only small children and beggars stood still on Sunday morning. Parents scolded the children, pulled them onward. No one scolded the beggars. They stood for as long as they wanted, extinguished like streetlights fired by the dawn and rehired by the evening. Nofar knew she was too old for a parent to come and take her by the hand. Although she wished for that. She watched the crying toddlers, flinging their arms about to escape the grown-ups' determined grip, and she thought about the blessing of such a tight grip. Someone else knew where you had to go. Someone else was responsible for getting you there. If only someone would grasp her like that, take her by the hand and drag her to the detective's office. But she was a seventeen-year-old in the middle of a busy street. She was in charge of her hand. She was free to go wherever she wanted. Free to stand still and say nothing.

★   ★   ★

The wind danced through the branches of the orange tree, and the branches replied with graceful bows. It wasn't clear why the tree had decided to grow in the alley, of all places, trapped between the backsides of buildings. Birds pecked at the oranges constantly, blessing their good fortune. And when the fruits finally despaired and fell from the branches to their death, the ants scurried over to the pecked oranges to suck out the marrow. So much life in a single tree, and no one knew. Only today did Nofar see the tree for the first time. Her overflowing emotions had pushed her legs from the main street, ordered her to find a quiet place where she could think. She hadn't been to the alley since discovering Lavi's betrayal. Now she sat down there, her legs heavy. This is where it all began. And in the midst of all that, despite all that, an orange tree. To think it had been there the entire time and she had never noticed it. Nofar stared at it intently now, not only because she wanted to escape her admonishing thoughts, but also because she wanted to make up for all the times she had passed it by without seeing it. A kind of green shiver ran through the tree, all the branches and leaves suddenly swaying. Faced with that green dance, the girl could not help but stop. Perhaps that was why she didn't notice she wasn't alone. She had lost herself in the tree and didn't see the other two eyes.

For the first time, Avishai Milner had the opportunity to look at her properly. Everything had happened so quickly that evening in the alley, and since then he hadn't had the chance to see her face. True, he could easily have found her on the TV screen and in the pages of the newspapers, but since his release from jail on bail, he had avoided, at all cost, what he called out-and-out slander. Now it was only him, the girl, and an orange tree. She was looking at the tree and he was looking at her, and just as she was fascinated by the infinite number of possible movements hidden in the tree, he was fascinated by the infinite number of possible actions he could take. But for now, he would only look. How enjoyable it is to observe another person who is unaware of you. How unbearable the vulnerability of the one being observed. If Avishai Milner had ever assaulted Nofar Shalev it was now, as he studied every quaver of her flesh, every quiver of her face, seeing her inside and out, and she didn't know.

Then she turned around and saw him, and at first she didn't seem to recognize him. She assumed he was someone who'd lost his way, or perhaps a gardener come to see how the tree was doing. Of course, she felt the natural fear of a young girl finding herself in the company of a strange man in a deserted alley. But the proximity to the busy midday street soothed her fear, and she gave him a small nod and stood up to find another place where she could be alone, when she suddenly realized who was standing before her.

The blood drained from her face. Her body was still there, but her mind had leaped out of her, the way a trapped burglar leaps from a window. For the first minute she feared for her life. In a moment she would feel his hands on her neck. Desperate people do desperate things—who knew that better than she? But then she asked herself whether it was Avishai Milner who frightened her or she herself, what she had done to him. The midday traffic was heavy, the main street still a scream away. And Avishai Milner did not seem capable of attacking. His tortured face looked at her with more weakness than hatred. No wonder she hadn't recognized him. All that was left of that smug, nasty customer was the shell of a person. Why did you come here now? he cursed himself. This chance meeting is likely to cost you dearly. But honestly, he hadn't

planned to see her. His feet had led him this way, and before
he noticed, here he was, at the scene of the crime. Here, his
former life had been stolen from him. Here, you could draw a
chalk outline of the body of the man he had been.

"Please," he said to her suddenly. "Please." Before he could
even think about what he was doing, his legs took over and
he knelt in the shadow of the orange tree, the damp earth
clinging to his pants, his hands spread to the sides, and there
he was, before her.

Nofar looked at him with wide-open eyes. "I'm sorry," he
said. "I'm really sorry." His face looked suddenly old, much
older that it had that night. There were blue bags under his
eyes. His cheeks were sunken and his voice was a hoarse
whisper. "I deserve to suffer for what I said to you. But not
like this." He shook his head and said, "Not like this" several
times with nearly closed eyes, his body swaying back and forth
in supplication, like a worshipper in a synagogue. "Stop this, I
beg you, stop it."

She wanted to look away, but couldn't. Reluctantly, she
looked at his drooping shoulders, the gray that had spread
through his hair with the speed of a disaster. But suddenly his
kneeling before her angered her. She wanted to grab him by
the shoulders and lift him up. Stand up now. Be cruel. Be that
man, the man who deserves it.

But Avishai Milner, as if trying to anger her, merely closed
his eyes, placing himself in her hands. He should stop, she
thought. He should get up right now. But he remained where
he was, still kneeling. The embarrassment he had felt at first
faded. It was not humiliation he was experiencing but the
opposite, the sort of spiritual uplifting he used to feel when he
woke up sick with a high fever, and instead of fighting it his
body simply sank pleasantly into its defeat. So it was now, on

his knees before her with his eyes closed. Let her do with him whatever she wanted.

The sight was so terrible that Nofar couldn't control herself and burst into tears. Avishai Milner opened his eyes. He hadn't expected that. "I can't," she sobbed. "I'm sorry, I just can't."

"But I didn't do anything to you."

She was sobbing so hard that she didn't hear him. It took a long moment for her to catch her breath. "If I say I lied, they'll never forgive me."

"I'll go to jail."

His voice trembled when he spoke, and she knew he was right, that he would sit in prison for five years. She pictured a dark cell with dangerous criminals in it, among them the innocent Avishai Milner. She heard the loudspeaker announcing the end of visiting hour, the clank of the lock on the large iron door. The face she saw before her would become wrinkled. The shoulders, already stooped, would stoop even more. And his parents—what do they think when they watch the news? What do they say to their neighbors? But she absolutely could not do it. Maybe she could have done it before, but now it was too late, and that's what she told him, "Now it's too late to say I lied. Now I can't anymore."

She expected him to plead. To shout. She was afraid he might slap her. Even hit her. But it never entered her mind that he would smile that way. A cold, contemptuous smile that reminded her of *that* Avishai Milner. No problem, he said, she didn't have to say anything. The recording on his phone would say it all. And if she didn't want the police to come for her, she should go to them first. Because he himself was planning to walk straight over to the station.

Now it was Nofar's turn to fall to the ground. There was a soft thud as her knees met the damp earth of the alley.

The leaves of the orange tree moved gently, as if the tree felt the switching of roles: a girl standing and a man kneeling, a girl kneeling and a man standing. And a moment later—a girl kneeling and a man who was no longer there, who had turned and gone, not smug, not fleeing, but walking with the calm, steady gait of someone who knew that, finally, his life was in his own hands.

Her stomach seemed to hurt. Seemed to, because the connection between her head and her stomach was only partial at the moment, as if someone had cut the ropes that joined her head to her body, leaving only a thin string barely able to do the job. She heard her breathing from a distance, rapid and shallow. Her tongue was heavy in her mouth, and there was not a drop of saliva in her throat now. Maybe she should run after him. But she couldn't move. She couldn't even get up. Maybe it really was better to stay there, in the alley. She would retreat to this place and cut herself off from the city, because she could never return to it again. And it was only a small step from retreating from the city to retreating from life itself, because it would be better to die than live there when everyone found out.

There was no way of knowing how far those thoughts would have gone if Lavi hadn't suddenly dashed out of the ice-cream parlor, grabbed her by the shoulder, and shouted, "Come with me!"

He chased him alone. Nofar was too shocked to move. She had stared at Lavi, her expression so tormented that the fire that had been blazing inside him grew a thousand times more intense and he shot out of the alley like a missile. His body felt stronger than it ever had before. As if during all the time he had been waiting, all the hours he had spent staring out the window in the expectation of seeing her, all the training with his father on the beach—he had been gathering strength for the moment when he could be her helpmate.

He found Milner at the next intersection, waiting for the light to change and putting his mobile phone in his shoulder bag. But Lavi had to follow him for a full nine blocks before he had an opportunity. Those thousands of points he had accumulated playing computer games and the hundreds of hours watching thrillers had not been wasted—the boy had taken a long course in the art of surveillance. He only hoped he had mastered the secrets of bag-snatching as well. Because Avishai Milner had finally come to a side street that was sufficiently unpopulated. Now he felt relaxed enough to slow down, and Lavi Maimon leaped toward the walking man and hit him in the stomach, making use of the one and only maneuver Lieutenant Colonel Arieh Maimon had succeeded in teaching him on the beach.

Sprawled on the pavement, Avishai Milner saw the boy run off with his shoulder bag and couldn't believe it. "Thief! Crook! Thief!!!" He managed to see him dash toward the southern part of the city before he was swallowed up in the throng of passersby. He stood up and tried to run after him, but the boy had completely disappeared. He cried "Thief!" one more time, then stopped. Someone might hear. A crowd of people might gather. And in Avishai Milner's situation, there was nothing more dangerous than a crowd of people.

Only after long minutes of running south, when he was completely convinced there was no one else around, did Lavi halt his flight and hail a taxi. The driver asked *where to?* and as he gave him the address Lavi checked on his mobile whether there had been any news reports of a robbery in broad daylight. Of course there hadn't been. The news doesn't report on bag-snatching unless an old lady is injured or a gun has been pulled. He jumped out of the taxi, left the change for the driver, and burst into the alley at a run. Nofar was still there, sitting on the steps, her head buried in her hands. He restrained the urge to kiss her and settled for handing her the bag in a gesture of victory. "Here. I brought you this." She raised her head and looked from Lavi to the bag, from the bag to Lavi. And once again, the boy discovered that there was nothing in the world as deeply blue as her eyes.

To hide the way he trembled at her closeness, Lavi quickly turned the bag over and emptied out its contents. A wallet. Three passport pictures. Two pens. A granola bar. A mobile phone. He checked the last recording: Avishai Milner singing a new tune he had written. The previous recordings were similar: melodies, lyrics. Lavi foraged around in the bag looking for another phone, urging his fingers to find secret compartments, hidden zippers. To no avail.

"Maybe he moved it to his pants pocket," he said in a worried voice. Because what other explanation could there be for the missing recording?

Unless there had been no recording from the beginning. Nofar raised that possibility in a whisper, but something in the tone of her voice indicated that she had been turning the idea over in her mind for several minutes. "Maybe there was no recording at all. Maybe he just said there was." She gave a precise account of that moment under the tree. How Avishai Milner had suddenly shifted from pleading to threatening. And how, despite everything, she had still felt his fear vibrating under every word he said. As if he were playacting, wearing a frightening mask. From moment to moment, the knowledge solidified in her mind. "There was no recording. He said that so I would be scared and confess."

Lavi breathed a sigh of relief. If that was true, everything was all right. Everything was truly wonderful. Here he was in the alley with Nofar, as they had been in the past, and she was sitting beside him, talking to him, knowing that he was willing even to snatch bags for her, and this wonderful girl was in no danger from that terrible person. But a quick glance at Nofar's face made it clear to Lavi that, for some reason, it wasn't enough. Although the threat of the recording had been removed, her eyes still looked haunted. Maybe because, unlike Lavi, she wasn't entirely sure who the terrible person in the alley was. Was it that man who had fallen to his knees in front of her, who had lied to her in the hope that it would finally prove his innocence, or was it her? And no matter how grateful she was to Lavi, who had put himself at such risk for her, she couldn't help wondering what would have happened if he hadn't returned with the phone.

Nofar didn't feel her body begin to tremble. She only heard the sound of her teeth chattering, and the sound seemed to be coming from someone else's body. For another minute she thought about Avishai Milner kneeling before her, pleading for his life, and the next minute she stood up and ran, leaving Lavi to wallow in his misery alone in the shade of the orange tree.

48

ON SUNDAY AFTERNOONS, the city's residents go to the park to run. Nofar stood out from the crowd. Not only because of her jeans and the backpack on her shoulder—it was something in her face. Runners have a goal—the fifth mile or the fortieth minute, whereas people running away from something don't care where they're going as long as it's far away. Nofar was running like a person fleeing. No wonder, then, that people turned to see whether someone was chasing her. But the person she was running from was the one running right there, in the park, wearing jeans and carrying a backpack whose weight she didn't even feel. She had been running from the moment she left the alley, along the bustling street, over the bridge, then through the park, and despite the pain in her sides, she kept running because that pain could not compare to the pain of Avishai Milner's pleas beating against her eardrums.

Finally she stopped and gulped down huge breaths of air. The park smelled fresh and green, but inside her was the charred odor that had come down from the roof with her the other night. Still panting, she took Avishai Milner's phone out of the pocket of her jeans. Maybe she should get rid of it, she thought suddenly. After all, anyone using sufficiently modern techniques to search for it could locate it and find her. But she knew very well that no one would find her. No one would look for her. And though that knowledge should have reassured her, for some reason it only frightened her more.

With a trembling finger, she wandered through the contents of the stolen phone. Why did moms always ask the same questions: *Are you coming for dinner tonight? Why don't you call? Should I bake that cake you like?* There was a message from his grandmother too, terribly long and full of typos. "Be strong, my boy, we're all behind you, all you need is hope and faithh and we'll wait until the storm passes. Granspa sends his regards, when are you coning to visit." There was a message from Ronen the psychiatrist about the prescription left in the clinic for him, and a message from Adido asking if he felt like babysitting Gali. And another message from Adido with a picture of Gali, and another one saying that even if he didn't feel like babysitting his niece, she still wanted him to call. She was worried about him, she hoped he was able to sleep and he was eating something, sorry she sounded like Mom.

Nofar stopped looking at the phone. Reading his messages didn't make her feel better. But a moment later she reached out again, almost against her will. The woman in that picture had to be Adido. She had a nice smile. And there was Gali again, with Avishai Milner swinging her in the air. You could see she was a bit heavy for him, but he made the effort. There were also pictures taken at the Dead Sea, everyone's faces covered in mud. She could barely recognize him but she recognized Gali easily. Most of the pictures were of Avishai Milner hugging his dog. He had a small brown dog with folded ears.

49

HE WAITED IN the alley until the sun set and everything lost its shape and color. The sounds of cars and people came from the street. His mother had already called three times. Laundry was hanging on the floor above him, the socks dripping on his head, and he didn't move. The alley cats rubbed lightly against his legs and went on their way. Lavi Maimon remained sitting.

She'll come back. She has to come back. Now that she knows what he's ready to do for her, she'll surely forgive him for that picture of Maya. But the hours passed. His limbs ached from sitting so long. He heard the sound of her steps in every passing noise. She'd be there any minute now and thank him for the bag he snatched from Avishai Milner in order to protect her. How did you manage to get it? I ran as fast as I could. You can run that fast? That fast, for you. And when you finally caught up with him, how did you get hold of the bag? I did some hand-to-hand combat moves on him. He almost beat me, but I fought like a lion. He had an iron bar in his hand, or a large knife, or a gun, and I had nothing. The whole street stopped to look at us, and the falafel guy called the police, but they were afraid to step in. They saw us reach the fountain, trying to drown each other. The water was red with his blood, but in that blood I remembered—what did you remember?—the apricots of your laughter—I don't understand—but I do, and I want you to know that it was only because of your apricots. When he escaped to the roof of the tallest building, I ran up the stairs after him to the twentieth floor, and there, on the roof, we kept fighting, right on the edge. Weren't you afraid to fall? It wasn't falling I was afraid of. I was only afraid that I'd return to the alley and you wouldn't be there.

A figure moved in the darkness. Lavi leaped up with joy. A homeless guy appeared in the passageway between the buildings and urinated in the bushes. Lavi watched him as he stumbled on his way, muttering incoherently. The alley reeked of disappointment and urine. He kept hearing the sound of her steps in the night noises, but it was actually the sounds of her absence.

He trudged up the stairs to his apartment, every step up a step down. He opened the door. His father was sitting in front of the news, arguing loudly with the analyst on the screen. His mother was putting on her makeup in preparation for her Pilates class. "Where were you?" she asked. "What a load of crap!" his father thundered at the analyst. "Why didn't you answer your phone?" his mother asked. "National irresponsibility!" his father griped. "You're not planning to answer me?" "I have nothing to say." "We'll talk about it tomorrow, because I'm in a hurry now," his mother said. Lavi went to his room and closed the door. Thousands of bats of agony were hanging from the ceiling.

The knock on the door came two hours later. From where he was sitting on the couch, his father roared, "Who is it?" and Lavi, who heard the knock and the roar, ran out of his room faster than any of the soldiers in the elite combat unit had ever run. A delivery boy who had come to the wrong door. A member of the Boy Scouts asking for donations to help the hearing-impaired. A package of women's clothes ordered from China. As long as the door was closed, all options were open. He stood there for another moment before he grasped the handle.

When he opened the door, all the owls took off at once. In the fluorescent light of the corridor he could see that she had been crying. Her face was red and swollen, but to Lavi she looked like a wonderful grapefruit. Avishai Milner's phone was in her hands. There was something in the way she stood that made Lavi hesitate.

"A bunch of nothings!" Arieh Maimon shouted, pressing the remote with a strong hand, and the news analysts on one channel were instantly replaced by news analysts on another. Like their predecessors, these too spoke with total confidence, and Lavi tried to adopt some of that confidence for himself as he took her hand and said, "Come in!"

He pulled her to his room, skipping over the formal introduction—Dad, this is Nofar. Nofar, this is my dad— perhaps because he didn't exactly know how to introduce her, what she was to him, what he was to her. Dad, this is Nofar. She was the reason I stole a bag from someone in the middle of the street. I would have killed him if she'd asked me to. She's the reason I screwed up on the math exam, because I multiplied everything by her. But I can tell you exactly where every freckle on her face is located, and that's just as important as solving an equation with two unknowns. And I can tell you that the thing she's doing with her hands, running them through her hair and then pulling it out, is something she's never done before.

As Lavi was still pulling Nofar to his room, Arieh Maimon turned to look at the girl. What could he say, she was definitely cute. Plump and pleasant. A bit swollen from crying, but the lieutenant colonel had already seen enough crying clerks in the army to know that he had to subtract the miserable expression on their faces from the final calculation. The door closed and Arieh Maimon turned back to the analysts on the screen. To their utter surprise, he winked affectionately at them.

On the other side of the door, the girl and the boy were face-to-face. Where were you, in the park, what were you doing in the park, running away, so why did you come back, to show you his phone, look at the pictures, and you're saying that this changes things, I'm not saying anything, but I hoped you'd say something, what should I say, tell me to stop, stop, you'll pull out all your hair, I'm not talking about my hair.

She was quiet for a moment, and then she told him about the roof. At first he could really see her there, with the lighter and the notebook, could see the street stretched out below, and goose pimples rose on his skin. She didn't notice that, but told him about what her mom said she should do. Talking about her mother, she was very embarrassed, as if more than anything else she was ashamed for her mother. Lavi, who knew exactly what being ashamed for your mother meant, wanted to touch her, but he wasn't sure it was allowed. He saw her fingers reaching out for her hair again and again. When had that habit been born? Before burning the notebook or after? He didn't know. He'd been without her for too many days. And if Avishai Milner hadn't appeared in the alley that day, she wouldn't be speaking to him now either. When you think about it, he owed him everything.

That movement again, the fingers reaching for her scalp, and this time Lavi couldn't restrain himself, he reached out to stop her. Nofar was surprised to discover how well she remembered his hands, despite all the days that had passed. Here were his fingers, so familiar, which only a few weeks ago had cupped her breasts for the first time, but they had been very warm then and now they were almost frozen. Here was his scent, which she had inhaled from his neck during those long nights and had inhaled from her memory since they'd been apart. Maybe the smell of him would help her finally forget the scorched odor that had been with her since she came down from the roof.

But the smell of the fire was still there. She began to think it would be part of her forever. Avishai Milner would stick to her the way leftover rice sticks to the bottom of a pot. You can't remove it. His face, when he fell to his knees in the alley. The desperate way he spoke. Lavi saw Nofar's eyes fill with tears. They were sitting on his bed, both silent, and in that silence he told her that he couldn't help her now. That he had no intention of making her confess for real. Because if there's no secret, there's no blackmail, and without the blackmail he was afraid he wouldn't know how to speak to her. That thought gave him chills, and it's no wonder he reacted that way—love is a very delicate thing. The truth can trample it like a hippopotamus running wild.

And yet, when he saw her crying like that, sobbing on his shoulder (the girl's sobbing could be heard clearly in the living room, and Lieutenant Colonel Arieh Maimon interpreted it his way, and swelled with pride), and yet, when he saw her crying like that, Lavi's entire body trembled. "I have to tell them," she said, "but I can't." Her body was racked with sobs once again, and this time she put her head in her hands, pulling at a clump of her hair as if she were about to wrench it out. Lavi couldn't bear to see her sobbing any longer. The ends of her hair were wound around her long fingers. Her entire body shook on the bed. And before he realized what he was doing, he heard himself say, "You have to tell them tomorrow. Or I'll tell them myself."

50

AREH'LE WANTED THEM to go to his wife's grave to tell her they were moving in together. It wasn't to ask permission, he said, only to tell her, so she wouldn't have to hear it from someone else. Raymonde wore her nicest clothes, the way she had when she went to meet Victor's mother for the first time, put on her eye makeup and her lipstick, and even wound Rivka's pashmina scarf around her neck. Areh'le didn't speak much on the way to the cemetery, and Raymonde thought he must be thinking about his wife. "She'd be happy to know you're from Theresienstadt, too," he said suddenly. "She always said that the greatest victory over them is that we continue to love. And look, you and I are continuing." Raymonde said nothing, Rivka's light scarf as heavy as a rope around her neck.

When they reached the cemetery, the clouds dispersed and the sun tanned the white headstones. Areh'le told her that it had rained constantly on the day of the funeral, and even though, sometimes, rain at funerals adds a kind of sad festivity—even the skies are weeping—on that day it didn't seem as if the skies were weeping. It seemed as if someone had flushed a toilet and flooded everything all at once. When Esther was lowered into the grave, everyone stood there in rain-soaked shoes, and Areh'le knew that was what they'd remember about her funeral, not her death but their freezing feet, because no matter how sad and terrible death is, there's nothing more alive than a damp foot inside a wet sock.

Raymonde let the sun warm her. She wanted Areh'le to stop talking about wet feet and about Esther, so she suggested that they take a little stroll on the boulevard. They walked with the sort of silence that follows a visit to a cemetery, and sat down in a park. Filipino aides were pushing wheelchairs, not a pleasant sight. "Look at that, Rivka," Areh'le said. "In this city they separate the old people from the young ones with a wall of people from another country. They bring them especially from the Philippines because the young people here don't like to look at the faces of old people like us. It reminds them of what's in store for them. And old people like us don't like to look at the faces of young people because it reminds us of what we will never have again. Only really small children, the ones too young to understand how young they are, only they still smile with their smooth faces at our wrinkled ones."

Raymonde covered her head with Rivka's scarf. She looked like Jacqueline Kennedy now. They stopped near a murky pond with goldfish in it. The sun hid behind the clouds once again, and Areh'le took off his jacket and put it around her shoulders. "Those little children, when they taste their first kiss, you and I will be tasting the dust of the grave. But listen, Rivka, the children know that childhood is eternity, and we know that childhood is fleeting, and we are both completely right, because time lies to all of us."

Water lilies and several snack wrappers floated in the pond, and that's where she told Areh'le everything. At first she tried to skirt around it, the way you would around a muddy puddle in the middle of the street, careful not to wet your high-heeled shoes, but in the end she simply told it like it was. Buses passed on the nearby street, making a racket, and

Raymonde hoped he might not be able to hear her, but she saw his eyes and knew that he heard her very well. His clear, alert eyes looked directly at her, and then moved on to the Filipinos and the old people sitting around the pond. The old people stared with empty eyes, and the Filipinos passed their phones around, showing each other pictures of their families. Suddenly, Areh'le said they would eat lunch at a Polish restaurant he knew.

"Did I tell you about the waiter there?" he asked.

"Did you hear what I just said?"

"I asked if I told you about the waiter there."

"That he looks just like the brother you once had? You told me."

Raymonde already knew that the waiter in the Polish restaurant looked exactly like Avram, who was Areh'le's little brother, the one they took in the first *aktzia*. And although, at their age, everyone was allowed to tell a story twice, even three times, it still seemed strange to her that now, of all times, Areh'le had started with that. They might have known each other for only two months, but in that short time Raymonde had already understood that Areh'le had the sharpest memory of anyone she had ever known.

"When I told the waiter there that he looks like Avram, he didn't understand at first. Then he told me that his grandfather immigrated to Israel from Katowice. He might even recognize the family name, it—"

"Did you hear what I said before?"

"Grunfeld, that was his name. Grunfeld. I asked him if his grandfather knew the Kanzenpold family, but he said that his grandfather had already died and—"

"Areh'le!"

An empty Coke can floated in the pond, and an ugly black

raven pecked at it with his beak. Again, Areh'le looked at the old people in their wheelchairs, and then turned to look at her with his clear blue eyes. "At our age, our memories are not so good anymore. Most old people don't have the privilege of deciding for themselves what it suits them to forget and what they want to remember."

"Areh'le, did you hear what I said before?"

He shifted his clear glance to the murky pond.

"I don't remember."

51

AT THE BOTTOM of page 21 in Tuesday morning's news-paper, there was a 200-word article. The singer Avishai Milner would not stand trial. The complainant had recanted her accusations. They didn't even print his photograph. The editor preferred the picture of the largest Purim cookie in the country. After all, this was holiday time. The Purim-cookie picture had been relegated to the back of the paper because of the operation on the northern border, but its place was guaranteed. Not so with Avishai Milner.

Months had passed since the scandal had broken and was featured on the front pages. Public attention had wandered onward from that sex scandal to other sex scandals, and from them to the operation on the northern border and the winds of war blowing from the east. Those bastards had begun cut-ting off the heads of their victims. What with all those severed heads, the thick mane of the wrongly accused singer was for-gotten. And the accuser who recanted, well, she was a minor, which dramatically reduced the possibilities of coverage. The story had been born in an alley, had burst into a run that resounded throughout the entire country, and had now taken its last steps and fallen. And died.

The earth did not open its mouth. The sky did not fall. But between the ground and the sky was the city. Walking in the neighborhood became unbearable. And worst of all was school. Shir moved to a different seat. Nofar's name screamed at her from the bathroom doors, from the blackboard in class, from the wall in the gym, where graffiti had been sprayed that the custodian was in no hurry to clean off. After the graffiti, she stayed at home and refused to go out. She banished herself to her room, but Lavi came every day. At first he knocked at her bedroom door, and then sat down in the hallway. Finally, he told her that if she didn't open the door, he would climb in through the window. Since she lived on the fifth floor, that was truly dangerous, and she opened the door. Instead of hugging her, he pushed a pile of textbooks into her hands and said they had to begin studying for their end-of-school math exams. She didn't have to go back to school—he would teach her himself. And she would help him with literature. They had no problem with English, because of TV.

Then the war came and washed away everything in a carnival of air-raid sirens and missiles. Demonstrators took to the streets, their shouts deafening the shouts of her father in the living room. Then a heavy silence fell upon the building. But just as in a cement mixer, where nothing stays where it is, the movement of time is slow and continuous. The Givon boy from across the street was killed in battle, and for several days the neighbors spoke only of that. And when the week of mourning was over, the investigation was made public—friendly fire, attempts at whitewashing. People stood in the supermarket and said it was disgraceful how the army lied to us; if even the IDF lies, then really, you can't trust any-one. During an especially long shower, Maya told Nofar that her period was late. After her next shower, she said everything was fine, she got it, and between those two showers lay a small abyss, a broken tile in the middle of the apartment that Nofar was careful not to step on.

When it finally happened, Lavi asked her how it was. And

she almost told him it was wonderful, because that's what girls said on the TV shows she watched. But in the end she didn't say it was wonderful. She said it hurt. Really hurt. And Lavi caressed her shoulder and her back and her stomach, and said he was sorry. Maybe it would be better next time. And it really was better.

They agreed that she would keep lying to him. She had a new story in her arsenal every time. About what happened on the beach. About what happened to her on the bus. About what she told her mom. The more complex her lies became, the more he loved her. He admired the attention she gave to the small details. The way she guided the story to its glorious end. How beautiful she was when she spoke with shining eyes about the things that existed only in her mind. "Write them down," he told her. "You have to write them down. I've never seen anyone make up things like you do."

"But who should I write for?" she asked.

And he, with the arrogance that comes with his age, said, "For me."

"And what should I write about?" she asked.

And he, with the bliss that comes with youth, said, "About us."

"But we're not interesting."

"Write about them. Only we will know it's about us."

That evening, in her room, she took a new notebook out of her bag. Identical to its predecessor, only its pages were blank. She took the blue pen and placed it at the top of a page. An ink stain pooled where she wrote the first letter. Anything was possible.

About the Author

AYELET GUNDAR-GOSHEN is the winner of the 2017 JQ Wingate Prize for *Waking Lions*. She is a clinical psychologist, has worked for the Israeli civil rights movement, and is an award-winning screenwriter. She won Israel's prestigious Sapir Prize for best debut. *Waking Lions,* her first novel published in the United States, has been published in seventeen countries and was a *New York Times* Notable Book.